# yberian Affair

Mark A Pryor

Author website: www.pryorpatch.com
Email: mark.pryor@pryorpatch.com

Cover design by:
Mark Pryor: www.pryorpatch.com
Katherine Schumm: www.schummwords.com

To Diane

*My wife, my best friend, and the love of my life,
who has stayed by my side and encouraged me
through the good times and the bad.*

I am the luckiest man in the world.

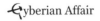

Acknowledgements

To my family and friends for their encouragement and support.

To my fellow writers who reviewed my early drafts and supplied valuable criticism—especially:

David Bishop, Christie Seiler-Boeke, Judi Ciance, Chris Coward, Ray Flynt, Bev Johnson, John Mallon, Katherine Schumm, Phil Walker, the Wannabee Writers, and the Oxford Writers.

To Katherine Schumm, one of my fellow writers, who helped me design the cover of this book.

To my wife, Diane, who has always been there for me.

And most of all to you, my readers.

Contents

Cyberian Affair

Part I: Payback

Russian Money
Chapter 1

Kozel Action Center —Ashburn, Virginia

Beads of sweat formed on Niko's forehead.

Sokolov's gonna be pissed.

Niko copied the next account number on his list and pasted it into the welcome screen of the National Bank of Cyprus. Then he entered the stolen password and transferred five million rubles into a Cayman Island bank account. This amount, less than $90,000, wouldn't trigger any reporting alerts within the government of Cyprus.

Nervously tapping his fingers on the table, Niko waited for the transaction to clear. He half expected someone to break the door down and arrest him.

It cleared.

He checked the remaining Cyprus balance—nearly one hundred million rubles. Niko ran a program to make twenty-two more transfers, each into a different Cayman Island account.

At the console next to him, Joey was removing money from Seychelles Islands Bank and Trust. Joey's curly blond hair and boyish looks contrasted with Niko's dark military haircut and rugged build. It made them an odd couple when they hit the bars together.

But tonight, the bars would have to wait. They had a special assignment. A Russian billionaire would pay dearly for meddling in the American mid-term elections.

Their boss, Marko Kozel, a tall, muscular man, graying at the temples, urged them on. "Keep it up, guys. Drain 'em dry." He stood at the front of the Action Center, a room with seats for twenty operators—all but two of them empty.

He pointed to the large screen which displayed charts of the increasing amount of money transferring out of each bank. "Sixty million rubles—over a million dollars—but we've got a lot more to go. We need to wrap this up before ten o'clock. That's five o'clock in Moscow. The early risers will start checking their investments by then. Our unlucky billionaire might notice his missing cash."

Niko looked at his watch. *Quarter after eight.* He chose the next account number. The password started with the letter "A." He had to use his ring finger to stretch across the keyboard because of the brutal lesson he received a few years ago. He should be happy the man only took his little finger.

Marko interrupted his thoughts. "Something wrong, Adam?"

Adam. That's what Marko called him, but to everyone else he was Niko, like the guy in the video game, *Grand Theft Auto.* Adam felt a kindred spirit with the character in the game, so he chose the nickname as his online "handle." Adam was a name from Niko's Ukrainian past—a past he preferred to forget.

He looked at Marko, the only father he'd ever known—the man who'd turned his life around. "I volunteered for this assignment because we need to stop the Russians. But those assholes can be truly brutal. Hell, I'm not even sure what our own government would do if they caught us."

Joey playfully punched Niko in the shoulder. "C'mon, man. We agreed to do this. It's no big deal." He turned back to his console and continued typing. "Now stop whining. Let's move the money."

It was a game to Joey, but he was right. They'd both agreed to do this, and it was too late to back down now.

Marko took a seat next to Niko. "You know I'll take the blame if our government finds out." A smile lit up his face. "We're the best security experts in the world. That's why Kozel Group won the contract to stop Russian meddling. No matter how much they object, the NSA knows we can't just play defense—simply sticking our finger into the dike every time it springs a leak. Besides, when we stop the Russians, no one'll complain about our methods."

Niko nodded and turned back to his computer to select the next account. "Twelve state primaries next week. Time to defend the will of the American voters." As corny as that must have sounded, he meant it. In the last two months, thousands of registered voters had been turned away from the polls in key precincts because the Russians deleted them from the voter rolls. *No more of that shit.*

He stopped briefly to stretch and looked up at the chart. They had stolen fifty million dollars so far. "We could use some help here. I thought Vyper would join us. I want to meet this super hacker."

Marko shook his head. "As I've told you before, some people don't work well with others. Vyper supplied the passwords and procedures for the banks. You guys handle it from here."

"You said no one else can access the accounts tonight. Did Vyper take care of that, too?"

Joey spoke up. "Niko, you might be able to talk a nun out of her habit, but you're not getting the boss to spill details about Vyper. He's—"

A high-pitched warble drew Niko's attention to the screen. A red stop sign shape flashed at the peak of the chart. Sweat dripped from his forehead. "No more Cyprus transfers. Everything's on hold. They're onto us."

On the screen below the chart appeared a flashing message:

AWAITING CONFIRMATION.

Marko placed a hand on Niko's shoulder. "We're cool. Stick to the plan. You're just pulling off another con. Vyper told us to expect this. It's normal."

Another con. Niko shook his head. He grazed his finger on the stump where his pinky used to be "Russians don't play games. They kill people. You don't know what they're like."

"You're in America now. We've covered our tracks. Remember, the Russians don't know what we're doing. The banks simply need approval because the number of money transfers exceeds the default limit. Vyper will redirect the call to us shortly."

The phone rang. Niko answered in his native Russian tongue. "*Allo?* ... One moment, I will transfer you."

Marko waited ten seconds before picking up the phone. He spoke in an authoritative Russian voice. "*Allo?* ... *Da,* this is Sergei Orlov ... *Da,* I approve for Alexei Ivanovich Sokolov ... password *Indrik.*" He hung up.

One minute passed, then another. Finally, the flashing message on the screen disappeared.

Niko looked at his console. "We're good!" He let out the breath he didn't realize he was holding. "Transfers are going through now." He picked up where he left off, entering more wire transfers to move funds out of Cyprus.

It felt good stealing cash from this man. Marko had told him Vyper traced the Russian hackers and their money back to Alexei Sokolov, a Russian oligarch on the sanctions list. Apparently, the Russian believed he could swing the American election to favor politicians who would end the sanctions against him—perhaps even promote trade with his technology and weapons companies. In addition, Vyper discovered where Sokolov stashed his cash.

By 9:30, they had stolen over two billion dollars and deposited it into Marko's temporary accounts. Niko had settled into a rhythm, preparing to enter each new piece of data as soon as the computer responded. Then he noticed the system at the was bank slowing down.

The warbling alert sounded once more. On the screen below the chart, a flashing message appeared:

DISTRIBUTED DENIAL OF SERVICE.
CYPRUS AND SEYCHELLES BANKS.

DDoS! Someone was flooding the bank servers with hundreds of network messages—too many to handle. This was not a coincidence.

Marko spoke first. "They're onto us. These attacks are the fastest way to stop our transfers. Move the funds out of the Cayman accounts NOW."

The race was on. The banks would soon be forced to tell the Russians where their money went. They could also block all access.

Niko began at the top of the list of Cayman accounts—the ones where he deposited the stolen rubles. He transferred the entire balance into a backup account in the Bahamas. This wasn't the time to worry about reporting limits. He and Joey continued to work their way down the list.

They had moved nearly the entire two billion dollars before Niko's access was blocked. "I can't get in."

"I'm locked out, too," said Joey.

Marko waved his hand. "Abandon the remaining money. We took enough. Start the laundry."

Niko ran Vyper's *Kleener* program which controlled a few hundred "bots"—robotic programs that rapidly moved funds through several accounts. They methodically transferred millions of rubles in small batches to hundreds of accounts in Panama. Once all the money was in Panama, the bots moved it through more banks in Eastern Europe.

Joey leaned back in his chair and watched the charts on the wall, tracking the laundering progress.

Niko couldn't relax. "The Russians caught us in the act. Are you sure they can't find us?"

A smile crossed Marko's face. "Don't worry. They can't trace us through the dark net, and all the bank accounts were registered under fictitious names." He turned his laptop toward Niko. "Help me out here. Your Russian is better than mine. Proofread this email. I'll be sending it anonymously to our unlucky billionaire."

Niko read it once, then again. *Holy shit! He's stirring up a hornet's nest.*

> *Spasíbo* for your generous involuntary contribution. We have removed over 100 billion rubles from your banks in Cyprus and the Seychelles.
>
> These are the funds you preferred to keep secret. We also know where you keep the rest of your cash. If you move it, we will find it. If you do not do as we demand, we will take all your money, your family's money, and your friends' money—every ruble.
>
> We know what you are doing to the American election. You have 24 hours to stop. If we detect any interference after the deadline, we will destroy your comfortable life.

> We will monitor the CONTRIBUTIONS post
> on the XIRO.COM website waiting for your
> reply.

Niko looked up. "The language is clear. So is the message." He hoped this would stop the attacks. But he also worried the Russians might discover who took their money.

Marko sent the email.

Once the laundry operation was complete, Niko and Joey scrubbed all traces of their activity from the computers. Only the three of them—plus Vyper—would ever know who did this.

Before they left, Marko checked XIRO.COM, a website used for anonymous communication. "We received a message. Take a look."

Four words appeared on the screen:

I AM NOT AMUSED.

Joey stood and grabbed his coat. "Well, I'm amused. Let's go get a beer."

"A beer sounds good," said Niko. "But I'm pretty sure Sokolov just threatened to hunt us down and make us pay. I'll need at least two beers."

Go Deep
Chapter 2

Kozel Action Center: Eight months later

Niko looked up from the console and raised his voice so everyone in the room could hear. "It's Sokolov again—this time in Virginia. He's probing Fairfax County servers, doing port scans, looking for a way in."

Russian meddling in the election had stopped after Marko stole their money. Now that the election was over, Sokolov must have directed his hackers to a different target.

Niko shook his head. "I don't get it. Why is he going after local government servers? It won't get his sanctions removed, and it doesn't bring him new business."

Marko looked at Niko's console. "A lot of government experts are wondering the same thing. We believe the Russian intelligence agencies may have subcontracted this work to Sokolov." He pointed to the front of the room. "Display the Fairfax data on the big screen. Which servers are they targeting?"

Niko tapped a few keys. A network diagram appeared, large enough for everyone to see. In the center, the images of three computers were highlighted in red. "Looks like the public safety servers—9-1-1 dispatch, police, and fire."

Every seat was full today, all eyes fixed on the screen. Next month there would be even more people—once they relocated operations into a larger building with tighter security. Marko needed the new center to support Kozel Group's newest contract, protecting the nation's critical infrastructure.

Across the room, another operator announced, "Same thing's going on in DC. Definitely Sokolov."

This is what Niko hoped for. The team had monitored these hackers for months while they probed local government systems in other cities. Vyper always made sure they couldn't break in. But today, Sokolov's folks targeted DC and several nearby counties, including locations where Vyper's traps were deployed.

"Let them break into Fairfax this time," said Marko. "We're ready for them. They won't get any sensitive documents, and Vyper's tracker will infect their computers. If things work as planned, the tracker will communicate with us from the hackers' sites."

Two more operators entered the room. Marko checked his watch. "Second shift's arriving. Let's bring them up to speed. We need them to watch for feedback from the tracker."

Twenty minutes later, Niko got ready to leave with the rest of the first shift. He was heading directly home, no stopping for a drink. Bar-hopping and socializing after work ended for him five weeks ago when someone stuck a knife in Joey and vanished into the middle of the night.

"Wait." Marko grabbed Niko's arm. "Do you have plans this evening?"

"Plans?" He shrugged. "I guess not. Not since Joey..."

Marko nodded. "Would you like to join me for a beer or two at Alpha World? Happy hour starts in ten minutes. I'm a regular there on Mondays."

An evening with Joey had always been fun—two young studs on the move. But no matter how much Niko admired Marko, they were from different generations. The idea of a night at a brewpub with the "old man" promised to be awkward.

He looked down at his feet. "I don't know..."

"C'mon, you need a night out."

It did sound tempting. "Any hot women there?"

"All the time. Maybe you can hook up." Marko smiled. "I know this isn't like a night out with Joey, but I don't think you've been out with friends even once since he died."

"Murdered, you mean. Damn it, Marko, you know it wasn't a mugging."

"You're right, but there isn't much we can do about it. I guess you need more time."

Niko was disappointed with himself. He was alienating his friends, and it wasn't good for his own health. He hurried to catch up with Marko. "On second thought, Alpha World sounds good. Okay, I'll meet you there."

When Marko left, Niko grabbed his laptop and coat, and handed them to the security guard. After a quick check, the guard motioned him to pass.

Niko ventured out into the cold and walked across the lot to his blue Camaro. He turned the key, hoping the engine would turn over. *Need a new battery.* When it finally started, he turned on the heater, and crossed his arms. With his hands in his armpits he waited until the heater warmed the car and the defroster cleared the windshield. The Alpha World brewpub was on the other side of VA-625.

Gotta move to Florida.

Niko spotted Marko's Porsche, parked two spaces from the door of the pub. No more spots up front, so he parked around the side. The frigid air hit him when he opened the car door and walked to the front of the building.

When the sliding glass doors opened, warm air and the inviting aroma of pizza and beer washed across his face. He didn't see Marko at any of the tables, so Niko headed toward the bar. Working his way through the crowd, he spotted the back of a tall man with a beer in his hand.

There he is.

Marko turned suddenly and glared at an old woman standing behind him. They had a short exchange before the woman shook her head and walked unsteadily away.

Niko waved. "Leave any beer for me?"

Nodding, Marko grabbed a pint glass filled with black liquid from the bar and handed it to him. "I know you prefer it warm. This is their imperial stout."

The hop aroma was inviting. He smiled at Marko and took a sip. "Very good." He pointed to an open table with short benches on each side. "Let's grab a seat."

Marko sat down and stuck out his left leg to inspect it. He lifted the pant leg and looked at his calf.

Niko tried to see what he was looking at. "What's wrong? Something happen?"

"I don't know. An old lady bumped into me and I felt something sharp. She apologized, but my leg still hurts." He shook his head. "No blood, though."

"I saw her behind you at the bar. She appeared tipsy." Niko looked around. "But I don't see her now."

"The hell with my leg." Marko sat up straight. "They're tapping a special cask-conditioned double IPA at seven o'clock. You'll love it."

They talked about beer, football, and women. When Niko bought the next round, he changed the subject to Joey. "The cops are full of shit. It was a professional hit."

Marko's eyes scanned the room, his head barely moving, speaking in a faint voice. "You think Joey might have told someone what we did?"

Ever since the murder, Niko had pondered the same question. "He knew better. Sometimes he drank too much and bragged a bit. But, shit, not about that. No way."

Even though the room was cool, sweat formed on Marko's brow. He wiped it off and leaned forward. "I've had my suspicions about Joey's death, too. Maybe we're being paranoid, but if the Russians got Joey, they'll come for us."

"I know about Russian assassinations—like the Bulgarian writer in London. Someone stuck him in the leg with poison. Used an umbrella."

"That was the Soviet Union," said Marko. "Fucking KGB. You weren't even born then."

"Soviets, Russians. All the same. They're ruthless."

Marko wiped more sweat from his forehead. He lifted his leg onto the bench and looked at his calf. A circular area about an inch in diameter appeared pinker than the skin around it. He poked at the center.

"Are you okay? You don't suppose—"

"Shit! The old woman." Marko clutched his chest "My heart. It's too fast. Call 9-1-1." He handed his phone to Niko, then lowered his leg and laid his head on the table. "Use my phone, not yours."

"Your heart?" Niko reached for the cell. It slipped from his fingers and dropped to the floor.

Calm down.

He picked it up and punched in the number, speaking as soon as an operator answered. "This is a medical emergency. I'm at Alpha World Brewpub in Ashburn. My friend ... I think it's a heart attack."

Marko waved his hand and spoke, his voice weak. "Hang up."

Niko ignored him.

"Hang up," Marko demanded.

Niko ended the call. "What's wrong? They had more questions. They'll call back."

Shaking his head, Marko whispered, "First Joey, now me. You're next. The ambulance will come. Turn off my phone. Leave now. Go deep."

Go deep?

All of Niko's training kicked in. *Focus!* Extreme measures were required when clandestine operations went bad. That's when you go deep. Disappear. No phone. No credit cards. No car. No home.

He turned off the phone and took Marko's hand. "You're not going to die. I won't let you."

A young man in a jogging suit rushed over and looked at Marko. "Is he okay?"

"It's his heart. I called 9-1-1." Niko struggled to remember what he knew about heart attacks. "Do you have any aspirin?"

The man rushed back to his table. A woman rummaged through her purse.

Marko grabbed Niko by the shirt and pulled him close. "Get out of here now! Go deep. Call the emergency number from a burner phone." His eyes fluttered. "Use the pass phrases."

Niko had memorized the number. It was part of his training. Also, the two-part pass phrase: *I'm calling from Provo ... I'm The Pythia.*

The man returned with pills. Marko chewed and swallowed them, then lay down on the bench in obvious pain.

At the sound of a siren, Niko turned toward the door. "It's coming! You'll be fine, Marko. You'll be fine."

Through the glass doors, he watched the ambulance arrive. Two people in blue uniforms jumped out. They opened the back of the ambulance, removed a stretcher, tossed a red duffel bag onto it, and rushed inside.

Marko spoke in a weak, yet forceful voice. "Go! Now! Don't try to contact me—or the hospital." He turned his head and threw up.

Niko stepped out of the way to make room for the emergency responders. More people gathered, all of them staring at Marko except for one middle-aged man who seemed interested in Niko. *Russian?* He had a squarish face and a long, bulbous Slavic nose.

Can't stay here.

The Slavic man stood at the back of the crowd. His eyes shifted away when Niko spotted him.

Time to go deep. Niko ran out the door, straight for his Camaro. Glancing over his shoulder, he saw the Slavic man running outside with a phone to his ear.

Gotta be Russian.

Niko jumped into his car and sped toward the highway. In the mirror, he saw a dark BMW pull up next to the Russian man who hopped in.

As Niko approached the intersection, he glanced back. Under a streetlight, a blue BMW appeared, approaching fast. He turned right without slowing down.

The Russians followed, two cars behind.

At the next intersection, Niko turned left through the yellow light. The car behind him stopped, blocking the Russians.

A heavy truck pulled into the intersection. In the mirror, Niko saw one car, then another, go through the traffic light behind him. Neither was a BMW. He turned at the next street and pulled into the lot of a shopping mall. Racing to the side of the building on the end, he drove behind it. Niko spotted two delivery trucks parked at a dimly lit loading ramp. He backed into the shadows between them and shut off the engine and lights.

No way they're gonna find me here.

Niko grabbed his phone, then stopped himself before making a call. *Go deep.* Marko had told him his cell was like a flashing beacon to electronic surveillance equipment. Its constant communication with cell towers meant spies could locate his phone. Niko powered it off and removed the battery and SIM card. He hoped he'd done it soon enough to shake this guy.

A few minutes later, the BMW appeared ahead on the right and drove slowly past the loading ramp. Niko's heart pounded. He held his breath while the vehicle moved out of sight. Then he spotted lights—white lights.

He's backing up!

Niko turned the ignition and waited while the starter cranked, but the engine refused to start. When it finally turned over, he punched the accelerator to the floor. His tires squealed as he raced out of the slanted loading ramp. Not letting off the gas, he rounded the building, nearly skidding into a wall as he raced toward the exit at the highway.

The BMW raced up from behind.

Niko yanked the wheel to the right, directly in front of a truck.

The truck swerved, tires squealing, as it narrowly missed a car in the passing lane.

A loud bang came from outside as cracks burst across Niko's windshield on the passenger side, spreading out like a web from a small hole. The passenger window shattered, glass fragments flying at him.

Niko turned the wheel sharply. A second bang and a second hole.

The Pythia
Chapter 3

Holy shit! Niko jammed his foot against the gas pedal, darted into the passing lane, and picked up speed. He jerked the wheel and pulled into the right lane to swerve around the car in front of him. A moment later, he cut back to the left, only to switch and pull around another slower car. A traffic light in the distance turned red.

No tail was visible in the rearview mirror. *So far so good.*

The traffic signal ahead spread its red light through the spider-webbed glass around the bullet hole in the windshield.

Niko sped toward the intersection without slowing down. He leaned on the horn and drove into the intersection to the sound of squealing brakes. Halfway through, a pickup clipped the left side of his Camaro and spun him half around. He jerked the wheel to aim the car forward, punched the accelerator, and steered into the right lane.

Shit. I can't see the Russians. Where are they? Where the hell are the cops?

Niko hit the accelerator and took a hard turn at the next intersection. He spotted headlights behind him coming out of the turn, speeding closer. *Shit!*

The passing lane ended. Only one lane each way. A line of trucks appeared ahead, backing up as they approached Route 7. He drove on the shoulder to pass them, but it narrowed abruptly. Behind were the Russians' headlights. Niko pulled back onto the road between two trucks. A blaring horn and squealing tires signaled the driver's rage.

For a moment, no cars approached in the oncoming lane, so he turned into it and passed two trucks. He would reach the red light in seconds.

Change. Damn you. Green. Come on.

Niko yanked his wheel hard to the right and cleared the front of a truck, sideswiping a Toyota. His car fishtailed as it merged onto Route 7. *Okay, assholes, catch me if you can.*

Tires squealed, and drivers honked their horns. Cars swerved to avoid hitting each other while Niko forced his way onto the divided highway. The Camaro shimmied. It took all his strength to hold the wheel steady.

A break in the tree line appeared on the median strip a few feet ahead. He cut the lights and turned left across three lanes. Then he drove onto the grass beyond the trees and downshifted to reduce his speed and maintain control of the Camaro on the frozen ground. In another fifty feet, Niko circled around the trees and came to a stop facing the opposite direction. He shifted into neutral and kept his foot off the brake.

His heart raced as he twisted around to watch out the rear window, hoping to see the Russians drive by.

If they spot me, I'm dead.

A dark-colored sedan swerved along the highway. Brake lights came on briefly when it changed lanes. *There they go. Didn't see me!*

When the Russians disappeared into the distance, Niko pulled forward off the grass and onto the shoulder of Route 7. He saw an opening and turned on his lights, pulled out, crossed to the right lane, and turned at the next intersection.

He drove into the lot of a shopping village, came to stop next to a Dumpster, and killed the engine.

The frantic chase and the events of the night caught up with him. Niko gripped the wheel. Life as he knew it was over.

Go Deep. Disappear. Leave the car. Never go home.

He'd done it before when he fled from the Ukraine. Marko had prepared him for this possibility—something he never expected would happen. *Goddamn Russians.* Niko had to do this alone.

From the warmth of his car, with his breath fogging the cold window, he studied the signs on the shops. Clothing stores, restaurants, coffee shop ... *Starbucks.* That would be a warm place to plan his next move—and to call the emergency number.

Niko checked the glove compartment to be sure nothing personal was inside. Then he grabbed his laptop case and got out. He spotted a large dent on the back quarter-panel of the car. He unlocked the trunk, but it wouldn't open. He struggled to force it, but it didn't budge. He kicked it—once, twice. On the third kick, it moved. One more kick and it popped open.

Exhausted, Niko sat on the edge of the trunk. He removed the panel over the spare tire and retrieved a gray gym bag. Marko called it a *go bag*—told him to keep it ready for emergencies like this.

He unzipped it and took a quick inventory. Water bottles, energy bars, a change of clothes, and a 9 mm Glock with four fully-loaded clips and extra ammunition. But the most important items were three pre-paid throwaway phones, false ID, and a bank card. He put those items in his pocket, re-zipped the bag, grabbed his laptop, and abandoned the car.

Niko used the bank card to make a three-hundred-dollar withdrawal from an ATM near Starbucks. Marko had never told him whose bank account the money came from, but he was glad to see the cash. With only forty-three dollars in his wallet, and unable to use his own cards, he would have run out of money quickly. Stuffing the bills into his pocket, he walked into the coffee shop and looked around.

The young woman at the counter smiled. "Can I help you?"

Any other day, Niko would compliment her. He loved to talk to pretty women. But tonight, he just nodded. The coffee smelled great and he needed something warm. "Anything strong and black. No special flavors."

"We have a dark roast. What size do you want?" She pointed to a row of cups on the counter.

Niko read the label on the big cup, "Venti."

While waiting, he eyed an unoccupied spot in the corner away from other customers. When she brought his coffee, he took it to the table and sat with his back to the wall.

Niko set his *go bag* on the floor between his chair and the wall. He removed the laptop and mouse from their case, put them on the table. He thought about plugging it in, but the wall plug was too far away, and his battery was fully charged.

The warmth of the coffee cup was welcome, and he held it with both hands. The first sip started to take the chill from his body. He set the cup down and opened his laptop—one Marko had hardened against attack. This computer would not be an easy target for anyone who tried to penetrate its defenses, or to identify the owner.

Usually, Niko used an encrypted connection to a private network in Ashburn, but tonight he chose a network in Los Angeles. That would make it even more difficult for anyone who tried to identify or track him.

He took another sip of coffee and searched for information on Marko. Despite using his best computer skills, none of the emergency alert or local hospital systems gave up any confidential information. Too bad he wasn't a super-hacker. Vyper would know how to find out, but Niko didn't know how to contact the computer wizard. The only alternative was to call each hospital in the area and pretend to be a relative. That would take a while, and he didn't want to attract unwelcome attention from Starbucks patrons.

Niko needed a safe place to stay tonight. He'd have to find a hotel—one that accepted cash. More important was the emergency number. Marko told him to use it. He could call from here, but he'd have to be careful about what he said.

He grabbed his phone and punched in the number.

An eerie voice answered. It sounded electronically altered. "Hello."

Niko took a breath. "I'm calling from Provo."

"Provo? ... Give me a few minutes. Don't hang up. I will be back."

Someone's scrambling their voice. Why?

Niko looked around. No one seemed to have any interest in him. Three minutes passed with no noise on the other end. He checked to see if the call was still active. It was.

The strange voice returned. "Sorry for the wait. Please hold a bit longer." The phone went silent again.

Marko had told him to call this number, so the person on the other end must be someone he could trust. Niko hated sitting there and waiting. *Maybe I should have mentioned The Pythia.*

A sudden response from the same unnatural, mechanical voice on the phone startled him. "You do not have a camera. I cannot see you."

Camera? This person hacked into my phone? Niko wanted to hang up. *No. Marko trusts this person.* "I'm using a flip phone. No camera. What—"

"No problem. You are in Starbucks. Look up at the man in front of you. The one holding a cell aimed in your direction."

What? How? Two tables away, a man was totally absorbed with something on his phone. Maybe the guy was texting or playing a game. The back of his phone pointed toward Niko. *Shit!* Was he using it for surveillance? This didn't make sense.

Before he could say anything, the mechanical voice continued. "Good. I needed to see your face."

"Is that man working with you?"

"Certainly not. I just used his phone."

Niko knew how to hack computers—not phones. This mysterious voice must belong to someone who could hack both. Despite his technical curiosity, he had to focus on priorities. It was getting late, and he had to find somewhere to hide and sleep tonight. "I need—"

"No explanations yet. Tell me who you are."

"Niko ... I mean *The Pythia*."

"*Pythia*? ... Certainly. Wait there. Someone will come for you immediately." The phone went dead.

Vyper
Chapter 4

From his seat at the back of Starbucks, Niko peered through the windows at the well-lit shopping plaza. No sign of the Russians.

So far, so good—gotta leave soon.

While waiting for his mysterious contact, he tried to focus on another hacking trick—attempting to break into the emergency dispatch system. He needed to know how Marko was doing.

EMTs got there fast. He'll be okay.

He started uploading a file to gain root access to the system when his burner phone rang. Only one person should know this number—the one Niko called half an hour earlier. Even so, he answered cautiously. "Hello?"

A female voice responded. "I am calling from Provo. Who are you?"

Provo. Marko's contact. "The Pythia. Are you—"

His phone chirped.

"No conversation. I just sent you a code. Enter it into the form."

Niko looked at the screen. An unfamiliar program appeared with a highlighted text box. He copied the code from the message and pasted it into the box. "Is this for encryption?"

"Quiet. Give me a minute."

Damn. The Russians were looking for him, and this woman wanted him to wait. *Who is she?* Her voice was flat and emotionless.

She spoke once more. "We are secure. Take everything you have. Walk out the front door. Turn right. Get in the passenger side of the dark green Ford Taurus."

"Who—" The call ended. Niko shook his head. *Gotta trust her, whoever the hell she is. No other options.* He stuffed the laptop in its case and grabbed his bag.

Outside, he spotted the Taurus in a dimly lit section of the parking lot. When he opened the door, no light illuminated the inside of the car. A woman, probably in her early twenties, nodded from behind the wheel. Her dark, shoulder-length hair was either curly or dirty, maybe both. A gray, loose-fitting sweat suit hid her shape.

Tires squealed from the far side of the parking lot where Niko left his car. A quick glance revealed headlights racing toward them. *Russians!*

"Get in, now!" the woman insisted.

He jumped into the Taurus, slammed the door behind him, and threw the bag and laptop case onto the seat. "We're dead if they catch us."

The mystery woman hit the gas, turned the Taurus away from their pursuer, and sped toward the shopping center exit.

Niko looked back. It was the familiar dark BMW. Cars parked in the Starbucks lot blocked its way, so the Russians had to drive around them.

Without a word, Niko's driver took a sharp right turn onto the highway, darting into the left lane. Horns blared. The tires of the Russians' vehicle squealed as it slid around the end of a row of cars.

The woman pointed to the glove compartment. "Inside. Get the laser."

Laser? He opened the compartment and grabbed a silver cylinder. It looked like a light saber. He waved it toward the driver. "This it?"

"Stop!" She switched lanes, cutting off the car on her right, and raced forward. "Be careful with the beam. Open your window. Point it outside. Activate it with the button."

Niko pointed it at a billboard, and a blue dot appeared. "I got it." He glanced back at the headlights switching lanes in pursuit. "What do I do now?"

"When I tell you, aim at the driver's window. Move the dot around until the driver reacts."

The Russians passed the last car separating them, closing the gap.

"Now!" demanded the woman.

He leaned out his window and pointed the laser where the driver's head should be. He moved the laser up a bit, then down, then left. The BMW fishtailed. Niko did his best to keep the laser pointing at the same spot while the Taurus followed the highway as it entered a wide curve.

The BMW swerved before smashing into the post at the end of a guardrail. The rear end of the car raised up and flipped over the front.

Niko stared in disbelief. "It worked!" He closed the window. "You're an amazing driver." He held up the laser. "I gotta get one of these."

The Taurus moved into the right lane and slowed to the speed limit. The dark-haired woman looked at him but didn't make eye contact. She seemed to be studying his face. "Tell me your name."

She spoke in a flat, emotionless voice—no obvious regional dialect. Maybe he could figure her out as she talked more. "I'm Niko—uh, The Pythia."

She nodded. "I trust you because you are The Pythia. But, your name is not Niko. It is Adam Zima. You are from the Ukraine."

"What? You already knew my name—my *real* name. Did Marko tell you?"

She glanced at him. "Your face ... from Starbucks ... I had time to identify you from your face."

"You know my name. So, what's yours?"

She didn't respond.

Niko let the silence hang in the air, waiting for an answer.

"Vyper. The name's Vyper." She turned into a parking lot and made a U-turn facing the highway. "Watch for a tail." She headed back in the direction they came from.

Vyper! Finally, we meet. He scanned the traffic. No vehicles made an obvious attempt to follow. Now that the Russians were gone, Niko decided to ask for help. "Is it safe to talk here?"

"Yes. I sweep for bugs regularly. But you must answer my question first. Where is Marko? I cannot locate his phone."

She doesn't know? "He was poisoned. I think it caused a heart attack. I don't even know if he's alive."

Vyper was silent, hands on the wheel. She kept driving while rocking her head and shoulders back and forth—in a rhythm.

"Are you okay?" Niko touched her arm. She jerked it away.

Her reaction reminded him of an autistic girl he knew back in the Ukraine, but he didn't think anyone with autism could drive a car and hack a computer. *Strange.*

She turned into a strip mall and parked in a remote area. "I do not understand. Marko's phone is not active on the network, and you say he was poisoned. But he sent out an alert to the entire first shift, telling them to return to the Center immediately."

"What? I didn't receive the message." Niko raised his voice, nearly yelling. "Marko was lying on a stretcher heading to the hospital before I ditched my phone. He wasn't in any shape to send a message."

Vyper gripped the wheel and continued rocking back and forth. "Tell me what happened."

Niko described the incident with the old woman in the brewpub. "Is there any way you can obtain the security videos from Alpha World?"

"Of course. But first, tell me everything."

He detailed the events—from Marko's reaction in the brewpub to the high-speed pursuit by the BMW.

Vyper never met his gaze. She continued rocking. This cool-as-ice woman, super hacker, evasive driver with a laser weapon, shut down as soon as she heard about Marko.

But Niko needed answers. "At Starbucks, I tried to get information out of county dispatch. None of my hacking tricks worked. Can you help?"

She stopped the rhythmic movements. "You will never break into Loudoun County Dispatch. I put protection into their systems. Marko told me to secure them three weeks ago as part of the new government contract." She reached behind the seat and retrieved a laptop. "Give me a minute." She opened it up and typed a few keys at a blazing rate. A second later, she typed another burst of keystrokes, then another.

Niko watched while Vyper skillfully worked her way through all the security barriers. As soon as one screen appeared on the laptop, he tried to make sense of it, but before he could, a new screen appeared. After a minute of trying to follow her actions, he gave up.

Vyper shook her head. "No. No. No!" She typed in a flurry of bursts. "He was non-responsive in the ambulance." She started to rock again. "No. No. No!"

A Sterling Hospital logo appeared on the next few screens, followed by text and computer code.

She stopped typing, closed the laptop, and wrapped her arms around the steering wheel. In a soft voice, devoid of emotion, she whispered, "He is dead."

Critical Threat
Chapter 5

Niko stared at Vyper, who was still hunched over the steering wheel. Her words screamed inside his head: *He is dead.*

Shaking his head, Niko tried to deny the facts. "Marko can't be dead. The ambulance arrived. The EMT's treated him right away and took him to the hospital."

Vyper released her grip and her hand went limp. Then she flapped it up and down before doing the same thing with her other hand.

Niko instinctively edged toward the door. "How do you know Marko's dead?"

Pressing one hand to her cheek, Vyper gripped the wheel with her other hand. Her voice shook as she answered. "They summoned the coroner."

It's true! Russians killed him ... Joey, too. I'm next. Gotta hide. Start a new life—alone.

Vyper slipped the car into gear. "Marko was my friend. He changed my life." She pulled out of the strip mall and onto the highway.

Niko looked around. They were still in Ashburn, turning onto Route 7. "Marko changed my life, too. He told me to go deep. Can you take me to the Metro station in Reston?"

Vyper shook her head. "You cannot take a chance. The Russians will look for you. You must stay at my place ... for now."

"You sure?" Niko didn't think she'd be able to handle someone in her home. "Why don't you drop me at Tyson's Corner? The Russians can't stake out all the Metro stations."

"No. You will stay at my home. You are in danger." She pointed to the glovebox. "Break down your burner phone and take one of mine."

"Okay." Niko disassembled his phone. "If I'm going to stay with you, I'd like to know your name—your real name."

"I used to be Lydia Harris, but now I am Vyper. Only Marko knew my real name."

Niko suddenly realized something that sent a chill through his veins. "Marko didn't send that message to the Action Center staff—but someone did. Someone who wants both shifts together in the same building. We've got to alert them."

Vyper snapped her phone into a holder on the dashboard. "I will send the alert." She tapped on a red shield-shaped icon before speaking. "Code Omicron. Critical threat alert. Marko is dead. The message recalling first shift is bogus. Suspect Russians. Repeat, this is a critical alert." She ended the call.

Niko shook his head. "I don't get it. The Action Center staff wasn't part of our classified operation—they don't even know about it. It was only Marko, Joey, and me."

"I know that, but the Russians do not. They will want to eliminate everyone."

I warned Marko about them. Joey, too.

Niko took a burner phone from the glovebox. "Franklin's in charge. Marko trusts ... uh, trusted him. Franklin will respond to the alert."

Vyper nodded. "I hope you are right." She slowed the car and turned onto a private road leading to a tall building. Across the top story, red neon letters spelled out the word *Umber.*

Niko stared at the building—a corporate office of some kind. "What's with this place?"

Vyper drove into a multi-level parking garage. "The Russians know my car now. We need a replacement." She parked in a dark corner on the third level. "Gather your belongings and get out. Leave nothing behind."

No one was around. Only a few vehicles were parked on this floor. When they stepped out of the car, he could see Vyper more clearly. Despite the baggy sweat suit, she was an attractive woman. She wore no makeup and didn't smile much, but he found her button nose and mysterious eyes captivating. Something about those eyes—not blue, not dark—perhaps hazel.

Niko helped clean out the Taurus, putting everything in a bag. As Vyper walked away at a brisk pace, he followed her and whispered, "Where are we going? Do you plan to steal a car?"

Vyper kept walking. "Marko rented space here. Other garages, too. A replacement car is on the second floor."

"Replacement? How could Marko afford that?"

She opened the stairway door. "Money is not an issue. Especially after the Russian operation earlier this year. He told me to prepare for anything."

When they got to the second floor, Vyper walked up to a blue Toyota Prius and squatted down behind the liftback. She retrieved a small plastic container attached to a magnet. Inside was a key fob and a battery. She inserted the battery and unlocked the doors. When they both got in, she drove away heading south on Route 7.

For the past two years, Niko had assumed the legendary Vyper was a man. Marko always said he trusted Vyper completely, but he'd also warned the computer wizard "doesn't work well with others."

She's different. Hyperactive? ... or batshit crazy?

Vyper headed south and turned into a Walmart lot, driving through and exiting east into an industrial park. A few blocks later, she entered a residential area with ranch homes lining both sides of the road.

"You live here?" asked Niko.

"No. Just cautious. Do not want Russians following us to my home."

A highway came into view. According to the sign, they'd returned to Route 7. Vyper crossed the highway, entering a neighborhood like the one they just left.

Niko watched her out of the corner of his eye. She answered every question he asked, but nothing more.

Is she angry with me? The quiet type? Or just plain weird?

When stressed, Niko talked. "Marko found me when I was at my lowest." He held up his left hand, showing four fingers and a stump where his little finger had been. "He took me to a doctor and paid for everything ... I miss him."

Vyper glanced at the hand and kept driving.

Tightly packed residential duplexes gave way to expensive homes tucked back in a wooded area. As the road narrowed, the woods became thicker and the houses farther apart.

Niko rubbed the end of his stump. "I worked for a mob boss in Philadelphia—thought I was smarter than him ... I wasn't."

Vyper didn't respond so Niko continued. "Marko took me in. Sent me to study at George Mason University. Taught me to make an honest living."

This one-sided conversation was frustrating. Niko wasn't even sure she was listening. "Are you angry with me? Did I do something to piss you off?"

Vyper shook her head. "I am not angry. I trust you completely."

"I'm glad you trust me, but you're so quiet. Is it something I said? Something I did?"

Silence filled the air for a few seconds that felt like minutes. Then she responded, "Marko always told me I need to improve my people skills ... I am autistic."

Now the awkwardness and odd gestures made sense, but an autistic girl Niko remembered from his youth had needed constant supervision. No way she could hack into a computer or drive a car.

"I didn't realize you have autism."

"It is not a disease. I am autistic—just like you are Ukrainian."

"Sorry for prying. I'm a jerk."

The woods thinned out. Modular homes dotted both sides of the road. Vyper slowed and turned into a driveway leading through a line of trees. A green modular ranch home appeared in the clearing, situated on a small plot of grass, surrounded by mature oaks and pines.

Vyper clicked a button on the visor. Her garage door opened, and she parked inside. "Bring everything into the house."

They walked through the laundry room into the dining area. The kitchen appeared ahead, and the living room was to the left. Vyper pointed to the right. "Drop your belongings in the bedroom at the end of the hallway. I will connect to the Action Center."

Niko dropped his things on the double bed and returned to the living room where Vyper sat on the end of the couch, a computer on her lap. An oversized sweatshirt exposed one shoulder, and her stringy black hair covered the other.

He sat on the opposite end of the couch and studied the images on the large wall-mounted TV. It displayed four separate live videos of the Center where he had worked in Ashburn, each filling a quarter of the screen. Two cameras covered the operations area from different vantage points. A third showed the front of the building and the fourth showed the roof.

Niko stared at the people in the room. "It's crowded. Looks like both shifts are still there. Didn't they get your message? Why didn't they go to the safe room?"

On the screen, Marko's second-in-command, Franklin, stood before the group. Vyper turned on the sound. "... want to know as soon as the tracker communicates. We need to find the Russians as quickly as—"

Vyper interrupted. Her voice, altered by the computer to sound eerily mechanical, demanded the attention of everyone in the Action Center. "Code Omicron. Get out of there now. You are at risk."

Everyone in the Center spoke at once.

Franklin held up his hand. "Attention. Attention everyone."

The staff faced their boss.

"Marko warned us. He said our communication has been compromised. Our security team called for backup. They confirmed—help is on its way. Pay no attention to the voice on the PA. The Russians are trying to stop us. As Marko always says, we have a job to do. Do not abandon your station."

Niko turned from the screen to look at Vyper. "They should be okay. We use Parthian Security, and they always respond quickly."

Vyper didn't smile. Instead, she stared at the computer, unleashing one rapid burst of typing after another. She shook her head, then spoke into the microphone again, her electronically modified voice interrupting the staff. "Parthian never received your request. The Russians must have intercepted it—no one's coming. Get out. Now!"

A warbling alert sounded inside the Center, followed by an announcement, "Airspace breached."

The roof camera displayed a drone, illuminated by a spotlight, descending toward the building.

"Everyone out. Now!" announced Franklin, as he ran toward the door.

The video from the roof camera showed an octocopter, a drone with eight spinning propellers, holding a package below its belly. Behind it, two more drones followed.

The first one dropped to the roof. A flash appeared on the screen, followed by a loud bang. Smoke obscured the view on the video.

Niko looked at the interior Action Center videos where chunks of the ceiling fell onto the people below, blocking their way.

Another bang followed, and the rooftop video went black.
The second drone.

Flames engulfed the screaming men and women, struggling to escape.

The third octocopter appeared dimly through the flames. Another bang, followed by a fireball, then both interior videos went black, and the sound of screams abruptly stopped.

The outside camera continued to monitor the attack. The fireball from the third drone blew the front doors open, shooting flames across the parking lot.

Prixster
Chapter 6

Vyper's Home—Sterling, Virginia

Niko sat on Vyper's couch, eyes on the TV, studying the video for any sign of people escaping the building. Everyone he worked with, including his friends Rocky and Gato, were inside. Flames expanded and enveloped more of the building.

No one's coming out!

At the other end of the couch, Vyper's fingers hammered away at her keyboard. This was the same woman who freaked out at the news of Marko's death, but she didn't react to this attack. Everyone inside the building—maybe thirty people—could be dying ... or dead.

She's autistic. Not good with people.

Niko fished his phone out of his pocket. "I'm calling 9-1-1."

"No! Do not call. Russians hijacked the Loudoun County emergency phone numbers. No 9-1-1 calls from the county are going through. They have all been redirected to other numbers. County Dispatch cannot receive them. They commandeered Parthian Security's numbers, too."

She's right. Franklin called security. No one came—only the drones.

Niko stared at the video. No emergency vehicles in sight. "Do something, Vyper. We can't just watch them die!"

"I sent an anonymous message to County Dispatch operations and Ashburn Police. They will respond." Vyper grabbed a second laptop from the coffee table and handed it to

Niko. "The Action Center's system is not accessible—probably shut down before the attack. We must use backup data."

"You mean the copy we send to our backup site? That won't show the drone attack. It's got to be a couple of hours old."

"The official backup site isn't our only copy. There is another server that replicates everything in real time." Vyper scribbled on a piece of paper and handed it to him. "Use this password to login."

While Niko waited for the laptop to start up, he couldn't take his eyes off the video on the TV. The fire had spread, with flames coming from the roof and the front door. Two police cars arrived, but no other emergency vehicles.

They're still in there. Rocky, Gato—everyone.

For now, Niko had to push the deaths out of his mind.

Something else bothered him. As a security guy, he instinctively distrusted strangers. But Marko had given him Vyper's number, so he should trust her. Niko watched her type away in rapid bursts.

Autistic or not. She's a security geek.

He had to know. "Why do you trust me?"

She looked up from her keyboard. "Marko told me to trust and assist anyone who identifies themselves as *The Pythia*."

Niko's laptop displayed a small set of icons. "Where's the other backup server?"

She pointed over her shoulder. "The den—my computer room. But you access it here from your laptop. It is the blue icon. Use the password I gave you."

Niko double-clicked a small blue picture of a lock. He glanced at Vyper's screen and noticed the logo of EMS Telecom. "You broke into the phone company? They've got tight security."

"Have you ever heard of Groper?"

"Sure," said Niko. "Used to be one of the most dangerous hacking tools in the world. But all the security vendors have learned how to block it now."

"I keep improving Groper. My latest version can penetrate most systems."

"Your version? Everyone knows the mysterious Prixster created it."

"I was Prixster."

Holy shit!

Among Marko's staff, Vyper's reputation was legend. But the entire computer world knew Prixster was unmatched in her hacking ability—the creator of some of the most dangerous software ever unleashed upon the cyberworld.

"I thought Prixster disappeared—dead or hiding."

Vyper smiled. "Russia came after me. FBI, too. Criminals, hackers—everybody wanted to find me. When Marko discovered my identity, he protected me—took me deep. Taught me to use my skills to help our country. Prixster no longer exists."

Flashing lights on the TV screen captured Niko's attention. Police cars and fire engines parked haphazardly in front of the building. A ladder truck pulled up followed by emergency medical vehicles.

He looked at Vyper and pointed to the TV. "Maybe it's not too late."

She shook her head and continued typing.

He hated to admit it, but she was probably right. Everyone inside—Rocky, Gato, and the others—were likely dead.

Niko signed in and located the video files on the laptop Vyper gave him—the one labeled "Roof." He pressed REWIND until it reached the time when he left Starbucks. Using fast-forward, he watched the sky above the building. Suddenly, the video shifted.

Camera's linked to radar?

He pressed PAUSE and backed it up.

Vyper interrupted. "Someone at EMS Telecom reassigned the county emergency phone numbers. All 9-1-1 calls have been directed to Fairfax Hospital."

Niko paused the video and looked at her. "What? Can you imagine how confusing it is for the callers ... and the folks at the hospital? I guess confusion is part of the plan."

"A Loudoun County administrator must authorize all changes to the phone system, but any customer service representative at EMS can alter it—whether authorized or not. The transaction was performed by someone with the login name of *fancy*."

"The Russians must have planted someone inside the phone company."

Vyper's fingers danced across her keyboard. "I just sent the time-stamped details anonymously to the security team at EMS. They will know who *fancy* is, and they can arrest him ... or her. I also sent it to Loudoun County dispatch."

It wasn't a surprise that the Russians had an agent inside EMS—probably more than one. But they hijacked all 9-1-1 calls to the county, redirecting them to a hospital.

All those lives at risk ... what do they care? They're killers.

He pressed PLAY on the roof video, zooming in to view the approaching drone, then slowed it down to view frame by frame. It was an octocopter carrying cargo below its belly—something flat, but thick.

The drone reached the building, hovered for a few seconds, then dropped rapidly toward the roof. He paused it at the last minute. The cargo wasn't flat. A thick hoop sat on a thinner base. He played it forward through each frame until a fireball and smoke covered the video.

The hoop. It's the explosive.

Niko restarted the video, located the second drone, and zoomed in close. It carried a different package. Something the shape of a pizza box hung below the blades. As it approached, he got a clearer view of the box, formed of long, light-colored bricks.

Looks familiar. C-4 explosive!

Before it reached the roof, the smoke from the first drone obscured the view. A few frames later a bright flash cut through the smoke just before the video went black.

He backed up the video again and found a third drone. Zooming in as close as possible, he studied it as it approached. The recording ended before showing any detail.

Niko found another file, this one called "Outside." Before watching it, he turned to Vyper. "It looks like each drone carried a different type of explosive."

She stopped typing. "How do you know about explosives?"

"I learned a little when I worked for an arms dealer in Philadelphia. It seems each of these drones had a different purpose. The first one had some kind of explosive hoop. It might have been the kind of shaped charge they use to cut through metal. Looks like it blew a hole in the roof. The second one was C-4. I guess they figured this drone could drop its explosive through the hole in the roof and do more damage. I didn't get a good look at the third."

Vyper nodded and pointed to her laptop. "I learned more at EMS. Have you ever heard of an app called Telegram?"

"Sure. Used to send encrypted texts. Popular with people who want to keep their messages secret."

"Yes—like terrorists and spies. *Fancy* sent and received several encrypted messages using the Telegram app today. I believe this person is an agent."

"We've got to tell someone, but I'm not sure who. Marko once told me the White House won't authorize active measures against Russia. Defensive action is fine, but nothing aggressive enough to actually stop them."

"Marko told me the same thing. I will send the information to the FBI, but they might not follow through."

Niko slammed his fist on the arm of the couch. "That's not good enough. Marko, Joey, and everyone else are dead. I'm a loose end for them. They won't stop looking for me."

Vyper looked up from her laptop. "Marko was the only friend I had. I am angry, too. Do you have any ideas?"

"First, we have to tell someone who will force the government to act ... the press. Like Watergate. *Deep Throat's* inside information led to the resignation of the president. Maybe we could do the same thing and take down Sokolov." Niko struggled to turn his instincts into a real plan. "You need to be a new *Deep Throat*. We'll call you *Trotsky*."

Vyper shook her head. "I know computers, not people. I do not know what to say, who to talk to."

"Then I'll be *Trotsky*. I'll figure out what to say, who to tell."

"I agree. But it will not stop the Russians. It is not safe for you to leave my home. Not until they are stopped. Do you have any more ideas?"

"I'll think of something. Sokolov's doing this. We stole his money. He's looking for me—maybe you, too."

"How can we stop him?"

"Right now, I don't have a plan. But we need a brilliant hacker willing to do unethical things online. Someone like Prixster."

Falcon
Chapter 7

Niko waited anxiously for an answer. He couldn't take down Sokolov alone, but the best hacker in the world sat on the couch next to him. They could do it together.

She nodded. "You are right. I will be Prixster once again, but I will not use the name."

"Great. Working together, we have a fighting chance."

The live video feed on TV showed the outside of the burning building. The fire department had contained most of the flames while the EMTs stood around. No sign of anyone coming out.

Vyper set her laptop on the couch. "We cannot help them. The emergency responders will do that."

"We don't know..." Niko thought of the people who were in the Center earlier in the evening after first shift left. "Maybe Rocky or Gato survived."

"I am monitoring the dispatch system. If something significant happens, I will get the details. For now, we need a plan. Marko knew a lot more about the Russians than we do. I have his files on the backup server."

Niko accessed the server from his laptop and studied the directory. Next to the video files were twenty folders, each one labeled with unintelligible names consisting of random numbers and letters. "What am I looking at?"

Vyper pointed to one of the folders.

Niko selected it and entered the password Vyper gave him. A list of clearly labeled files appeared, with the newest dates on top. One name was familiar. "I'll start with the file on SOKOLOV."

"I will look at the latest information on security incidents." Vyper began typing on her laptop.

The Sokolov file summarized information about the billionaire who was recently named the CEO of Rusmir, the largest computer services company in Russia. Before that, he held a government position as Director of Communications, IT and Media—probably a reward from the Russian president for assistance in the Crimean intervention.

Crimea! That's where Niko grew up—in Sevastopol. Scanning quickly past the first few pages, he found confirmation of his suspicions. Sokolov had been a suspected enforcer in the Ukrainian Mafia.

Niko thought back to his teenage years in Sevastopol. He wasn't proud of the work his gang did for the Mafia—collecting and delivering protection money.

He turned to Vyper. "I might have met Sokolov when I lived in the Ukraine."

She looked up from her laptop. "Earlier this evening, I searched for your name and learned where you are from. You have more insight into Sokolov's background than I do."

On the TV, the live video showed an ambulance driving around the side of the building where the flames had been extinguished.

Niko jumped up and pointed at the screen. "Someone's alive! Maybe there's more."

Vyper kept typing on her laptop. "They are reporting one survivor—a man. He requires an ambulance. No name or description of injuries yet."

Niko thought about the Action Center. "Maybe the survivor was inside the datacenter. It's physically isolated. It could have protected him. The others were unprotected in operations, where the drone exploded." He looked at Vyper. "Have you learned anything about the hackers?"

"They are not done yet. It is a large team, and they are now probing Fairfax County systems, looking for weaknesses. The probes are coming from the dark net. If they find a vulnerable server, they might take more aggressive action."

"Can you protect the systems they're targeting?"

"Yes, I will, but it will not stop the Russians from probing other systems. I plan to configure a few decoy servers so they appear to have weak defenses. Once the Russians access the decoys, I will track them backwards."

"You said the hacks are coming from the dark net. You can't track anything through that network."

"So far, the only dark net traffic I see comes from the TOR network. It is only a minor problem because I know the vulnerabilities of its Onion routers. When I was Prixster, I infected over a thousand of them. Each time I see an attack coming from an Onion router, I install my software on it and spread the infection. Over time, I have been able to trace many attacks back to the source."

No one can crack the dark net ... except Prixster.

Niko felt giddy, like a fan at a rock concert. "I'm going to learn a lot from you."

"I am not a good teacher, but you may watch."

"Vyper." Niko waited for her to look in his direction. "Can I ask a personal question?"

"You can ask me whatever you like."

"Where were you born?"

A wrinkle formed on her brow. "Utah. Why do you ask?"

"Your English is so precise—so formal. I thought maybe it wasn't your first language."

"What do you mean? What is wrong?"

"Nothing. But I don't think I ever heard you use a contraction. You say, 'What is wrong,' not, 'What's wrong.' It's just ... like I said, it sounds formal."

"That is how I learned to speak. Contractions sound like slang to me. It is ... It's ... just the way I speak. Does it bother you?"

"Absolutely not. You have a lovely voice. It was a silly question."

A glance at his watch showed it was nearly 4 a.m. He could barely spell Sokolov at this hour. "I'm going to bed. My mind works better after a few hours' sleep."

"You are right. I need my sleep, too." She closed her laptop and stood. "See you in the morning."

It was too late for a shower. Niko moved everything off the double bed in the guest room. He stripped off his clothes, turned out the light, and crawled under the sheet. As tired as he was, sleep should come easily, but he feared a repeat of his recurring nightmare.

***

Adam Zima was eighteen again in Sevastopol, a few weeks before he changed his name to Niko. He knew it was a dream, but everything felt so real. He stepped out of the pub into the warm night air, carrying a valise full of protection money. He turned right and spotted his friend Yuri standing on the corner.

Yuri waved. "*Pryvit!*"

He was speaking his native language. "*Pryvit!* Is something wrong? Skorpion is expecting me."

Yuri's expression turned serious. He motioned Adam closer and lowered his voice. "Skorpion is dead. Shot full of bullets outside his house."

Holy shit! The man in charge of protection couldn't protect himself?

Adam whispered. "When? Who?"

"Two hours ago. No one said who did it—not out loud—but Falcon's taken his place."

"Did Falcon kill him?"

Yuri shook his head. "People like him don't do their own killing. They order the hit, and someone does it for them."

"Who collects the money now?" Adam held up his valise. "Falcon?"

Yuri smiled. "Yeah, but I don't think it would be a good idea to ask him if he killed Skorpion."

"Where do I find him?"

"At the warehouse. He's taken over Skorpion's office. Go in as though nothing happened. Hand over the money and leave."

When Adam arrived at the warehouse, he knocked and entered. Skorpion's bodyguard stood inside the door as usual. *Big lunk must have been in on the hit.* Inside the room, a man in a white shirt, with closely cropped, dark hair, sat at Skorpion's desk.

Gotta be Falcon.

Adam handed the bodyguard a slip of paper and the valise—just like he did every week. Then he turned to leave.

The man at the desk spoke. "Are you Adam Zima?"

"Yes. I'm Adam."

Falcon stood up. He was shorter than Adam expected. He looked like Kasparov, the chess master. "Come here, boy. I want to meet you."

Adam stepped closer, stopping in front of the desk. The man's eyes looked evil. His irises were black, the same color as his pupils. Adam's heart raced as he stared into the soul of the devil. He waited for the man to speak.

"They tell me good things about you. How loyal you are—how strong." He walked over and put his hand on Adam's shoulder. "We should be friends—loyal friends. Can I count on you?"

The man's touch made Adam's skin crawl. This stone-cold killer was demanding absolute loyalty. Only one answer would let him walk out of here alive. "Of course, sir."

Falcon walked back and sat behind his desk. "You collect Melnik's payments, don't you?"

"Yes, sir."

"They say he's behind a few months. That true?"

"It is. He's paying now, but there were two months when he didn't. It's all in the paperwork I turn in every week."

An evil smile spread across Falcon's face. "Well, Adam. You're no longer just a delivery boy. From now on, I expect you to collect all money owed to me. If someone refuses to pay, you won't accept their answer. You're a strong boy. They'll listen. Understand?"

Sweat formed on Adam's brow. He didn't want to shake people down. If he could refuse and leave right now, he would, but no Mafia leader would let that happen. "Yes, sir. I'll talk to Melnik. He'll pay."

Falcon shook his head. "He'll pay all right. Be a lesson to others. No one holds out on me. No excuses."

Shit! This is a test.

Falcon grabbed the tire iron resting against his desk and handed it to Adam. "Give him twenty-four hours to pay. Show him you mean business." Those black eyes bored into Adam. "Make sure he never walks again."

For the first time since leaving his mother's house, Adam regretted the life he had chosen. He didn't want to do what Falcon ordered, but now was not the time to resist. "I understand, sir." He took the tire iron and walked out the door.

Adam shivered from the cold, but his face was hot. His stomach cramped, and he thought he might puke. He wanted to run—and keep running. But Falcon's men would find him and bring him back. This was a test, and Adam was on a short leash.

Gotta get out of town. Head for the docks. Join a crew. Sail for America.

Right now, he had to shake anyone who might be tailing him. He walked two blocks and turned into his favorite pub. There were a few open stools at the bar.

The bartender spotted him. "Hi, Adam. Beer?"

He waved and kept walking. "Of course. Be right back. Gotta piss."

Adam walked down the dimly lit hallway past the men's room, opened the back door, and stepped outside. Five feet in front of him was the last man he ever wanted to see again. *Falcon*! No way to get around him. *Falcon*!

***

A woman's voice called out. "Niko! Wake up."

Falcon's jet-black eyes bored into him.

"Wake up," the woman repeated. "You are dreaming."

Niko shot straight up in bed, soaked with sweat, the sheet twisted around one arm. As he freed himself, the sheet pulled away, exposing the lower half of his naked body.

Vyper stood by the side of the bed, wearing a T-shirt with the cartoon Linux gnu over baggy pants dotted with small penguins, her breasts larger than he remembered, her nipples erect against the fabric.

He grabbed the sheet and quickly covered himself.

She appeared oblivious to his stares and the brief exposure of his manhood. "Are you all right? You woke me up. What were you speaking? It sounded Russian."

"I had a dream about my life in Sevastopol. The language was Ukrainian."

"You yelled about Sokolov, or maybe Sokol."

"*Sokol*. That's *falcon* in Ukrainian." Now it all made sense. "I knew Sokolov as Falcon. We've got to stop him!"

Tracker
Chapter 8

Niko awoke to the smell of bacon and eggs. Sunlight seeped through the closed shades, brightening an unfamiliar room. This was Vyper's home, not his. He would never see his own apartment again—the *Last Jedi* poster, his mug collection, or his favorite recliner. He would never see his friends, either.

Then he remembered the nightmare.

Sokolov ... Falcon. He did this. Killed Marko. Killed everyone in the Center.

The clock on the dresser read 11:45. After Vyper woke him out of his dream, he'd managed to sleep soundly through the night and all morning as well. A robe lay across a chair and Niko slipped it on. After a quick stop in the guest bathroom, he followed the sizzling sound and inviting aroma to the kitchen.

Vyper stood at the stove, facing away, spatula in hand. Her beautiful black hair, still moist from a shower, flowed down the back of a gray sweatshirt. Her pants revealed little of her shape

Niko cleared his throat. "Good morning. Did you sleep well?"

Her breasts moved freely when she turned. He remembered last night, when her nipples had pressed firmly against her tee shirt.

She placed a knife and fork on the table. Her hazel eyes never met his. "Yes, except when you started screaming about Sokolov." She turned off the stove and slid two eggs onto a plate. "You should take a shower. I will make you breakfast when you are done."

"Did you find out anything this morning? How many people survived the attack?"

"Only the one in the ambulance last night. We can talk about everything while you eat breakfast."

Niko went to the guest room and unpacked the only clothes he had in his "go bag." He stepped into the shower and turned on the hot water, letting it run over his body while his thoughts drifted to Marko, Rocky, Gato, and the others.

One survivor. Who?

Later, refreshed and wearing clean clothes, Niko went to the dining room.

Vyper sat at the table in front of her laptop. She looked up. "How do you like your eggs?"

"Over easy."

She stepped into the kitchen and began preparations. "Have a seat. How many eggs?"

"Three would be great." Niko sat at the table. "Do you know who survived?"

Vyper walked back to her laptop and located a picture. She rotated the screen toward him, then went back to the stove.

Niko recognized him right away. "Gato! That's Gato!"

"His name is James Harper. He is in Sterling Hospital, being treated for smoke inhalation—no other injuries reported. The datacenter damage was not as extensive as the rest of the building, and James was found inside. Your friend will be fine."

Niko read the report on Gato. He found two more articles by other news sources, but they added nothing. "I'm going to call him. See how he's doing. See what he knows."

"You cannot make contact. The Russians are still out there. They will try to find anyone who contacts James ... Gato." Vyper set a plate in front of him—eggs and three strips of bacon. "Do you want coffee or orange juice?"

"I'd love some juice." Breakfast looked great, smelled good, too. But eating was the last thing on his mind. Only Gato survived, and Niko couldn't even speak with him.

Vyper poured a glass of juice and set it before Niko. She took a seat at the table in front of her laptop. "Eat your eggs. We both need energy and clear heads to deal with the Russians. First, they must believe you are dead. I have already taken care of that—at least for a couple of days. Do not let them know otherwise."

"Dead? You took care of it? How?"

"All records in the action center were erased as required, following established emergency procedures. The only official records that remain are on the backup server in Beltway Recovery Systems. I modified the security data on the backup server. Records now show you entering the building before the attack."

"Vyper, you're amazing. I thought the Russians would never stop looking for me." Niko bit off a piece of bacon followed by a forkful of eggs. "You're a good cook, too." That first bite reminded him of how hungry he really was, and he ate like he'd been starved for a month.

She smiled and turned away. "The Russians might still be searching for my Taurus to find out who was driving. I fixed that. If they ever find the car and look up the registration, one of the action center operators is listed as the owner. The security data shows the two of you returning to the center at nearly the same time."

Niko finished the last piece of bacon. "You think of everything." He carried his empty plate and juice glass to the sink. "Are you and I the only people monitoring the nation's critical infrastructure?"

"You know who Cybercade is?"

He nodded. "Marko beat them out for the big contract. They were our biggest competitor."

"NSA engaged Cybercade to take over from Kozel Group. Their personnel have already begun downloading data from Marko's backup server. Of course, it will take them a while to get up to speed, so the infrastructure depends on you and me for now. Remember, no one knows about us—not Russia, Cybercade, or our anyone in our government. We cannot reveal our existence."

Vyper selected a file on her laptop. "I downloaded the archived security video from Alpha World. It shows the person who poisoned Marko." She pressed PLAY.

Niko pointed to the screen. "There's Marko. The camera's above the end of the bar ... and that's the old woman."

"It is a man." Vyper pressed PAUSE. "Facial recognition software from two video feeds agree. There is a 92% probability this is a man."

"She ... uh, he ... looks like an old woman."

"My software is not confused by a disguise. His head and facial data points strongly correlate to a man. The poor lighting and angles made it difficult to identify him. His face may not even be on file." She pressed PLAY. "Watch the purse."

When the "woman" got close to Marko, the large purse bumped into his leg, causing him to turn suddenly. Niko felt sick. "Sonofabitch! She ... he did it. Poisoned Marko ... killed him! The purse ... it hit his calf, same place as the sore spot. Marko showed me where it hurt."

Neither of them spoke for a long time, even after the video clip ended. Sadness and anger paralyzed Niko until the logical part of his brain regained control. "No one will suspect murder. We can't let the Russians get away with this."

Vyper shook her head. "I can send this video to the police anonymously, but they may not see it as murder."

Niko replayed the video in his head. "Something had to penetrate his pants leg creating a hole. It should line up with his sore spot. We have to tell them to look."

"We cannot tell them. We do not exist. You said we had to leak the information to the press—like Deep Throat. You agreed to be Trotsky. It is time for Trotsky to send out his first communication."

Shit! She's right. Mourn Marko later.

Niko stood up. "I'll draft something right away." He went to the bedroom, grabbed his laptop, and returned. "I prefer to use my computer. Can you help me set this up on your network?"

"Sure." Vyper took the laptop from him, configured the network, and installed additional software before handing it back to him. "You are all set. Now you can be Trotsky."

Niko had always known how to tell a convincing story. His mother had been a grifter, always working on schemes to con people out of their money. She taught her son well. Here in America, Niko applied his manipulative skills to social media— first to convince gullible victims to send him money, then later to do legitimate intelligence gathering for Marko.

He leaned on the arm at the end of the couch and began to compose Trotsky's first anonymous leak, starting with the facts. He omitted the clandestine theft of Russian money and any reference to himself or Vyper. He read his first draft, made some changes, and read it once more. Surely, a good investigative reporter would feel compelled to follow the facts and verify the story.

Vyper interrupted him from the other end of the couch. "One of our trackers reported in. It looks like a Russian hacker violated security and logged into FANTAZIJA.COM, a gambling site for auto racing."

"Auto racing?"

She laughed. "Apparently it is a big thing. Very popular."

"What did the tracker tell you?"

"The Russian computer remained on an isolated network for several hours. My tracker software recorded information but could not call back until the Russian got the urge to gamble."

Niko glanced at her laptop. "Can you trace him backward from the gambling site?"

"Better than that. My software was running on the Russian computer for hours before contact. This hacker used the Far Eastern University network to access FANTAZIJA.COM. Far Eastern is located near Vladivostok, Russia."

Niko closed his laptop and set it on the coffee table. "That's far eastern Siberia—near the North Korean border. I expected the hacker team to be in Moscow or St. Petersburg." He leaned back to process the information. "How does this help us? The guy could have been an innocent student whose laptop was infected by a hacker."

"For one thing, I collect unique information from each computer that responds—CPU ID, motherboard serial number … and a few other items. It is like a fingerprint. I will recognize it if I ever see it again. But you are right—until we receive evidence of more tracked computers reporting from the same region, we cannot be sure this person is a hacker."

Vyper logged into FANTAZIJA.COM. Athletic-looking men in colorful clothes stood next to race cars of all kinds. "If one of the Russians likes the site, I imagine some of his friends might visit it, too. When they come to gamble, I will infect their computer, and then trace them back through the network as far as possible. Often a pattern emerges. I expect to see visitors from Siberia."

An instant message popped up on Vyper's screen. She clicked on it, and the screen displayed more information. "It is about your friend Gato ... I'm sorry ... he went into cardiac arrest."

"Impossible!" said Niko. "He's not even thirty."

Trotsky
Chapter 9

Niko stared at his laptop screen, willing a message to appear. The people in the Center had been his only family, and now they were dead ... except for Gato ... if he survived.

Finally, a news alert flashed on the screen—the victim was stable but comatose.

Gato's still alive!

Niko knew something about comas. Years ago, his mother had gone into a coma after an overdose. Eventually, she woke up confused, and remained that way until she died. The same thing could happen to Gato.

Vyper sat at the other end of the couch. Niko had known her for less than twenty-four hours, but they'd been through a lot together. She was an amazing woman—good-looking, but all business.

She reached out and touched Niko's arm—something she hadn't done before. "I am sorry about your friend."

He gently touched her hand and gazed into her eyes.

She looked away but didn't recoil from his touch.

Niko took this as a positive sign. "Gato's the last friend I have ... at least from my past life. I feel so alone."

Vyper's eyes connected briefly with his. "Marko was my only friend. You are my friend now." She turned to her computer. "We must fight back. You are Trotsky now—tell the world what the Russians did."

All things considered, her warm response was a breakthrough. With any other woman, this occasion would merit a hug ... or more. But she was different.

Niko searched online for press coverage of yesterday's events. Most of the major news services carried the story distributed by *National Press*:

> DEADLY EXPLOSION AT GOVERNMENT FACILITY
>
> *Monday evening, an explosion and fire destroyed the Kozel Group Action Center in Ashburn, Virginia. Authorities fear dozens of casualties. One survivor was taken to Sterling Hospital where he is reported to be in serious but stable condition. Recovery teams, including canine units, began searching for bodies Tuesday morning. The cause of the explosion is under investigation.*

Niko checked the *Loudoun County Times* website. Their coverage was more extensive. It mentioned the CEO of Kozel Group suffered a heart attack and died the night of the explosion.

Damn right! Russians killed him.

The *Times*, in a separate story, reported emergency responders were delayed because the county's emergency phone system failed.

Failure? Russians rerouted the number.

Niko filled Vyper in on the limited news reports before updating his Trotsky message. If the reporters couldn't connect the dots, he'd do it for them. He also included a short clip from the Alpha World security video, along with a description of the injury on Marko's calf.

Vyper angled her screen toward Niko. "Those Russians chasing us on Ashburn Ridge Road died. Here's the accident report."

Dead? Niko had done many things in his life he wasn't proud of, but he'd never killed anyone. This was self-defense, though. "If I hadn't pointed that laser in the driver's face, no telling what would have happened."

Niko skimmed through the report. Both victims had Russian names, but he didn't recognize either one. He considered including this in the Trotsky communication, but decided it would be an unnecessary distraction.

Niko began building a list of people and organizations to receive his anonymous messages—the *Loudoun County Times,* the *National Press,* maybe someone in the government. If Marko were alive, he'd know.

"Vyper, do we have access to Marko's archived email?"

She gave him the link. "You should add the Cybercade security manager to your Trotsky contact list. I sent you his address."

Niko found several emails addressed to a DHS agent, and a few others to an FBI agent. He added them both. "My Trotsky message is ready. Will you send it anonymously? It should go to two reporters, two government agents Marko trusted, and Cybercade's security manager."

"Sure thing. But add a signature word on the DHS and FBI communications. Like a secret identity that only they know. Do not give it to the reporters or to Cybercade—they would not keep it secret."

"Okay. I'll add the name *Mercader.* He's the man who assassinated Trotsky."

"Appropriate name." Vyper smiled. "I also have some good news. Marko's killer is dead."

"How do you know?"

"One of the victims who ran into the guard rail had a mug shot, so I ran facial recognition on it. The video image of the killer in the brewpub was a match."

"At least we got justice for Marko." The vision of the BMW swerving and crashing flashed through Niko's mind. "You know, those two saw me, but now they're dead. All the other Russians involved in the attack probably believe the reports of my death. I don't have to hide anymore."

"I agree, you do not have to hide your face—only your friend, Gato, will recognize you. But everyone believes you died in the fire, so you cannot use your real name and you cannot go home."

Niko tried to make sense of everything that happened, and he decided two heads were better than one. "Tell me, do you have any idea what the Russians are up to? Are they simply probing our systems for intelligence, or are they planning a serious attack?"

"I am good with computers, not with human motives. The Russians are gathering data from emergency services computers in Fairfax County."

"I figure Sokolov needed to eliminate the threat from Marko's team—for fear we'd take his money—so he'd have to hold back on any planned cyber-attack until he could neutralize the threat. My friend Joey sometimes bragged a bit too much when he drank. He probably led them to Marko. If they learned he was in on it, they could have traced him to the Center."

Vyper set her laptop aside. "If he attacked the Center immediately, he only would have killed the staff on second shift. That is why they sent out the false message from Marko, calling in the day shift. It would not work if Marko was in the building at the time, so they poisoned him."

"That makes sense—Sokolov had to kill all of us. The drone attack was a surprise, but the Center should have had time to engage security. That's why the Russians had to intercept the call for help."

"And they hijacked the 9-1-1 phone number so police would not respond quickly."

Niko nodded. "When they went to Alpha World to kill Marko, they spotted me with him. I became a loose end, like Gato is now, so they tried to kill us both. This is the first time we've lined up all the pieces. With Marko's Action Center out of the picture, the Russians still face a threat from the team that replaced us—Cybercade. Sokolov might assume Homeland gave them access to Marko's information."

Vyper typed rapidly on her laptop. "Cybercade servers are being probed right now. It appears to be the same methods we saw the Russians using against us. I think they are gathering information to attack Cybercade."

"They used drones on Marko's action center, and it worked. They'll probably do it again." Niko opened the security video from the attack and fast-forwarded to the first drone. He zoomed in for the highest resolution view before the explosion. "It has eight pairs of blades. I'm not familiar with the shaped charges it's carrying. Hard to judge the weight."

He zoomed in on the second drone. "Looks like the same model. This one is carrying C4—eight sticks. That would be about ten pounds, plus the camera."

"I found the drone." Vyper entered a few commands on her laptop. "It is a DSI Heavy-8 octocopter. Their smaller models could not lift that weight. Maximum flight time is twenty minutes. Maximum range is five kilometers. The pilot had to be at least that close—to minimize the drone's travel time to the building."

"Can the signal from the remote pilot be jammed?"

Vyper tapped away at the keyboard. "It uses spread spectrum on the 2.4 gigahertz band. A jammer broadcasting across the entire band will interrupt communication, creating an error condition for the drone. It will either return to the pilot, or hover in place until it runs out of power."

"We've got to tell Cybercade. I'll alert them, and I'll include the video of the attack. They need to set up a jammer."

Vyper gently grasped Niko's arm. "I am sorry. A medical report arrived. Gato had another cardiac arrest. He is dead."

Christmas Eve
Chapter 10

The setting sun peeked through the trees, casting long shadows across the snow. Niko turned onto Vyper's driveway and pulled into the garage. It had been good to get out, even if it was for groceries, computers, and electronics. With all the holiday shoppers, Niko decided to get a card for Vyper. She never mentioned Christmas, but he wanted to be prepared in case she gave him a card.

Niko took the bags from the trunk and carried them into the dining room. "I got a battery pack for our jammer. It'll last more than an hour."

Vyper began putting the groceries away. "I think we will need it. Cybercade has installed drone detection systems, but they have not decided how to defend against an attack. Fairfax County will not allow them to fire weapons or use omnidirectional jammers because it would affect neighboring businesses. Cybercade's latest request is for permission to train their security team to use jammer guns."

"So, they can detect drones, but they can't stop them. For the last two weeks, every media outlet has been talking about the drone attack and the suspicious deaths of Marko and Gato."

"Cybercade understands the urgency. They cancelled all holiday time off when the White House announced a heightened alert. It's the county that is dragging its feet."

Niko grabbed the battery pack and headed toward the front of the house. "I'm going to make sure the jammer works with this—unless you need your phone or the internet right now."

"Go ahead. I will heat up the pizza."

Niko stepped onto the raised floor of Vyper's den—built out like a small datacenter. Racks of computers and networking equipment lined every wall. The room was cool because of powerful air conditioning that constantly forced air under the floor and up through the equipment cabinets, even during the winter.

In the middle of the room, sitting on a table, was the jammer—a black box that looked like an expensive stereo receiver. A foot-long vertical antenna was attached. A much smaller box sat next to it.

Niko unplugged the jammer from an extension cord and plugged it into the battery pack instead. He turned it on and picked up the smaller box, watching the signal strength meter. Slowly, he walked around the table, watching the movement of the needle.

Satisfied, Niko turned off the jammer and returned to the dining room. "It works with the battery pack—same power as when it's plugged into the wall."

Vyper glanced at her watch. "Pizza will be ready in ten minutes." She sat on the couch and opened her laptop. "I have been analyzing financial transactions, trying to follow Sokolov's money. We are fortunate Marko copied data he acquired when we worked with Treasury and NSA. I can track money travelling through the US, but I am having problems accessing the SWIFT transactions monitored from Belgium."

"Problems?" Niko sat on the couch and grinned. "I find it difficult to believe you can't get into the European network."

Vyper snapped her head up and glared at Niko. "I did *not* say that. I told you I was having problems getting in."

He didn't expect such a strong reaction. "I'm sorry if you misunderstood me. I tried to make a joke."

She locked eyes with him, a quizzical look on her face. Then she looked away. "I am not good at reading other people. It is difficult for me to know when you are telling a joke and when you are serious."

"I care for you, Vyper ... you're my friend." He took her hand and gave it a friendly squeeze. "I would never say anything to hurt or make fun of you."

She didn't move her hand while they sat silently. When the buzzer went off in the kitchen, she stood. "Pizza's ready."

While they ate, Niko brought Vyper up to speed on his activities, searching the internet for the current whereabouts of known Eastern European hackers. "At least a dozen of them simply disappeared. Maybe they gave up hacking, or perhaps someone hired them for a project."

"Like a cyber-attack team in Siberia?"

"That's what I'm thinking." Niko popped the last bite of his pizza into his mouth and carried his plate to the sink. "I chatted with some of the people who are still active. A couple of them remind me of hackers I used to know years ago, but they use different names now. One's called Zatan. He seems to be the most respected within the group."

"Does he know you are Niko?"

"I use another name. I keep bragging that I know Prixster. It seems to pique his interest."

Vyper took her dishes to the sink. "I can build a program that Zatan might want. Perhaps something that discovers parts of the dark net. I will make sure it has the usual signs of my Prixster tools."

"Perfect. If he eagerly installs your software, we won't need to break into his computer. I presume you intend to add something he doesn't expect—something he won't notice."

"I have many tricks no one has ever detected. Zatan will never spot anything wrong."

Niko opened his laptop to catch up on the news. One headline grabbed his attention:

KOZEL GROUP CEO MAY HAVE BEEN POISONED

Quickly scanning the article, Niko spotted the detail he was looking for:

> A reliable source inside the Loudoun County Medical Examiner's office verified previous reports that Marko Kozel, CEO of Kozel Group, may have been intentionally poisoned. Toxicology results are not expected for several weeks, but a suspicious wound on Kozel's leg seems to indicate poisoning.

Even two weeks after Marko's death, these details brought back feelings of anger and sadness.

When he told Vyper, she closed her eyes and held her hand to her cheek. "Did you see a needle mark in Marko's calf?"

"At Alpha World, I saw a sore spot, like a bee sting. I didn't have a chance to study it up close."

Vyper rocked her head back and forth, much as she had done when she first heard about Marko's death.

Niko read through two more reports on the poisoning, then his thoughts drifted to another victim. "Gato suffered a heart attack—two heart attacks—in the hospital. Those bastards could have slipped him the same poison."

He looked up from his computer and saw Vyper, curled up in a ball at the other end of the couch, holding her cheeks in her hands, her head rocking back and forth.

Niko couldn't bear to see her in such pain. He wanted to help but wasn't sure how. The last time she acted this way, she recoiled from his touch.

"Are you okay?" He set his laptop on the table. "What can I do?"

She didn't respond. The rocking continued.

He reached for her left hand, still firmly pressed against her cheek. When he touched her, she pushed him away. "Leave me alone."

Niko backed off but didn't move from the couch. He sat silently, trying to think about something else—the Russians, Zatan, and Sokolov. But his eyes never left Vyper. He would wait and be ready for whatever she needed.

Several minutes passed before the rocking stopped. She moved her hands from her face and looked at Niko. "I will be fine, now."

He wanted to reach out—to hold her—but didn't want to spook her. "I miss Marko, too."

She sat upright. "It is Christmas Eve."

What? Christmas is special to her. It wasn't special to Niko. He spoke softly. "I wasn't sure what you did for Christmas, but I got you a card." He stood.

Vyper took his hand and pulled him back on the couch. "Marko always came over for Christmas Eve. He was my only family."

"You and I can celebrate. I'll buy a tree. We can decorate it."

She shook her head. "No tree. I do not want one in the house."

"They have artificial ones. No mess."

"You do not understand. When I was a child, I had a different family almost every year. When they gathered around the tree, it was noisy—everyone talking at once. Each time I tried to get away, to be alone, they would force me to come back."

"That must have been difficult for you."

Vyper studied his face. "Do not pretend to be interested. I know what you are trying to do. I will not have sex with you."

Niko didn't know what to say. Although sex was often on his mind, certainly when near a pretty woman, this was one time when it wasn't. He genuinely wanted to know her better. He wasn't trying to get into her pants—not right now, anyway. "You're a beautiful woman, Vyper, but I'm not attempting to seduce you. You once said you trusted me. Can you trust me now?"

Her eyes locked onto his. She seemed to be searching his inner thoughts. "People have warned me about men since I was a child. They trained me to be suspicious. I have also learned about men the hard way ... but you have treated me well for two weeks. Marko trusted you ... I will, too."

Niko relaxed. "I'm glad we trust each other. I truly want to know about your life. Not everything ... but I'd like to know about all those families you lived with. Were you an orphan?"

"My father left us when I was very young. I think it was my fault. Autistic children can be stressful for a family—for a single parent, too. When I was twelve, my mother took me to an overnight stay facility and did not return. I never saw her again."

Niko wanted to reach out. To hold her. Stroke her hair. But he resisted his instincts, keeping his distance. "It must have been hard to understand at that age. Were you adopted?"

Vyper shook her head. "No one adopts autistic children, especially at that age. They placed me in one home, then another—and another. This was Salt Lake City, so the families were large. Lots of people. No privacy. And I knew nothing about their religion, which was important to them."

"There's one thing I know about you. If you want to learn something, you'll study it. Did you learn how to be a Mormon?"

"I learned, but some things were confusing. When I asked questions, people became angry with me. I learned to keep quiet and study something I could understand—computers."

"We can celebrate Christmas without a tree—and I promise not to be noisy."

Vyper smiled. "How do you celebrate Christmas?"

"My mother never had a tree. Said it would bother her *customers*." Niko made finger gestures to give air quotes around the word *customers*. "She was a prostitute and a grifter. I don't know who my father was, and I don't think she knew either."

Vyper placed her free hand on Niko's arm. "Did your friends celebrate Christmas?"

"Sure, but in the Ukraine, they celebrate it in January. And it was more about religion, less about gifts. They do trees, which they decorate with spiders and—"

A warbling sound drew Niko's attention. A message flashed on his laptop:

FAIRFAX COUNTY EMERGENCY SYSTEMS UNDER ATTACK

Cybercade
Chapter 11

Niko studied the screen on his laptop. "It says Fairfax County's getting hit by a Denial of Service attack. With thousands of messages hammering their systems, they won't be able to respond to any emergencies."

Vyper typed in a few commands and pulled up a lengthy list of IP addresses. "The bogus messages are coming from all over the map. A large network of bots. It looks like the same botnet that attacked the banks when you were taking Sokolov's money."

"Cybercade's gotta be the target," said Niko. "They'll be preoccupied with stopping the cyber-attack on the county while the Russians come after them with drones. With County dispatch down, they can't send out help."

"There are many targets the Russians could attack in Fairfax County. I agree they are probably going after Cybercade, but we cannot be sure."

Niko stood up. "Listen. We both believe the Russians are about to attack somewhere, and we both agree Cybercade is the logical target. If we're right, we have to do our best to stop it."

Vyper began typing. "I am warning Cybercade. Reston is twenty minutes away if we take the toll road."

"I'm getting the jammer ready."

"Are you sure it will work from the car?"

"Only one way to find out." Niko ran to the den and grabbed the jammer, along with its antenna and power pack. Then he raced to his room and grabbed his Glock plus two full clips of ammunition. When he came back to the living room, Vyper was gone, and the door to the garage was open.

He carried the equipment to the Prius, where Vyper sat in the passenger seat, computer in her lap.

Niko placed the jammer carefully in the back seat, connecting the power pack and antenna.

"You drive," said Vyper. "I will monitor everything from here."

"You'll lose cell phone and internet access when we turn on the jammer."

She held up a phone, much bigger than her cell. "I will use satellite—phone and internet. The frequency is lower."

Niko started the car, backed out, and headed south. "Did Cybercade get your message? What are they doing?"

"I do not know, their firewall blocks my access, but they should have received the message."

They approached the highway to Dulles Airport, and Niko took it. "I didn't think any firewall could stop you."

"Cybercade's security people are good. It would take me a few hours to break in, and we do not have the time."

A chime rang on Vyper's laptop. "Something happened ... Active shooter at McLean Plaza Mall. A SWAT team is on its way. Maybe I can find out more." She began typing furiously.

Niko knew the mall. "Why would the Russians go after them?" He hit the accelerator. "It's Christmas Eve—full of shoppers. A couple of miles past Cybercade."

"Slow down. You do not want to be stopped by the police."

He eased off the gas. "We can't go to the mall. The cops won't let us anywhere near the place. Besides, we can't help—it's a shooter, not a bunch of drones."

A video appeared on Vyper's screen, then she switched to another and another. "I do not see anything unusual in any part of the mall. They must not know about the shooter ... uh, never mind ... now people are running."

There were too many things going on at once. Niko tried to make sense of it all. "How did Fairfax County dispatch the SWAT team? Their computers are under attack."

"Loudoun County responded. They must be assisting Fairfax while their computers are out of service."

Niko thought about turning around at the next exit but changed his mind. "Any news of casualties? Anyone spot the shooter?"

"Nothing so far. Just people running away and police rushing to the scene."

The toll road was directly ahead. Niko followed the ramp and took the EZ-Pass lane onto the highway. "What if this is a distraction? It's a perfect time to launch an attack on Cybercade."

"It started." Vyper tapped away at the keyboard. "Someone rerouted the 9-1-1 calls. Just like they did with the Action Center attack. Calls are not going to the county, and I do not have time to fix it. I will send EMS Telecom a message."

Niko stepped on the gas. No need to worry about being stopped. Any cops in the area would be speeding to the mall, lights flashing. "Is there any place in the Cybercade parking lot where cameras won't see us?"

"No. But there is a restaurant just across the road. Their parking lot is less than one hundred feet from the back of the Cybercade building. Take the first right after the Shell station."

He pulled off the toll road, paying in cash, and spotted his turn. "Can you access their cameras?"

"Their network is secure. All I can tap into is their email."

Niko turned right and drove toward the restaurant. He turned off his lights and drove into a dimly lit section of the parking lot. Before he had a chance to park, a spotlight on the

Cybercade roof cut through the twilight darkness in the southern part of the sky.

"They spotted a drone." Vyper grabbed her cell phone and pressed a number. "If your phone responds, no one is jamming. They will be vulnerable."

The phone in Niko's pocket vibrated and rang as he pulled to a stop. "Turn on the jammer. Put the antenna on the roof."

While Vyper reached into the back seat, a drone appeared above Cybercade, dropping rapidly. It hit the roof with a bang, and a fireball erupted from the top of the building.

Vyper barely flinched as she retrieved the antenna and stuck the magnetic mount on the roof of the Prius.

Niko jumped out of the car and searched the sky. The faint sound of an electric drill—or angry hornets—drew his attention to the right, where an octocopter holding a package hovered a hundred yards away.

Vyper rushed over to him. "The jammer is working. It looks like this drone is programmed to stop when it loses its signal. If we turn off the jammer, I believe it will continue its attack."

A siren wailed at Cybercade, overwhelming the buzzing of the octocopter. Niko peered through the tree line. He saw dozens of people running from the front door. One woman held her cell phone to her ear, then glanced at the screen and put the phone back in her pocket. Two men did the same thing.

Vyper shook her head. "Cell phones, security cameras, nothing will work. Emergency responders will not come."

"I can shoot it down," said Niko. "But I'd rather avoid that in this neighborhood. Maybe we should let it hover until it runs out of power. How long do you think it'll take?"

"Hard to say. Maybe up to fifteen—"

A metallic boom came from the building. The drone broke apart and fell.

Through the tree line, Niko spotted two men in guard uniforms aiming rifles at the sky. A broken drone lay on the parking lot a dozen feet in front of them.

Outside Cybercade, everyone tried to start their cars at once, like the beginning of the Indy 500. Horns blared, and tires squealed, as cars darted to the exit, narrowly avoiding collisions.

Niko searched the sky in the area he believed the other octocopters came from. "They used three drones on the Action Center, but I don't see another one. We have to get out of here soon. Let's turn off the jammer and watch."

He reached into the back seat and flipped the switch. Less than a minute later, a buzzing sound announced the approach of another drone. It stopped the second he turned the jammer back on.

A second gunshot hit the drone, knocking it out of the sky.

Niko turned off the equipment again. They waited one minute, then another. After five minutes with no sign of a drone, Niko pulled the antenna off the roof and tossed it inside the car. He ran to the driver's side and jumped in behind the wheel. "Let's get out of here."

"Hold on," said Vyper. She opened the back of the Prius and removed a license plate from the spare tire compartment. She attached it magnetically on top of the existing plate before getting in the car.

Niko backed out and drove to the road before turning on his lights.

"Take the parkway back," said Vyper. "Traffic cameras recorded our arrival. The Prius will look suspicious if it is seen arriving and leaving the area within a short period of time."

"You changed the plates. Besides, there are a lot of light blue Priuses on the road. Aren't you being a bit paranoid?"

"I am cautious."

On the way to the parkway, Niko tried to make sense of the chaotic day. "The Russians weren't successful in taking out Cybercade. And they'd be nuts to try again."

"If no one steals any of their money, perhaps they will assume the threat is over."

A chill shot up Niko's spine. "Then they're free to execute their plan. But we don't know what it is."

Profiling
Chapter 12

As soon as they arrived home, Niko flipped on cable news and sat on the couch. Funny, he'd come to think of Vyper's place as *home*. She insisted he stay until they eliminated Sokolov as a threat.

The TV screen showed a live aerial view of the Cybercade building surrounded by fire engines, police cars, and other emergency vehicles. Below the images, a Breaking News chyron announced:

ANOTHER DRONE ATTACK ON GOVERNMENT BUILDING

Vyper sat next to Niko and opened her laptop. "They say the same kind of drones were used in both attacks, but no one mentions Russians."

The woman at the anchor desk announced the latest:

> "... so far, no deaths have been reported. Emergency medical personnel are treating the injured in the parking area. At least five people were transported by ambulance to area hospitals. A Fairfax County Police spokesman said the injuries and damage would have been much higher if not for the heroic efforts of two security guards who shot down the drones. For more—"

Niko stood. "We were lucky. No one died. And it appears no one noticed our car." He headed toward the garage. "I'll put the jammer away."

After moving the equipment to the computer room, Niko flopped on the couch. "I still don't think we're safe. If Sokolov ever realizes I'm alive, he'll come after me. That means you could be in danger, too."

Vyper nodded. "That is why we must do something to neutralize him."

"What about his money? Marko threatened to take it all. Let's take it."

"Marko was smart, but he was bluffing. I gave him the only information I had on Sokolov's accounts. I do not know where that murderer keeps the rest of his money."

That was our ace in the hole. Now it's gone.

Vyper closed her laptop and turned to face him. "You are surprised. I thought you knew." She placed her hand on his. "We can stop him—you and me. We agreed. I will use my Prixster tricks, and you will be Trotsky."

Her touch felt warm. Her eyes, light brown with gold flecks, held his gaze. All the awkwardness between them was gone. Even with all the tension, Niko had the urge to put a move on her. Kiss her.

Too risky. Could spook her. Take it slow.

"Okay, but you found Sokolov's money before. Can you do it again?"

"It will take some time, but I can do it—thanks to Marko. He did not always follow the rules. We recently performed a vulnerability assessment of the US Treasury systems, and I made an unauthorized copy of suspicious account reports. I also know a back door into the European SWIFT system."

"Holy crap. You can do that?"

"It is necessary. Marko would understand."

"If you get caught—stealing data from Treasury and breaking into SWIFT—you could go to prison. Are you sure you want to risk it?"

Vyper removed her hand and straightened her back. "Marko is dead because of Sokolov. I will do anything to destroy that man."

"I feel the same way." Niko grabbed his laptop. "I'll try to trace him through my contacts with Ukrainian hacker groups. I'm sure Sokolov himself never used a computer on the internet—he'd have people take care of those menial tasks for him."

"I have a database of millions of Facebook users. Would that help? It includes their bio, their friends, and everything they ever typed or clicked on."

"You're amazing. I don't know whether to call you Vyper or Prixster. Sure, this'll help—a lot. At least for people who use Facebook."

"I have Google, Twitter, and Amazon, too. They all sell marketing data. Most of their clients are not tight on security. I have been collecting it for a couple of years. All the data is in the computer room." She pointed to the den. "You can access it from your laptop."

The possibilities made Niko's head spin. Nearly everyone who went on the internet used Google or Facebook—or both. And everything was recorded—from their first naïve years online. The amount of data available was mind-boggling.

For the last two weeks, Niko had been digging for clues to identify Zatan, but he came up with very little. He'd been doing this the hard way. Everything he learned was recorded on the one-page document displayed on his screen.

Niko turned his laptop toward Vyper. "I think this hacker works in the Siberian 'research firm' financed by Sokolov. How much can you find on him?"

Vyper tapped away on her keyboard, then shook her head. She typed some more. Finally, her fingers stopped, and she turned the screen so Niko could see it. "I can only find his Google searches—all originating from the dark net. The oldest one is from four months ago."

"Amazing." Niko hadn't expected to find anything on the mysterious hacker. "I'm sure there's a lot more information on normal people. Most of them pay no attention to security issues, but Zatan does." He scanned through the report. "Interesting. Even these few searches tell me something about him. This hacker probably created the Zatan persona four months ago. The problem is, even though he speaks English, I'm sure he spends more time on Russian sites."

"Like Yandex and mail.ru? I have those, too, although I do not speak the language. Marko requested it."

Niko scooted closer to her. "Marko thought of everything. Since I know Russian, we can do a search."

Vyper typed something into her computer. "I will show you how to search the databases." The TV on the wall turned black, ending the network news program. The image of a computer screen appeared on the right side of the TV. "Each side is set up as a remote display. Project your laptop to the left side."

Niko located the settings and selected it. Now his screen was projected on the left, with Vyper's on the right. Following her directions, Niko ran the Russian search tool. The same program appeared on Vyper's side of the TV, except everything was translated to English.

Her mouse pointer moved to an empty box. "Here's where you enter Zatan. I have no idea how to do that with Cyrillic letters."

He typed "Затан" and hit ENTER. A few seconds later, a report filled his screen—much more than the meager list of Google searches from the English database. It appeared to go back only four months, but it still represented a wealth of information about the mysterious hacker.

"I could spend days going through everything here." Niko scanned through the sections of the report. "We're still missing a lot. This guy must spend most of his time on the dark web—hacker stuff, black market ... well, you know. I don't suppose it shows up here."

"No dark websites."

"Okay, I think there's enough here to develop a detailed psychological profile on him. If I learn enough, I'll be able to con him into doing anything we want. Well, not quite *anything*—but I could get him to share information, maybe even trust your software."

"You mentioned profiles," said Vyper. "There are computer models that do the work for you." Her screen changed to a list of files. "The one on the top is supposed to be really effective. It was used to micro-target voters with political ads—our election, Brexit, some others."

Niko felt like he was drinking from a fire hose. "That model will create the psychological profile I need?"

"They call it psychographic. It is not my area of expertise. You understand people better than I do."

He couldn't believe the wealth of data and tools at his disposal. "I've got my work cut out for me, but you certainly made it easier."

"If you learn the names of associates, or if you discover any of his previous internet identities, you should search for them as well." Vyper started to rock. "We have to get to Sokolov. Stop him. Ruin him."

Niko took her hand. "We're going to get this guy. He's going to pay for Marko's death."

Vyper's eyes began to water.

"What's wrong? ... Are you okay?"

She wiped her eyes. "I miss Marko. Especially tonight."

"What did you and Marko do on Christmas Eve?"

"We played video games." She wiped away a tear and smiled. "I always won."

"You got video games? I'm pretty good. Know why I chose the name Niko?"

"Of course—*Grand Theft Auto*. You think you are good? You will learn why I am called Vyper."

Zatan
Chapter 13

Niko sat next to Vyper, studying his computer screen. "Here's a job I could do. They're looking for a programmer. It's contract work, all online. No need to go to an office. I don't think they'll report my income to the IRS, either."

"Why are you looking for employment?" Vyper set her laptop down. "Taking down Sokolov is a full-time job."

"I've been living in your home for nearly two months, eating your food, and spending money from Marko's bank card. It's not fair to you, and the bank card won't supply cash forever."

"I do not understand," said Vyper. "I told you, money is not a problem. I manage the cash Marko kept off the books. Most of it came from Sokolov. The bank card will not run out."

"You manage his money?" Niko walked to the kitchen. "That doesn't matter, I still need a job. I can't put a deposit down on an apartment using cash from a bank card." He grabbed a paper plate, bread, and lunch meat.

Vyper stood and turned to him. Her head moved slowly back and forth. "An apartment? Why leave?" She pressed her hand against her cheek. "We work well together."

"I don't want to impose any more than I already have. I've overstayed my welcome."

She took a step closer to him. "I want you to stay." Her hazel eyes began to water. "Please don't go."

Sadness and desire gripped Niko. He set his plate down and gently rested his hand on her shoulder, resisting the urge to embrace her. "I won't leave you. I—"

Vyper reached out and wrapped her arms around his waist. She pressed her head against his chest and squeezed him close. "I am glad."

For a second, surprise froze him in place. Then his hands met at the small of her back and he pulled her close. Her hair had a faint scent of coconuts. Her soft breasts pressed against him.

Niko stroked her hair and tucked a strand behind her ear. He pressed their hips together so she could feel his arousal.

Almost immediately, Vyper released her hold and stepped back, an awkward smile on her face. "I will have a sandwich, too."

Damn. I spooked her.

Niko moved to the kitchen table, blocking her view of the bulge in his pants.

Her eyes never left the plate while she made a sandwich.

"Are you sure you want me to stay?" asked Niko.

She looked at him and raised an eyebrow. "I thought we agreed. Did you change your mind?"

"No. I just thought ... uh ... we held each other ... I didn't mean—"

"We are friends. I needed a hug." She grabbed her plate and headed to the couch. "I want to see the news."

Niko sat next to her as the news anchor teased about an upcoming official briefing on the recent attacks at two government facilities. Then the show broke for a commercial.

He pointed to the TV. "That briefing's going to be about the action centers. I think the FBI ran out of leads after they found the dead Russians in the car crash. They can blame them for Marko's murder, but not the Cybercade attack."

Vyper flipped her laptop open. "Marko's killer and the driver—they shared an apartment. The FBI searched it, but they never told the public what they discovered."

"Look at the TV. They're showing what they found in the apartment. A drone, exactly like the ones that attacked the Action Center."

On the screen, an FBI agent stood behind a table used to display evidence from the search. Vyper stared at the dark coil next to the drone. "Is that an explosive?"

"That's the shaped I told you about. It blew a hole in the roof."

The television briefing continued. A government official requested northern Virginia residents to call if they saw a similar drone or explosive material. When a reporter asked for information on the poisoning of Marko and Gato, officials repeated the statement that toxicology results were not yet available.

Vyper tapped away at the keyboard. "An unnamed reliable source claims the police found digoxin in the apartment. It is made from digitalis."

"That should make it clear, even to the FBI—they killed Marko. The media says nothing about Russian involvement despite my Trotsky messages. Are they blind or stupid? How much evidence do they need?"

Vyper turned her screen toward Niko. "I just received another tracker report from FANTAZIJA.COM. This is the third one—all from Vladivostok. Does the name look familiar?"

He nodded. It was one of the top Eastern European hackers Niko had identified. Each of them had disappeared from sight around five months ago and appeared online later with a new name. Vyper had used her magic to correlate the old names to the new ones.

But Zatan wasn't on the list. He hadn't visited FANTAZIJA.COM, or perhaps he avoided being infected by the tracker. Nevertheless, Vyper had discovered his former computer identity, one Niko remembered from his youth. Back then, the man who had become Zatan used his computer skills to manage the books for Falcon—aka Sokolov.

A smile appeared on Vyper's face.

Niko knew why. "You cracked your way through more of the dark net, didn't you?"

She nodded. "This guy connected to FANTAZIJA using two of the Onion routers I already control. He also accessed two routers I had not seen before, so I infected them."

"Haven't you spread your software across the entire dark net yet?"

Vyper giggled. "It is on twenty-five percent of the Onion Network. I only have a partial view of the network traffic."

"You never cease to amaze me. No one else has penetrated it like you."

"You are wrong. The NSA has been doing this for much longer than I have. They monitor most of the traffic on the dark net."

"What?" Niko's pulse raced. "The government knows what we're doing? They know you're breaking into financial records? They know where we are?"

She shook her head. "You realize everything about security is risky. Nothing is one hundred percent safe. But we take precautions—encryption, false identities, private networks. We make it hard for NSA to break through our defenses, but they can find us if they really want to."

"I thought my secrets were safe behind the dark net, but now you tell me the NSA can see anything they like." Niko shook his head and went to the kitchen. "You thirsty?"

Her only response was the sound of tapping on the keyboard.

He selected a pale ale from the refrigerator and grabbed a glass. "Have you found Sokolov's money yet?" He set the glass next to the couch and took a seat.

"Making progress. I discovered a bank account tied to Sokolov's nephew. He is the owner and the only employee of a business called Altai Associates. For some reason, Russia's GRU pays Altai over two billion rubles each month."

Niko did a mental calculation. "That's thirty million dollars from Russian military intelligence. What does Altai do?"

"It is a service provider, but there is no mention of the type of service. Of course, it does not make sense for a one-man company to deliver any service worth that much money. It must be a shell company—used to launder or funnel funds secretly."

"Where does the money go?"

"I am still trying to figure that out."

"I hope NSA doesn't realize what you're doing." Niko turned to his laptop when it beeped. "Zatan just appeared online at his favorite dark web site—Runion."

"That is a dangerous site. Hackers and con artists lie in wait for newbies."

"Hackers and con artists? Like the two of us?"

Vyper smiled. "Which one are you?"

"Definitely the con artist." Niko projected the image of his laptop screen to the TV. "Zatan believes I'm a naïve newbie. The only reason he talks to me is because I know Prixster. You'll find our conversation interesting. We always meet up in the public chat room. They speak English there."

A message appeared on the screen:

Zatan666: u there anarch?

"He saw me come online. My handle is Anarch. I'll see what he wants."

Anarch13: u bet
Zatan666: private

"This must be important. I have to join him in our private chat room. We speak Russian, so I'll translate for you as we go."

Although Niko spoke fluent Russian, sometimes his grammar and word choices reflected his Ukrainian roots—even in text. Zatan didn't disguise his disdain for Ukrainians.

Vyper set her laptop aside. "What does he want?"

"Last time we chatted, I gave him your list of Onion router nodes near Sevastopol. He told me I was full of shit—these couldn't be real. Well, he checked it out, and now he's asking where I got the information."

Niko typed a response. "I told him I used Prixster's program to search for Onion routers."

When Zatan's response came back, Niko burst out laughing. "He said, 'Give me the fucking thing.' I'm going to tease him a bit. When I finally give it to him, I want his hungry anticipation to overcome his instinctive suspicions."

"Do not overplay it," said Vyper. "We need him to accept it. Once he does, my spyware will give me control of his computer, and he will never know."

"Let me show you how a con artist sets the hook. I'm going to tell him Prixster does not share with strangers." He typed it in.

The response came back immediately. "He says, 'Prixster doesn't have to know.' I'm going to play hard-to-get."

A few minutes later, Niko decided he had played with him enough. "That's it. I made him promise not to share it, show it, or say anything to anyone. Zatan agreed and I'm sending it to him now."

Vyper's face lit up. "You did it! We are a team. We will get Sokolov. I am so glad you decided to stay." She wrapped her arms around his neck and kissed him on the lips. Then she stood and walked to the kitchen.

Although the kiss lasted only a few seconds, the warmth of her body and scent of her hair lingered. As she walked away, he whispered under his breath, "I love you."

Weaponize
Chapter 14

Fresh from his shower, Niko slipped on his BVDs and a pair of cargo pants. He pulled a T-shirt over his head. He remembered the end of his dream last night. Vyper was playing a video game in the nude, then they made love.

One day...maybe.

Niko heard footsteps in the other room. No surprise, Vyper always got up early. Maybe she received a message from the spyware they planted on Zatan's computer. It should have responded by now. After all, Niko gave him the program two weeks ago.

He entered the kitchen. His heart warmed at the sight of Vyper. Her silky black hair draped over her green track suit, the zipper on her top resting low, showing cleavage. "You look beautiful this morning. Your outfit brings out the color of your eyes."

"You are sweet." She smiled and grabbed two cups. "I made coffee. You want some?"

"Sounds great." Niko settled in at the table and opened his laptop. "Anything from Zatan's computer yet?"

Vyper handed him a cup of coffee and sat in front of her computer. "Yes, I received the first communication early this morning. Extracting data from his system is a slow process, but this transmission included information about more Onion routers on the dark net."

"I thought you had full control of his computer. What's taking so long?"

"He knows security, which makes it more difficult. The program you gave Zatan was simply a beachhead. Its main job was to discover unprotected methods to communicate—and to do it without being detected. It sent a few documents. Once I study them, I will modify the spyware."

"Did the documents tell you anything of interest?"

"Give me a minute." She typed a few commands. "Zatan's computer is on a network in Vladivostok—at a major internet connection point near Eagle's Nest Hill. It seems he is less technical than you thought. His job is supervisory and financial."

"That's perfect." Niko opened his notes on Zatan. "Who did he supervise? What kind of financial stuff?"

"I am sending you what I received. There is a staff list, payroll, and financial spreadsheets. If we are lucky, he may have included bank account numbers. Perhaps some of the staff members will match the visitors to FANTAZIJA.COM."

Niko took a quick look at the documents. "I can't help you with this data. It isn't my strong suit." He glanced at his news feed. "And my Trotsky communications aren't working very well, either."

"What do you mean? The attacks were in the news for quite a while, and the police followed your leads."

"Yeah, but the investigation has stalled, and the attacks are seldom mentioned any more. The police and the media aren't treating this as a Russian attack. Their focus is on finding the missing conspirators, and they don't have any new clues."

Vyper took his hand. "How much more can you do? You are only one man."

"One man—that's it!" said Niko. "That's the problem. It's the old way of doing things. It may have worked for *Deep Throat* during Watergate, but modern communication doesn't work like that. Today everyone uses the internet—especially social media. It's time to weaponize Facebook."

"Like Russia has been doing with our elections?" She clicked away on the keyboard. "I've read about it. I understand the technology, but I do not understand what kind of messages to post."

"Leave it to me. First, we have to come up with a goal and a targeted marketing plan." Niko glanced through his Trotsky messages. "We need to convince the public that the Russians are bad, and they attacked the United States."

"Everyone already knows the Russians are bad."

"I wish you were right, but a lot of Americans don't seem to care about Russia—either way. We need people running around with their hair on fire, demonstrating against the Russians."

Vyper giggled. "Hair on fire? Why would anyone do that?"

"It doesn't matter, it's just an expression. I plan to engage the emotions of the public. Every time the word Russians is mentioned, I want everyone to think 'dangerous enemy'. I need to get them excited."

"How?"

"You gave me those psychographic models and all the Facebook and Google data. Now I have detailed information on the largest groups of like-minded people who are active on the internet. For example, there are those who believe the Russians threw our election, and there are others who believe a deep state is undermining the government. Some groups hate immigrants, others hate guns. There are people who believe in every tin-foil-hat conspiracy theory they see."

"Those people never agree on anything. Which groups do you plan to influence?"

"All of them." Niko smiled. "Those psychographic models reveal what their hot buttons are, what they already believe, what they *don't* believe, how they reach each other online ...

everything. I need to set up a few hundred identities—liberal, conservative, Christian, atheist—and become a member of each group. I can play on their hot buttons to gain trust, then build suspicions against Russia."

"I may be able to help. I have a few thousand identities online, and I have bots that can control them as a group. You can pretend to be thousands of people. You decide on the messages and the targets, and I will control them like sock puppets."

"Thousands of sock puppets? You can control that many? They'd look like a grass roots movement."

"Sure, let me show you." As soon as Vyper typed in a command, a warbling sound from her laptop interrupted them. She pounded her fingers on the keyboard in rapid bursts, glared at the laptop, and typed some more.

Niko peeked at the screen but couldn't make sense of what she was doing. When she finally stopped, he shook his head. "What happened?"

She looked up from the keyboard. "Someone was on an Onion router I just used—a hacker. It accessed the routing tables. I had to stop it and delete all evidence of my communication. Then I scrambled the system."

"You crashed it?"

"Actually, I bricked it. That router will not come back online any time soon."

Niko laughed. "I just thought about the poor guy who owns the computer you killed. He probably installed TOR software to pirate some music. I'll bet he doesn't even realize he's on the dark net. Then, unknown to him, two hackers sneak inside his computer and start a fight."

"If he did not want to pirate music, he would not get caught up in this."

"You're right, but I picture him sitting in his bedroom, playing a game, when the computer suddenly shuts down. When he tries to start it up, it just lays there like a brick."

"I am being cautious. Perhaps it is only a coincidence, but it makes me worry when I see a hacker rummaging through a router I am using."

"You're the expert." Niko scooted closer to her. "You were about to show me those online identities I can use."

Vyper typed a command, and the warbling sound interrupted them once more. "Not a coincidence," she said, as she bricked another router. "Someone is searching through the dark net, and they bumped into me twice."

"What can we do? Would it help to sign onto a different private network?"

"Yes. The person who is searching may be looking for Onion routers near the Los Angeles network I have been using. We should switch to Atlanta or Chicago. Better yet, use a different private network each time we go online."

Niko rested his hand on hers. "If you hadn't stopped them, could they have located you? Identified you?"

"It is possible. Depends upon who it is."

"Who could do this?"

"This is beyond most hackers. It was probably someone working for a government."

"Like Russia?"

Vyper's smile faded. "Yes. I believe Sokolov is searching for me."

"He doesn't even know who you are. Why do you think he's looking for you?"

"Last night, a system administrator at the National Bank of Cyprus died. He slashed both his wrists."

"We stole Sokolov's money from that bank."

Vyper nodded. "Two days before you stole it, I broke into the bank's system and retrieved the passwords to his accounts. They were encrypted, but not difficult to decode."

"You believe Sokolov sent someone to interrogate him?"

"It is possible. They may have thought he was in on it. If not, maybe they figured he knew something. I plan to search for employees of the Cayman banks and some of the other banks we used to move the money. Perhaps some of them suffered a similar fate."

"It might be a coincidence," said Niko. "It's only one suicide."

"It is not just one. I have been searching for hackers from my past—like we did with your past. I discovered that one of the better programmers from my Prixster days was a single woman in Boston. I learned her name and address."

"What happened to her?"

"She jumped from the balcony of her apartment last week— nineteen stories up."

"Wow. That takes some determination ... it could be another coincidence."

Vyper shook her head. "The police found her pet, a small Pekinese, dead in her apartment—neck broken. Someone must have tried to question her."

"Did you ever communicate with her as Prixster?"

"All the time. We were celebrities of a sort. Other hackers followed our chat room conversations. Our online relationship was well known."

"Prixster's been 'dead' for a couple years. It doesn't make sense for anyone to search for you." Niko took the empty cups to the sink. "Unless they had reason to believe you were alive— something I recently told Zatan."

Vyper walked to the living room and sat on the couch.

Niko followed. Normally, he would have taken a seat on the far end, hugging the arm rest, but today he decided to sit closer—just a foot or two closer. "You think Sokolov's trying to follow the money to you, and Zatan's trying to find Prixster."

She looked up from the computer, her hazel eyes locked onto his. "We are pretty sure Zatan works for Sokolov. They may have concluded I am the same person." Her hand started to flap. "If they find me, you will be in danger, too."

Niko leaned closer. "I love you." He reached out and held her head in both hands. "We'll stop them. I won't let anything happen to you."

Vyper's flapping stopped. She gave a weak smile then wrapped her arms around his waist.

He pulled her close and pressed his lips against hers. Sensing no reaction, he nibbled her lips with his, and teased them with his tongue.

Her eyes closed, and her mouth opened a bit, enough for Niko to reach the tip of her tongue. That must have flipped a magical switch. Her mouth opened wide, eagerly taking in my tongue and alternately reaching out with hers.

He wrapped one arm around her back, leaving the other free to settle on her breast. Even through the velour top, her breast was firm. Vyper's back arched when he caressed her nipple. She sank lower into the couch. Encouraged, he pulled on the zipper and slid it lower to expose more flesh.

Niko moved his mouth to her neck and ear, kissing and nibbling. He moved her top, exposing more skin. His thumb touched her nipple. She reached up, grasped his hair, and moaned.

He ravaged her breast with his mouth, lips, and tongue. One hand reached for the other breast, while his other hand reached down for her track suit slacks, where Vyper's hand was waiting.

He tugged lightly at the waistband, but she held firm. He tugged once again.

She sat up. "I am sorry. I cannot do this."

Niko released her. "Did I do something wrong?"

She zipped up her top. "No. I wanted to do this ... I thought I could ... but I am afraid."

"I love you, Vyper. I'd never hurt you. Can we talk about it?"

"I am not sure how to talk about it."

"You're afraid." Niko was sure he knew why. "Are you a virgin?"

Her eyes looked off into the distance. "No."

That wasn't the answer he expected. "Were you ever in love?"

Vyper's eyes met his. "My feelings for you are ... stronger ... than I have ever felt before. Maybe that is love."

He wanted to make love to her, but he'd have to be patient. "When you first had sex ... did you ... have strong feelings for the man?"

"No." Her hand began to flap. "I never wanted sex from any of those men."

Anger filled Niko's mind as he pictured a man—*more than one man*—forcing themselves on her. He rested his hand on hers. "Did someone rape you?"

Vyper's head rocked back and forth with no sign of stopping.

Niko knew he had to leave her alone until she snapped out of it, even though every instinct told him to take her into his arms. He waited silently but remained at her side.

When she stopped rocking, she placed her hand on his thigh. "You are very good to me ... but I will not talk about those men. I refuse to think about them."

He squeezed her arm. "I won't ask about them again. But I have a different question."

She raised an eyebrow but remained quiet.

"Someday, I would like us to have a physical relationship. How about you?"

Vyper glanced at the floor. "I want to ... but not today."

Niko gave her shoulder a playful shove. "That means we have something to look forward to."

Sock Puppets
Chapter 15

Washington, DC

Niko held Vyper's hand while they made their way toward the Capitol dome three blocks away. It stood proudly above the crowd on this beautiful March morning. A month had passed since Vyper's sock puppets began to spread anti-Russian propaganda, and it appeared this demonstration was a direct result.

The event was scheduled for 1:00, but thousands of protestors had already arrived—mostly young, more women than men, some with children.

Vyper slowed her pace and came to a stop. "Are you close enough to see what you want?"

Niko turned around. "I promised we'd walk along the edge of the crowd, and that's exactly what we'll do."

He led her north, maintaining their distance from the throng of people, many of them waving hand-painted signs. The messages were anti-Russian: "Evil Empire," "Beer not Vodka," and "Make Russia Pay."

"Impressive," said Vyper. "A few weeks ago, nobody was upset about the Russians. Now they are angry." She winked. "I never thought anyone would pay attention to your messages."

"I wasn't sure it would work either. It's amazing how easily people can be led when thousands of sock puppets keep pushing a common message. If the demonstrations in the other cities are half this size, we can call it a success."

A man nearby held up a sign that read, "Freeze their money."

Niko waved his arm in the direction of the sign. "I'm going to talk to him. Do you want to come with me?"

Vyper nodded and wrapped her arm around his as they walked over to the man.

"Excuse me," said Niko. "We're visitors here. What's with the crowd? ... the signs?"

"It's the Russians." The man set down his sign. "Embassy's full of KGB spies and killers. We gotta kick 'em out of the country. Freeze their money."

Niko smiled. "Thank you." He looked at Vyper. "Sweetheart, this is the demonstration we read about in the news."

After they walked away, Vyper whispered, "He said the KGB, but—"

"I know. KGB, GRU ... most Americans don't know the difference. It doesn't matter. He considers them killers, and that's what's important."

Niko pulled Vyper closer to the heart of the crowd where some of the demonstrators screamed wildly while others cheered them on. Organized groups chanted their messages: "Damn senators are paid off by the Russians," "They bought the damn election," and "What will they blow up next?—the White House?"

Three burly young men carrying red plastic cups approached, singing, "One bourbon, one scotch, and one beer." They shoved demonstrators out of their way. Some tried to flee, others stood their ground, trying to fight back, but the drunken trio kept pushing closer.

Niko tried to avoid the drunks, but the crush of people blocked his escape. The crowd pulled Vyper away. Her hand slipped from his fingers. Niko pushed and reached, touching but not grasping her outstretched hand.

Someone shoved him from behind, and he turned to see the tallest drunk push a woman aside. When the man began to take another step, Niko kicked the raised leg aside. He pushed hard on the drunk's chest, knocking him into his friends and spilling his drink.

The ebb and flow of the human wave pushed Niko away from the drunk. He searched for Vyper, spotting her a few yards ahead. A stroke of luck opened a small gap in the crowd, and Niko pressed through it.

Barely five feet away, Vyper appeared, panic in her eyes, reaching out. A surge of people pushed them together. Niko grabbed her arm and pulled her nearer. Another gap appeared, and he pulled her through.

They escaped the knot of people, held hands, and ran toward an open area in the grass. When it was safe, they stopped, and she hugged him tightly.

She didn't move—just squeezed him tighter—shaking and rocking.

Niko had wanted to see the demonstration up close, but he got more than he bargained for. He stroked Vyper's hair. "You're safe now. Let's get the hell outta here."

She released him. Her eyes were wet with tears. "I love you."

Niko kissed her. "I love you, too." They headed toward the parking garage.

When they reached the car, Vyper sat silently in the passenger seat. Niko got behind the wheel and headed south to the interstate. He glanced at her. "Are you okay? Did the crowd—"

She shook her head. "It was the big man. One of my fathers looked like him."

"Are you talking about one of the foster families you lived with?"

She nodded. "Each family had a father. Some were nice. This one was not."

Niko gripped the wheel tighter and almost missed his exit north. "You don't have to talk about it unless you want to."

"I was a virgin." Her hands flapped. "He said no one would believe a retard ... I never told anyone."

The car drifted onto the shoulder, and Niko steered it back onto the road. His anger focused on the face of the tall drunk at the demonstration—same face as her rapist.

This was a fragile moment. He fought to remain calm. "Couldn't you tell his wife? Or someone from social services?"

"He was right. They would not believe me"

"Your foster father was a monster. Most men are kind. I wish I could hold you and make you feel better." He took the exit north.

Her flapping started again but stopped when she placed her hands in her lap. "I used to wear baggy sweat suits, but it did not seem to help. He never gave up. Some of the other families had fathers like him ... and brothers. I just let them. No one would believe the retard."

Sonofabitch!

A horn blasted at him from the left. He jerked back into his lane. Niko squeezed her hand. "Those men were *wrong*! They should pay for what they did. You can speak up now, people will believe you."

"No! ... I want to forget them." She grabbed her laptop from the back seat and opened it. "I have more important things to think about—like Sokolov."

Niko wanted revenge, but she wanted to forget the men, so he'd try to put them out of his mind. Now he understood her fear of sex. He'd have to suppress his anger. Be patient.

Vyper tapped on her keyboard, then abruptly stopped. "I broke through Cybercade's firewall. They are not monitoring county services anymore. Apparently, the Russians moved on to another target. They are going after oil pipelines and refineries in Texas and Louisiana. Nothing active yet, just probing."

The sign for Route 7 was up ahead. Niko moved into the right lane. "That's alarming, but it's Cybercade's problem. We're after Sokolov."

"The hackers accessing the oil systems are coming through the dark net, using the same routes as Zatan's team in Vladivostok."

Niko turned into Vyper's driveway and raised the garage door. "Hmm ... another connection between Zatan and Sokolov. No doubt in my mind, they work together." He pulled in and closed the door.

Vyper went inside and headed directly for the kitchen. "You hungry? I'll make sandwiches."

"Starved. We should have stopped for lunch." He walked to the sink. "Want some water?"

She nodded. "I have been studying Zatan's spreadsheets. I think I figured out what is going on, but I need to look up some accounts. There might be more information on suspicious activity reports."

"What did you find?"

Vyper handed him a sandwich and sat down. "You have to wait. I will check it out after I take a shower."

"Would you like some company in the shower?" Niko grinned. "It saves water, you know."

"You are naughty. You can shower in the guest bathroom like you always do."

"Can't blame a guy for trying."

A shy smile was her only response.

Vyper had loosened up over the past few weeks. They loved to "make out," and she wasn't shy with her body around him. But Niko's naked body—a man's body—was off limits. She certainly had reason to fear men, and she always demanded he keep his pants on. Even though they kidded each other about it, she was dead serious.

After lunch, Niko took a shower. Then he put on a pair of gym shorts and a T-shirt before heading to the living room to join Vyper on the couch.

She adjusted the top of her bathrobe. "I do not want to distract you. I think we hit the jackpot with Sokolov."

"I love being distracted by you." Niko scooted closer and looked at the computer screen. "What did you learn about our favorite Russian?"

"According to Zatan's financial spreadsheets, he receives 650 million rubles a month from Altai Associates—the one owned by Sokolov's nephew."

"That's about ten million dollars a month. Sokolov receives thirty million from GRU."

"Right." Vyper pointed to a number on the screen. "This ten million comes out of the thirty that goes to Sokolov."

"Okay. I must be missing something. Sokolov spends one third of his GRU money on Zatan's team. That's a lot, but it could be legitimate."

"Look at this." Vyper's finger moved to another spot. "Zatan pays sixty-five million rubles each month to this account. The owner is Sokolov's nephew—the same nephew who owns the Altai account."

"Hmm ... smells fishy. The mysterious nephew is a front man for the GRU. Then Zatan sends this same nephew a ten percent cut. He's skimming money. Cheating his own government."

Vyper nodded. "I told you I hit the jackpot. If we can prove this, the Russian government will be angry with him."

Niko laughed. "This isn't a court of law. We have sock puppets. If our puppets post it, many people will believe it. I'm going to post the story as a fact and send it to my pro-Russia and pro-Ukraine followers. If they buy it, Sokolov could be in trouble. If not, we lose nothing."

After Niko drafted and refined the messages, Vyper configured her sock puppets, each one falsely identified as a real Russian or Ukrainian. After a thousand of them posted their messages, she directed a thousand more to post responses.

Before long, real Russian-speaking followers reacted, and arguments followed. The internet lit up, and the hashtag *#SkimmingScandal* topped the trending list.

Vyper threw her arms around Niko and kissed him. "We did it. We got him. All we have to do is wait."

"We should celebrate." He nuzzled her neck. "I have an idea."

She softly pushed him away. "I know your idea, but right now I want to play video games."

Niko went to the game console and brought the controls to Vyper. As she started it up, he walked to the back of the couch and kissed her neck.

She squirmed while clicking on the controller. "What are you doing?"

"I have a challenge for you. I'll bet you can't maintain your concentration while I kiss you."

"How silly. If anyone can concentrate, it is me."

"You're on." Niko opened the front of her robe and cupped her breasts while he nuzzled her neck.

"No fair." Vyper kept playing. "You said kissing."

He released her breasts and walked around, kneeling next to her so she could still follow the game on the TV. "You're right.

I said kissing ... well, fondling, too." He opened her robe, exposing her entire body, then he removed his shirt.

Vyper squeezed her legs together, but she continued playing. "Only kissing and fondling. Nothing more."

"I know. I'll keep my pants on." Niko's lips and hands roamed all over her body, teasing and squeezing.

She continued to play. Her hips moved rhythmically, her legs relaxed, and she arched her back. Then the game controller slipped from her hands.

Niko did everything possible to please her while keeping his pants on—and it was working. Her inhibitions washed away.

Vyper's hands gripped his head and she pulled him gently on top of her. "I want to make love." She reached down to the waistband of his shorts. "Take them off. Make love to me."

Niko rolled over and removed a condom from his pocket before slipping off his pants.

She grabbed the condom and tossed it on the floor. "I use birth control."

The woman was a mystery, but now was not the time for questions. He turned back and reached for her breast.

Vyper grabbed his butt. "I want you ... *now.*"

He began slowly, treating her like a virgin—and in a way she was. She responded to his moves and he responded to hers. They made love with abandon until she collapsed with a smile.

Her arms held him tightly for a long time. "This was even better than I imagined." She kissed him. "You have been so good to me. I hope it was worth the wait."

Niko raised himself on his elbows. "I would do anything for you."

A wicked smile appeared on Vyper's face. "It is your turn to play video games. Let me see if I can distract you. And you may *not* put on your pants."

Sokolov
Chapter 16

Vyper's Home—Sterling, Virginia

Even though Sokolov went into hiding after the successful internet campaign against him, Niko's nights continued to be plagued by frightening dreams from his life in Sevastopol, when he was still known as Adam.

***

On the bed next to Adam was a valise of collection money for Falcon. Beside it was a suitcase, packed and ready to go. Time to leave this dangerous life behind.

But first, he couldn't resist playing his favorite video game. Every time he played *Grand Theft Auto,* he became Niko Bellic—a hardened war veteran willing to do anything to make a buck. Right now, 'Niko' was running from the police. He turned the corner and—*shit*—one of them pointed a gun at him and pulled the trigger.

The game ended with a familiar metallic sound, followed by a groan and the word WASTED plastered across the screen. He could start another game, but not tonight. This would be his last for a long time.

Adam stood up, dropped the game controller on the bed, and opened the valise. It was a lot of money, and Falcon would never get his hands on it.

He started with the largest bills, stuffing them into pockets on the inside lining of his jacket. More went into his underwear, his socks—every place he could hide it. He checked himself in the mirror to see if any suspicious bulges appeared. Satisfied, he abandoned the remaining small bills, grabbed his suitcase, and left for the docks.

Straight ahead was the cargo ship Adam was looking for. The *Bolshoi* was headed to Odessa where he'd buy a fake passport. From there, he'd find a ship to Istanbul and eventually to America.

Adam walked up to a sailor who was barking orders to others. "You hiring?"

The man looked Adam up and down, then nodded. "You'll do. What's your name?"

Adam responded with the first name that came to mind. "Niko. The name's Niko."

"You can start right away." He yelled to a sailor on the upper deck of the ship. "New man coming up." Then he spoke to Niko and pointed. "Top of the ladder. We'll do the paperwork later."

The ladder, actually a steep metal stairway, was firmly attached to the ship. Niko climbed to the top.

The deck boss's on-the-job training was delivered with one terse command. "Do what they're doing."

Niko got right to work, moving barrels off pallets and muscling them down a narrow ladder, where he placed them next to dozens of other barrels. It seemed like the job would never end.

When he returned for more barrels, his boss yelled out. "Niko, the third mate wants to see you." He pointed toward the bow. "Take the forward ladder—two decks down."

Niko descended one deck and half of the next. Then he stopped abruptly.

I'm a dead man.

On the deck below was Falcon, an evil grin on his face. Next to him stood a large man, obviously an enforcer. Niko turned to climb back up, but another man blocked his way. There was no escape.

"Where do you think you're going?" asked Falcon, leaning on a metal table, fingering the handle of a meat cleaver.

Niko's heart raced. He felt the bile rise in his throat, but held back, trying not to puke. Nothing he could say would help, so he remained silent.

Falcon spoke to the man behind Niko. "Get him down here."

Niko quickly scrambled to the lower deck, trying to avoid being pushed off the ladder. He stopped in front of Falcon.

The evil man's black eyes never blinked. "You owe me a lot of money." He tilted his head briefly toward each of his enforcers. "Strip him."

One man pulled Niko's jacket from behind, pinning his arms against his body. The man in front removed Niko's shoes and socks, spilling cash on the deck. As the rest of his clothes came off, more cash appeared.

Falcon picked up the jacket and removed more money. "Tie him to the ladder. Tie his arms to the rails." He grabbed a meat cleaver from the table. "You know what happens to people who steal from me."

***

Niko sat straight up in bed, sweat soaked the sheets. "My hands!"

Falcon had disappeared. Vyper's hand was on Niko's shoulder. He reached out and hugged her naked body.

"You are shaking," she said. "Did you have the same dream?"

Niko's breathing calmed, and he released her. He nodded. "Sokolov caught me stealing. He threatened to chop off my hands."

"Lie down and relax." Vyper ran her fingers through his hair. "You let the death of Sokolov's nephew affect you. That happened a week ago. He is the one whose hands are missing."

"True. The Russians killed him, and we're the ones who exposed his role in the skimming scheme. He wasn't even in Russia. They tracked him down to Odessa. They took his hands! It was a message to people who steal Russian money—like we did."

Vyper kissed his cheek. "It is almost morning and I am awake. I will fix breakfast."

"We don't have to get up immediately." Niko wrapped his arms around her neck. "I'm not hungry yet ... not for breakfast."

***

When they arrived home in the evening, Niko followed Vyper into the bedroom they now shared. "You look amazing in that dress. And I wasn't the only one who noticed. Everyone in the restaurant checked you out."

"They were staring at my breasts." Vyper walked to the dresser. She pulled out a halter top and shorts. "Fancy clothes are uncomfortable. And I do not like strange men staring at me."

"All the women show a bit of cleavage." Niko picked out a T-shirt and cargo pants. "Did you enjoy the restaurant? Would you like to go back sometime?"

"I prefer eating here. The chef does not cook meat the way I like it." She removed her dress and held it in front of her. "It is pretty, but uncomfortable."

"Okay, you win." Niko changed his clothes. "I won't drag you out to dinner again ... at least not for a while."

Vyper got dressed and went to the couch. "Come on. We have work to do."

He joined her. "Sokolov's going to have a hard time finding you. Ever since his nephew was killed, he's been hiding. And I don't blame him."

"We cannot let up on Sokolov's team until they arrest him and put him away." Vyper tapped a few keys on her laptop. "It looks like Zatan's team is stealing data from pipeline and refinery systems, so someone must be paying them. I want to find out who it is."

Niko searched through news and online postings. He found a positive article about Sokolov, published by a Russian newspaper a few hours ago. The story made the billionaire sound like the savior of Chechnya. As the CEO of Rusmir, he had built a broadband internet service in Grozny, and extended it into the more rural areas of the country.

To counter this, Niko wrote an expose on Sokolov, starting with his time as a crime boss in Sevastopol. He added the story of the billionaire's role in money laundering and skimming. Once he was satisfied, he pushed the story using Vyper's sock puppets.

As people responded to his expose, Niko engaged more sock puppets to express outrage and to reinforce the negatives.

When he searched for more news, he discovered something that stopped him cold. He raised his voice. "Vyper! This is it! The news we've been waiting for!"

"What?"

"Sokolov and his wife were killed. Found a couple hours ago in a cheap hostel in Kiev." Exposing this powerful man had been their only focus for four months. Putting him away was their goal. Now the Russians found him—murdered him—his wife, too. Niko wanted to celebrate, yet he felt bad about the wife's death.

Vyper tapped away on her keyboard. "The official report says they were killed in their room by a team of violent criminals. Shot in the head. His hands were cut off—missing. The place was trashed. Nothing valuable was found in the room."

They stared at each other in silence until Niko finally spoke. "We have no reason to feel guilty. We probably saved lives."

She smiled. "I want to celebrate with video games. We can test your concentration."

***

Whoop ... Whoop ... Whoop

Niko bolted upright in the bed at the sound of an alert.

Lying next to him, Vyper grabbed her cell phone and the whooping stopped. "Armed men. Three in my driveway. There could be more."

Niko caught a glimpse of her phone—green video with dark trees, plus three light green figures moving slowly. Then the night light under the bathroom door went out.

"They killed power." Vyper sat on the edge of the bed. "We are on batteries now. Maybe thirty minutes before the generator starts up." She tapped on her phone. "This will encrypt all data, erase temp files, and shut down the computers. Whoever it is, they will get nothing."

Niko took her by the arm. "We don't have thirty minutes. They'll be breaking down the door in a minute or two. We could hide, but they're certain to find us." He snatched his Glock from the dresser by the bed and checked the magazine.

"No!" Vyper grabbed his wrist. "You cannot fight them all. They will shoot us both."

A loud bang came from the front of the house—then a second one.

Part II: Game Changer

Mr. Bodnar
Chapter 17

Niko jumped out of bed, Glock aimed at the unlocked door, waiting for the inevitable. Armed men were inside the house. Heavy footsteps—lots of them. He jerked his head toward Vyper. "Move away from me!"

"No shooting! We will die!" She slipped out of her side of the bed and grabbed a bathrobe.

A commanding voice somewhere in the house shouted, "Bedroom. Two targets." Bright lights moved back and forth under the door.

English! Police?

Niko set his gun on the dresser. He wasn't going to shoot it out with Americans—especially if they might be cops.

The door swung inward, hitting the wall with a thud. Two strong lights, one above the other, blinded him.

"Hands up!" yelled a commanding voice, as the lights separated to opposite sides of the room.

Niko raised his arms as a third light appeared. At least three different voices yelled out—some demanding cooperation, others giving status. He couldn't keep track of everything they said.

They weren't Russian, and Niko was alive, but he was still in danger. He didn't know who they were, or why they broke into the house.

His eyes adjusted to the light and he spotted three armed men in dark, SWAT-style clothing, wearing helmets with the visors raised. One man aimed an assault rifle at him. Another held his aim on Vyper, who stood shaking in her robe at the opposite side of the bed, hands above her head.

The third man tossed the mattress up against the wall and lifted the box spring. Then he announced, "Clear."

Unseen men throughout the house barked orders and responses to each other. Niko heard someone say, "Check in there. Some kind of equipment running."

The nightlight came on.

Power's back.

One gunman flipped on the overhead bedroom light, revealing a fourth man in SWAT gear entering the bathroom. His backpack displayed FBI in large letters.

Whoa!

Two men stood at the far corners of the room training their rifles on Niko and Vyper. The man who tossed the mattress seemed to be the team leader. He walked up to Niko. "What's your name?"

A gust of air reminded Niko he was naked. Then he realized what would happen if he told the FBI his real name. Adam Zima "died" in the fire at Marko's action center. There was also the electronic theft of Sokolov's money. He decided to remain silent.

The man turned to Vyper. "What's your name?"

She lowered her arms and flapped her hands.

The SWAT leader moved closer to Vyper, his face only inches away from hers. "Get those hands in the air, NOW!"

She flapped harder, and her head rocked back and forth.

"Stop!" yelled Niko. "She's autistic. She's having a meltdown."

The man froze for a moment, then raised his voice loud enough to be heard outside the room. "Get Jackson in here."

Several voices called out the name "Jackson" before a woman in SWAT gear entered.

The team leader hitched his thumb toward Vyper. "This one may be autistic. Process her in another room once it's cleared."

Vyper's rhythmic movements continued as the woman led her away. An agent with a rifle followed closely behind.

Niko let out a breath. This could have ended badly, but Jackson seemed to know what she was doing. Then a glance at the man aiming a rifle in his direction brought Niko back to reality—he might never see Vyper again.

The leader turned his attention to Niko. "I'm going to ask you one more time. Tell me your name."

Niko shook his head. "I don't have to talk. I want a lawyer."

"We'll learn who you are soon enough. The court will assign you a lawyer if you can't afford one." The SWAT leader pulled out handcuffs. "Turn around."

"Can I put some clothes on? It's chilly outside."

The man nodded and clipped the cuffs back on his belt. He inspected the clothing that Niko selected before allowing him to get dressed.

"Turn around. Place your hands behind your back."

Niko did as instructed. "Am I under arrest? What for?"

"We're arresting you on suspicion of murder and conspiracy."

"Murder?" *Holy shit!*

The agent snapped cuffs on Niko's wrists and recited the Miranda rights.

Niko had a million questions. *Murder who? Conspire with who?* He should wait for a lawyer. The FBI agent said the court would appoint one—if he couldn't afford it. The only way he'd be able to pay for a lawyer was to use Marko's money, but he couldn't let anyone know where it came from.

While being led away, he saw half a dozen people in assault gear searching the house. Niko asked the FBI agent, "Do you have a search warrant?"

"Of course. Are you the homeowner?"

Niko ignored the question and walked outside to the waiting vehicle.

***

At the DC Detention Center, Niko had refused to give his name, so the booking clerk designated him as John Doe. They took his mug shot, confiscated his clothing, gave him an orange jump suit, and fingerprinted him. It wouldn't be long before they found out who he was.

Now Niko sat on a thin mattress which covered a hard metal bed facing a toilet with a sink attached. A tray with the uneaten portion of his breakfast was on the floor. He wanted to know how Vyper was coping with everything. Did they put her in a cell like this? Did they charge her with murder?

Originally, Niko thought he'd been arrested for stealing Sokolov's money, or maybe for unauthorized access to a computer. But murder? Was this a mistake? Unrelated to the Russians? Not likely. The smartest thing to do was remain silent until he learned what he was accused of doing. He'd find out in a few hours when he appeared before the judge.

A uniformed officer stopped outside his cell. "Stand against the far wall."

When Niko complied, the cop entered, handcuffed him, and led him out of the cell block and down a long corridor. Near the end of the hall, he opened a door and led Niko inside, sitting him down in a folding chair. He attached the cuffs to a rail on the only table in the room.

Niko sat there alone, waiting for the inevitable interrogation. Vyper was probably going through the same thing. No telling how she would react to the loss of control—the handcuffs.

Waiting gave him plenty of time to think—Russians, murder charges, and jail. But mostly he thought of Vyper.

When the door opened, a tall man in a dark suit carrying a briefcase walked in. He stopped short when his eyes settled on the cuffs. He shouted a command loud enough to be heard outside the cell. "Remove my client's handcuffs."

Client? Niko didn't have a lawyer. "Who—"

The man held a finger to his lips, signaling silence, then turned around and raised his voice. "Are you deaf? I said remove these handcuffs—*now!*"

Niko sat silently as the uniformed officer rushed in, removed his cuffs, and left the room.

The lawyer followed him outside the door briefly and looked both ways. When he returned, he closed the door and walked back to Niko, his hand extended. "I come from Provo."

Provo? That's half of the passcode from Marko. Niko cautiously shook his hand. "Who are you?"

"I am The Pythia." He sat down. "But you may call me Mister Bodnar."

That was the proper response. Niko had to trust him. "Who sent you? How'd you know I was here?"

Bodnar smiled. "Lydia Harris sent me. I'm her lawyer."

Vyper! "How's she doing? Where is she?"

"She's doing fine. They're holding her in a cell like yours."

"Is she really okay? I mean ... she was upset last night. And she doesn't like—"

Bodnar held up his hand. "I've known Lydia for a few years, and I'm aware of her limitations. She told me she's being treated well. Her cell is small, but they never restrain her."

"That's great, but why did they arrest her?"

The lawyer set his briefcase on the table and opened it. "Before we discuss anything further, we need to settle something. Lydia would like me to represent you ... if that's your wish."

"Um ... yeah, but ... I can't afford a lawyer."

"No need to pay me a thing." Bodnar pulled out a small packet of papers. "I've been on retainer to Marko Kozel for years. His estate will pay for everything." He set the papers on the table facing Niko. "This is a standard agreement with an additional authorization for joint defense with Lydia. I will be able to share information with each of you about your cases. You can read the document, or I can explain it to you. If you're satisfied, sign at the bottom of the final page."

On the top of the first page was the name Ivan Bodnar, Attorney at Law. Niko glanced through the verbiage, written in legalese. He skipped to the last page where his signature was required. Under the line, someone had typed the name Adam Zima.

"Did Vyper tell you my name?"

Bodnar nodded. "Lydia said you prefer to be called Niko, but all legal papers reference Zima. I know you haven't revealed your name to the FBI, but they figured it out—I presume from fingerprints. Are you aware you were declared legally dead?"

Niko ignored the question and signed the paper. "Now can you tell me why they arrested Vyper?"

"She's been charged with murder and conspiracy—same as you. You'll receive the formal charges when you appear in court this afternoon. Lydia, AKA Vyper, is scheduled to appear later in the day."

"They told me what I was charged with, and it makes no sense. But Vyper? How can anyone think we're murderers? Who do they think we killed?"

The lawyer took the signed paper and placed it in his briefcase. "I don't know. I could only speculate. The formal charges will be more detailed." He stood up. "See you in court. Is there anything you want me to tell Lydia?"

Niko stood to shake Bodnar's hand. "Tell her I love her."

When the lawyer left, a guard returned Niko to his cell, where he sat alone with his thoughts for hours before he was taken to see Mister Bodnar again, and then the judge.

Niko stood in court wearing an orange prisoner jump suit, Bodnar at his side. His hands were cuffed in front of him.

The judge looked like someone's grandfather sitting at the bench. He spoke with authority. "State your name."

Since the court already knew the answer, Niko responded, "Adam Zima."

The judge began to read the formal charges. It sounded like legal mumbo jumbo. Then he got to the point, "... Adam Zima provided material support and resources to Alexei Sokolov ..."

No! I didn't help Sokolov.

The reading continued, "... the murder of Marko Kozel and the attacks on the Kozel and Cybercade action centers ..."

Niko couldn't believe what he heard. They got it all wrong. Why did they think he did it? It was the Russians!

Then the judge said something that made Niko's heart stop. "... conspired with Lydia Harris ..."

The rest of the reading went by in a blur. All he could think of was Vyper.

Gotta be a way to set her free.

Bodnar whispered into Niko's ear. "Time to enter your plea."

The judge glared down from the bench. "Do I have your attention now?"

"Yes, Your Honor."

"How do you plead?"

"Not guilty, Your Honor."

Evidence
Chapter 18

Sterling, Virginia

Niko had given up hope that he and Vyper would be freed any time soon. But Mr. Bodnar was a miracle worker. He made the case that the evidence was circumstantial, and he posted bond for both of them once they agreed to home confinement and electronic monitoring.

After he had been fitted with an ankle bracelet, Niko was directed to go immediately to his home of record, which he listed as Vyper's house.

When he arrived, he paid the Uber driver and walked up to the door. Someone must have replaced the old door after the FBI smashed it in last night. He pressed the bell and waited.

The door opened. It was Vyper, beautiful as ever, a broad smile on her face. She opened her arms wide.

Niko stepped into her embrace, buried his face in her hair, and inhaled her intoxicating scent. He whispered in Vyper's ear, "I love you so much. I was afraid I'd never see you again."

She tightened her grip. "I was afraid, too. We cannot let them separate us again."

Niko kicked the door behind him, shutting it with a bang. He looked into her eyes and brushed a tear from her cheek. Her lips were inviting, and he met them with his own, as their tongues wrestled playfully.

His leg bumped something hard near her foot, and he spotted the ankle bracelet. "I see they're monitoring you, too." He held out his own leg for her to see. "House arrest is better than jail."

Vyper stepped back and held a finger to her lips, then pointed to her ankle. "Mister Bodnar is wonderful. He replaced the front door and bought us computers and phones." She waved her arm toward the open door to the computer room. "The FBI took everything."

It had not occurred to Niko that these monitors could also be listening devices. On the dining room table lay a pad of paper and two pens. Next to the table was a shredder. He waved toward the table. "Bodnar should be here soon."

She took a seat, grabbed a pen, and wrote a short message on a piece of paper:

> Mr. Bodnar swept the house—no bugs—except ankle bracelets
>
> The internet is turned off—police will come here tomorrow and turn it on

Niko took the other pen and wrote on the same pad:

> Did you tell the FBI anything?

Vyper scribbled a response:

> No—but I told Mr. Bodnar everything—you can trust him
>
> I want to tell the truth—it was Russians—not us

Niko shook his head:

> Let's talk to our lawyer first—we stole money— hacked computers
>
> FBI may not believe us—we could go to jail— prison

The doorbell rang. Vyper inserted the paper into the shredder. Then she got up and opened the door. "Good evening, Mister Bodnar. Come in and sit down."

Niko stood and pulled out a chair. "I can't thank you enough, Mister Bodnar."

The lawyer nodded at Vyper, shook hands with each of them, and took a seat. "Mister Kozel always said great things about both of you. It's a pleasure to assist you in any way I can." He opened his briefcase on the table and removed a manila folder. "Please call me Ivan."

Vyper sat next to Niko so they could face their lawyer across the table. "I want to thank you, too."

Ivan waved his hand dismissively. "No need for thanks." He opened the folder. "We have a lot to talk about, but first, we need to discuss your GPS ankle bracelets."

Vyper pushed a small booklet across the table. "They gave us a user manual."

With a nod, Ivan continued. "We need to discuss privacy, something they don't mention in the manual. These bracelets use cell phone communication. As described in the manual, during an emergency you may use them to communicate with the police. When the police need to listen, they are supposed to vibrate the unit to make you aware. The problem is, they can listen without your knowledge. There have been incidents where they were caught listening covertly."

Niko smiled. "I'm glad you're as paranoid as I am."

Ivan reached into his briefcase and removed two bulky socks along with a couple of straps. "Police have no right to listen to communications between a lawyer and client. To ensure our privacy, you'll need to wear these soundproofing socks during our meetings." He stood and knelt next to Vyper. "Let me have your ankle."

She turned her chair and lifted her leg.

He grabbed her foot. "First we have to isolate your leg from the bracelet. Sound travels through your body, you know." He removed her slipper and wrapped a strap around her ankle, between her skin and the bracelet. "Now put on this sock. It blocks sound."

"This is heavy." Vyper pulled the sock up over her calf. "A bit too warm."

Ivan went back to his seat. "That's the price of privacy. Feel free to wear them any time, whether I'm here or not." He handed a strap and sock to Niko. "Put yours on, too."

As he put it on, Niko asked, "Does this block the signal to the police? Will it set off an alarm?"

"No, no." Ivan shook his head. "It only blocks sound. Electronic signals are not affected. You could wear these socks all day long if you could get used to them."

Niko rested his stockinged foot on the floor. "Can we discuss the case now?"

Ivan nodded. "No one else can hear us."

"So, how much trouble are we in?" Niko placed his hand on Vyper's. "How do we avoid going to jail?"

The lawyer outlined the charges filed against both of them. They were accused of conspiracy with Sokolov to kill Marko, and to attack both action centers. This meant they were accessories to the murder of everyone who died in the Kozel action center attack. They'd face many years in prison if convicted on all counts.

Vyper shook her head. "They are charging us with everything the Russians did. Why do they believe we helped them? How did they find us?"

"A government task force has been chasing Russian internet activities for a long time. In fact, they're still chasing the Russians—the attacks haven't stopped." Ivan glanced at one of the papers. "They discovered communication between Sokolov's Russian hackers and this house. When they investigated your home, they discovered an unusual pattern of internet activity—a heavily utilized high-speed connection with network traffic around-the-clock, all encrypted, most of it going to the dark net."

Niko exchanged a look with Vyper. "That must have been NSA tracking you on the dark net."

Ivan continued, "After they raided the house and learned Niko's real name, they used the information as corroborating evidence." He looked at Niko. "Specifically, evidence that you faked your death right after Marko was killed and the action center was attacked. They claim it proves you were in on everything."

The circumstantial evidence was piling up, but Niko had an idea. "They must think I'm the bad guy here. Can we convince them Vyper had nothing to do with it? Can we get her off?"

"No!" said Vyper. "I will not let you sacrifice yourself for me. We did not help the Russians! We have to prove it."

Ivan raised his hand. "Sorry, Niko. Even if you wanted to take all the blame, it wouldn't work. The FBI has documentation from Marko's original request to obtain a security clearance for Lydia ... uh, Vyper. It includes the reason she needed it. Marko cited her exceptional computer security skills."

All the cards were stacked against them. How could the evidence be so damning when they were innocent? Perhaps coming clean was the only solution. It was risky, but Niko was willing to discuss it. "Did Vyper tell you about our Trotsky communication?"

"She did." Ivan flipped through a few pages from the folder. "You gave anonymous information to media and law enforcement about the Russians. Are you thinking of revealing that to the FBI? Do you believe it will exonerate you?"

"I'm not sure." Niko turned his head away from Ivan and mouthed the word *money* to Vyper.

She nodded. "Ivan knows about Sokolov's money. He knows about the computers I have illegally broken into. Marko always trusted him. We can, too."

Niko faced the lawyer. "What happens if they listen to everything we tell them? Suppose they actually believe us. Would they let us go free? Or would they send us to prison for financial crimes and computer hacking anyway?"

Ivan looked at Vyper and back to Niko. "Marko always said you were smart. You should be a lawyer. The Justice Department would be inclined to charge you with your crimes and send you to prison—unless we negotiate a deal, which would probably take a month or more. It's quite possible that the best deal they'll accept will result in some prison time for each of you."

Vyper took Niko's hand. "We have no choice. We should negotiate a deal."

Ivan took a glossy flier out of his folder. The seal of Homeland Security was emblazoned on the top. "Negotiating a deal is the best *legal* alternative. But I'd like you to consider something that has nothing to do with the legal system."

Niko glanced at the paper in front of Ivan. "We know Homeland's still fighting off Russian cyber-attacks. That's what got us into this mess."

The lawyer turned the flier around so they could read it better. "Do you know what the government does with talented hackers after they're caught?" When no one responded, he continued. "They hire them."

Matter of Trust
Chapter 19

Standing on a ladder outside Vyper's front door, Niko disconnected the camera from its mount. None of the wireless surveillance equipment outside worked since the FBI confiscated the equipment that controlled them. One wired camera would have to be enough for now.

He fished a video cable into the laundry room, following the same hole used to supply power, then he refastened the camera and brought the ladder inside.

Vyper sat in the dining room. She looked up from the computer and waved silently. It wasn't safe to speak unless they both wore their soundproof socks.

Niko took the small TV out of his bedroom. It would make a good video monitor. He carried it to the laundry room where he connected it to the camera's cable. When he turned it on and switched the video source, a live image from the front door appeared. Then he carried the TV out and set it on the dining room table.

Vyper smiled and gave a thumbs up. She grabbed a soundproofing sock and strap, and fitted it on her ankle monitor like Bodnar instructed.

Niko fitted the other sock over his foot and took a seat. "What are you doing?"

She pointed to the screen. "Testing the program I wrote. It logs information about software installed by the police—their internet monitoring, too."

"But the internet's disabled."

"The police will turn on the internet and install their software when they arrive. I need to know what they are doing."

"I'm sure this is a silly question, but won't they notice your program?"

"It is a silly question." She pushed the laptop aside and replaced it with the second one. "Can you hook us up to the network?"

Niko went to the den and returned with two network cables. Once the laptops were connected, they played computer games. No sex, though—not until after the police visit.

In the early afternoon, Niko spotted movement on the surveillance camera. A dark blue Ford Taurus was travelling along the driveway.

They removed their "socks of silence" and put them inside a kitchen cabinet.

Niko carried the TV into the laundry room and returned to follow Vyper to the front door.

When the bell rang, she opened the door.

A smiling woman stood before them wearing a loose-fitting blue shirt with matching slacks. Her short-cut red hair was fringed with a hint of gray. "I believe you're expecting me." She reached for the handle of her wheeled travel bag. "My name is Lieutenant Green."

"Come in, Lieutenant." Vyper moved aside. "I am Lydia, but I prefer the name Vyper."

Green stepped inside, pulling her bag behind her, as Niko closed the door.

"I'm Adam, but please call me Niko." He waved his arm toward the dining room. "Have a seat."

The lieutenant glanced at the table. "Are those the only computers in the house?"

"Yes," said Vyper. "The FBI confiscated all our equipment. These laptops are brand new."

Niko offered Green a seat at one of the computers. Vyper sat next to her and Niko sat across the table.

The lieutenant reached into her bag, removing a folder and a USB thumb drive. She opened the folder and handed each of them a document. "This explains the details of what I'm about to tell you. Since you haven't been convicted—not yet, anyway— you have the right to use computers and access the internet— but there are restrictions." She paused briefly. "Let me see your phones."

Vyper and Niko pushed their flip phones across the table to the lieutenant.

Green opened one of them. "Good. You can't use smart phones. Do you have any more?"

Niko shook his head. "The FBI took the other ones."

The lieutenant nudged the laptop toward Vyper. "I'm going to install the software required by the court. I understand you're the computer expert. Please unlock this laptop and sign in as the administrator."

Vyper complied.

Green inserted her thumb drive into the side of the laptop. "We'll monitor your activity remotely. We can see all internet activity, email, chat—everything. And you won't know when we'll be checking."

While Green installed the software on both computers, Vyper's eyes never left the screen.

The lieutenant made a call on her cell phone. "It's Lieutenant Green. The computers are ready ... The internet cables are connected ... Okay, turn it on ... Good ... Just a minute." She typed a command on one laptop. "Okay." She typed on the other. "Thanks. We're all set." She ended the call.

It happened so quickly, Niko had to ask, "Does this mean we can use the internet now?"

"Yes, but wait until I leave. You're forbidden to use encryption. You also can't use any private networks. We'll monitor every site you visit—and don't access any dark websites." Green opened each phone and inspected it. "These must be brand new—no contacts, no calls. Don't use another phone without contacting us first."

The lieutenant returned the folder and thumb drive to her bag. "We monitor all calls and internet access from your service providers. If you violate the rules or break any laws, we'll know." She stood and grabbed the handle of her roll-behind bag. "A colleague of mine might pay you a surprise visit to inspect your equipment. You won't be warned in advance."

Vyper stood. "We will follow the rules. Let me see you out."

Once Green left, Niko carried the small TV back out to the dining room and watched the surveillance video as the lieutenant's Taurus pulled away from the house.

Vyper took the socks from the cabinet and sat at the table while she fitted one over her ankle bracelet. She pulled a laptop toward her and started typing.

Niko took a seat next to her and put on the other sock. "You checking out Green's program?"

"I am familiar with this software. I know what data it collects. If they install any updates, I will know." Vyper navigated her way through the computer configuration to turn off Wi-Fi and Bluetooth.

"What about the camera and microphone? The FBI could turn them on remotely."

Vyper smiled. "Now you are thinking like I do. I will get my tools." She went to the garage and returned with a small black case. She sat down and opened it, selecting a metal tool with a thin, flat end that curved a little. She used the tool to separate the top of the laptop screen from the lid. When she laid the screen down, she pointed to a small circuit board. "It is the camera and microphone."

"Very convenient. Looks like the connector simply slips off."

"You catch on quickly." Vyper disconnected the circuit board and pressed the screen back in place. "Can you fix the other laptop? I need something from my emergency kit."

"Sure." Niko pried the screen away from the second computer.

Vyper grabbed a screwdriver and walked to the living room where she squatted down in front of an unused wall plug. "This is where I keep my 'go bag'. She unscrewed and removed the wall plate, and reached inside, retrieving a small electronic device.

"Is that a satellite phone?" Niko asked, as he disconnected the circuit board.

She nodded. "The FBI can monitor our cells as much they want, but they will not be monitoring this." She reached inside the hole in the wall and retrieved a thumb drive. "And this contains some useful software."

"Aren't we taking a chance with the sat phone? Won't the FBI see the signal?" Niko snapped the back on his laptop.

"Not unless they search for it. Even if they detect a signal, it could be coming from any house nearby—this phone does not send location information." Vyper reattached the wall plate and stood up.

"The encryption on sat phones is so simple, even I can crack it. All they have to do is unscramble all the calls coming from this area."

Vyper sat next to Niko. "I know how to make secure calls. But first I will install my software." She inserted the thumb drive into her laptop and ran the installation software. "Whenever you use the computer, run the cleaner program afterwards. It is probably not necessary, but I do not want to leave any breadcrumbs for the police to follow."

She opened her toolkit and removed a short telephone cord. "We must to use this for private internet access." She connected the phone to her laptop and pointed to the screen. "Use this browser to visit forbidden sites." She dialed a number and waited while tones and warbling sounds came from the computer.

"I haven't heard modem noises for years. This is like the good old days."

"It will be slow, but private. I wonder if Mister Bodnar sent us anything." She logged into an email system. "Nothing yet."

Niko placed his hand on Vyper's. "Sweetheart."

She looked at him and smiled. "You have never called me that before. I like it."

"It suits you." He grasped both her hands. "We need to discuss Homeland. If Bodnar doesn't get them to agree to the deal, we'll both end up in prison. Even if he *does* get the deal, we still might go to prison."

Vyper shook her head. "Bodnar said Homeland would hire us. I thought that meant the FBI would leave us alone."

"Homeland will expect us to tell them everything we know, and they'll share the information with the FBI. Do you believe they'll offer full immunity for everything? We committed bank fraud and stole Sokolov's money. You stole financial information from Treasury."

"Bodnar said he would request full immunity."

Niko shook his head. "Do you trust Homeland or the FBI? I don't. Even if they promise immunity, nothing is guaranteed until we have it in writing. Even if Bodnar gets them to sign papers, they can claim we lied to them. One lie and we go to prison."

Vyper's hands began to flap. She clasped them together and looked up. "We cannot let this happen. Do you have any ideas?"

"We need leverage. You can demonstrate your value—creating software implants the Russians can't detect, tracking people through the dark net. But I'm not sure that's enough. We have to show we've got power over them."

"What power do we have? They are the government."

Niko thought about the scene from *The Godfather*. Don Corleone delivered one of the best lines of all times. *Make him an offer he can't refuse.*

Vyper raised an eyebrow. "How can you smile at a time like this?"

He opened a laptop and selected the special internet browser. "What kind of dirt can we find on Homeland—or any of the people in charge?"

Time Bombs
Chapter 20

Niko checked the surveillance video—no cars, no people. He typed a command on his laptop to sign onto a private network in the Cayman Islands. It felt good to be anonymous on the internet again.

Vyper sat next to him at the dining room table. "We should look through Marko's files. He supported Homeland and the CIA for years, and he saved all the dirt he came across."

"Where'd he store them?"

"Let me do it." Vyper slid his laptop in front of her, typed in a few commands, and accessed a dark website where she entered a password. "This is where I backed up his data." She scrolled down a list of directories until she reached one called RAINYDAY. "Marko always told me to prepare for the worst— and he practiced what he preached." She opened it.

Niko studied the titles of the first page of entries. "Everything looks like CIA stuff. We need something on Homeland."

Vyper moved to the second page and paused until they both had time to read through the titles before moving onto the next, and the next.

In the middle of the seventh page, Niko spotted something. "Look at this. Leonard Grimes ... he's the Secretary of Homeland Security. At least he is now."

Vyper opened the document. "He must have worked in the CIA five years ago."

Niko skimmed through the pages. "It's about torturing prisoners in Batman, Turkey. If Secretary Grimes was involved, I'm sure he wouldn't want his role made public."

"I thought it was illegal—even in Turkey."

"You're right. And the Turkish people would be pissed to learn their government was helping America like this."

Vyper pushed Niko's laptop back. "This sounds like the kind of dirt you were looking for. What do we do now?"

"I'll do some more digging—see how much I can learn about this place and what they did there. I also need to learn more about Grimes' CIA assignment."

"What should we do with the information?" Vyper tapped on her keyboard. "I can use my bots to spread the word—inside the US and also in Turkey."

Niko had the beginnings of a plan, but everything depended upon Bodnar's negotiations with Homeland. "Can you post something on the Homeland Security web page?"

"They will not like it." Vyper smiled. "But I can post whatever you want on their public web page and most of the internal pages as well."

The phone rang and Vyper answered. "Hello, Mister Bodnar ... Yes ... We will see you shortly." She hung up. "Bodnar is on the way over—maybe half an hour. He did not want to talk on the phone."

Niko continued his research while Vyper studied the Homeland web pages. They also tossed around ideas about how to leverage the dirt on Grimes and the CIA.

When Bodnar arrived, Vyper led him to the dining room table. He sat, opened his briefcase, and took out a small manila folder. "Homeland's interested in hiring both of you, but not without an interview. They weren't specific about what they want you to do ... 'Need to know,' I suspect. Since I insisted on tying the job to an immunity deal, they agreed to meet the three of us."

Vyper held Niko's hand and looked at their lawyer. "Does this mean we do not go to prison?"

Bodnar wrinkled his forehead. "I believe so, but I haven't seen the agreement. No one's signed anything." He removed a paper from the folder. "When we meet with Homeland, make no mention of Prixster or Sokolov's missing money."

"When do we speak with them?" asked Niko. "Where is this place?"

"The interview is tomorrow at two o'clock. They scheduled it for two hours. Homeland won't hire you directly—or authorize you to enter their offices. You're actually applying for a job at a company called Crystal Intelligence—near Reagan Airport. But don't be fooled, everyone in management works for Homeland."

Even though it sounded like a good deal, Niko still had reservations. "What happens if they refuse to give us full immunity? If we turn down their offer, we have no deal—and we risk spending a long time in prison."

"That's a legitimate concern. They hold all the cards. I think they realize you didn't work with the Russians, but they still don't approve of unsanctioned hacking."

Niko needed to prepare for the worst, so they had to let Bodnar in on their plan. "Vyper and I've discussed ways to mitigate the risk. If the government decides to screw us, we're prepared to play hardball. To be precise, as far as the government is concerned, I'll be the one that'll play hardball."

Bodnar raised an eyebrow. "Feel free to run your idea by me. I won't try to stop you, and I won't tell the government. I know Marko would want me to help you if I can."

Niko took a deep breath and slowly let it out. "You said the meeting starts at two o'clock and goes for two hours. We'll schedule a time bomb to go off at 4:15—releasing compromising information around the world. If the government decides to screw us, I'll go rogue around four o'clock—and you two need to act surprised and worried. On the other hand, Mister Bodnar, if the government decides to give us full immunity, you'll be able to stop it with a phone call or a text."

The lawyer leaned forward on the table. "I won't ask you what the compromising information is, but I don't see how it'll make them change their minds."

Vyper smiled. "There will be more time bombs, each one releasing additional information. The bombs will continue until told to stop."

Bodnar packed up his papers and set the briefcase on the floor, then he looked each of them in the eye. "Marko had confidence in both of you, so you can count on me."

They talked through the details of the plan, refining it, and talking contingencies.

The lawyer stood. "I'll pick you up tomorrow at 11:00." He picked up his briefcase. "We'll have lunch before the meeting."

"We'll be ready." Niko walked him to the door.

Crystal City, Virginia

The following morning, Niko and Vyper followed Bodnar into a courtyard surrounded by modern high-rise buildings, an unlikely location for the offices of Crystal Intelligence. They headed toward the glass and steel structures on the right. A fast food restaurant and a clothing store flanked a tall set of glass doors below the street address of the building.

Their lawyer held the door as they entered a small lobby with artificial potted trees on either side of a bank of elevators. They rode it up to the tenth floor.

The doors opened to a reception area that looked like the lobby of a fine hotel. They walked past a small unoccupied seating area, and approached a woman standing behind a desk.

She smiled. "May I help you?"

Bodnar nodded and handed her an identification card. "We have an appointment—"

"They're waiting for you in Conference Room B." She returned his ID and pressed a button. The door on the right clicked. Bodnar opened it, waving his arm to encourage Niko and Vyper to enter.

To their left was a double set of oak doors. Ahead was a bland hallway devoid of any pictures or plants, where a tall woman in a dark business suit stepped through a door on the right that displayed the letter *B*. She offered her hand to each of them. "Mister Bodnar ... Mister Zima ... Miss Harris." She waved toward the door. "Please come in."

The windowless room had a large whiteboard on the wall and a rectangular conference table in the center, surrounded by seven chairs, four of them empty. The woman closed the door and took a seat at one end, leaving three available chairs—all on one side.

Niko sat closest to the woman who appeared to be in charge. Bodnar sat on his right, leaving the remaining seat for Vyper. Across the table, they faced three men in dark business suits, each one holding a light-blue folder.

On Niko's left, the woman spoke. "My name is Victoria Evans. My associates are here to observe. We've studied your backgrounds and the recent events that brought you here. The security clearances you obtained at Kozel Group remain active, and they'll be sufficient for the briefing you receive today." She handed some papers to Bodnar. "Each of you need to sign this form before we proceed."

Bodnar quickly read through each document and nodded. "This is standard." He handed one copy to Niko and another to Vyper. "It says you can't repeat anything you learn today—ever. Go ahead and sign it."

Ms. Evans placed the signed copies in her folder and set three identical large color photos on the table. "This is Stepan Belenko, also known as Zatan. He's six feet tall, a hundred and ninety pounds. He runs a Russian cyber operation. As you know, his former boss and benefactor, Alexei Sokolov, is dead. Belenko seems to have another benefactor, since his operation remains active."

Niko had never known what Zatan looked like. He expected to see a young computer nerd, but this was a powerfully built man, with short blond hair and a long bulbous nose.

The men across the table stared at the three of them, like predators stalking their prey.

Evans leaned forward. "Several oil pipelines and refineries in Texas and Louisiana are experiencing cyber-attacks, and we believe it's Belenko. His team hacked into the administrative systems and stole personal information. They're probably behind the spear phishing campaign—system admins are receiving bogus emails demanding they change their password. We believe none of them have clicked on the false link. But our greatest concern is the probes of the operational network, where pipelines are monitored and controlled. So far, they haven't penetrated any of those systems."

None of this was a surprise to Niko. *What do they need us for?*

Evans raised an eyebrow. "I know what you're thinking. This is normal security monitoring and incident response." She took a sheet of paper from her folder and turned it for everyone to see. Names and logos of corporations dotted the page. "The pipelines, refineries, networks, and computers are privately owned by these companies. We've offered to inspect and defend their systems, but each company refused. They don't trust the government. They treat their corporate secrets like gold."

Niko pursed his lips to keep from smiling. Marko would never have let that stop him. If systems needed protection, Kozel Group would protect them, even if they refused assistance.

"The owners haven't granted us authority to perform penetration tests. We can't plant bugs on their networks to infect Russian computers." Evans sat back in her chair and swiveled slightly in Niko's direction. "We need someone else to do it for us. Someone who can do it anonymously. If these companies discover the intrusion, our government needs to be able to deny involvement."

Niko nodded. *It's all about deniability.*

Evans' eyebrows pinched together. "One more thing. We know you were trying to track down Belenko ... Zatan. We can't do it ourselves without illegally breaking into private computers, spoofing addresses, and leveraging uncooperative telecom company networks. We must learn where his operation is located. We need to plant bugs on his computers. But we aren't authorized—someone else must do it instead."

For the next hour and a half, the briefing went into details. Niko and Vyper engaged in the conversation cooperatively, asking and answering questions.

Niko glanced at his watch—3:45. No one discussed immunity yet. He nudged his lawyer.

Mr. Bodnar cleared his throat. "This has been a productive meeting. One I feel will lead to better safeguards for our country. My clients are prepared to work for you if they're granted immunity from prosecution as we previously discussed."

Evans set her papers on the table. "We've spoken about this with Secretary Grimes who's been in contact with the Department of Justice. They agreed to reduce the recommended sentence to a range from three to six months."

Niko looked at Vyper, her eyes beginning to water. He shook his head.

Bodnar fixed his gaze on Evans. "Our understanding was complete immunity—no prison time at all. Who changed their mind?"

"I wasn't aware of any earlier agreement. All I can tell you is Secretary Grimes won't reduce the sentence recommendation. He feels your clients broke the law with their illegal hacking and need to serve time."

"Do you realize how ridiculous this sounds? You want my clients to illegally hack on your behalf, so you have deniability, but they must serve time for doing the same thing."

They continued to argue without making progress.

At 4:00 as agreed earlier, Niko began to play hardball. "Why'd you ask us to come here if you weren't willing to grant full immunity?"

Evans shifted her gaze to Niko. "Would you prefer to spend twenty years in prison? That's your alternative."

"Lydia and I have cooperated. This meeting was productive. You know we could help keep the country safe. Is this the way you treat people who agree to help?"

"This is not negotiable. We treat all hackers the same."

"I'm surprised none of them have retaliated—sought revenge."

The men across the table glared at Niko. Even Vyper and Bodnar stared at him with looks of disbelief.

Evans's eyes narrowed. "Revenge? Are you threatening the United States government?"

"I was just saying. Lots of hackers have uncovered government secrets—black sites where prisoners are tortured, even killed. I could imagine hackers using information like that against the government."

Evans pulled out her phone and texted something.

Niko shook his head. "Of course not. I wouldn't do anything like that. Even if I wanted to, I've been under surveillance ever since my arrest."

The door opened, and two uniformed guards entered.

Evans looked at Bodnar. "Zima will remain here. You and Harris will come with me." She stood and faced the guards. "Don't let him leave."

Niko watched everyone exit the room, leaving him alone with the guards. His heart pounded. *Stick to the plan.*

In about five minutes, the first-time bomb was scheduled to go off. Thousands of bots were poised to distribute the exposé of the secret black site in Batman, Turkey, where captured ISIS fighters were held and tortured. Some were even killed. Niko had used Google to translate the exposé to Turkish for release in that country. The story would also show up on the Homeland Security web page, and Secretary Grimes would receive an anonymous email at his official and personal email accounts.

There was no backing out now. This was the only way he knew to keep Vyper out of prison. As far as the government knew, Vyper didn't participate in this 'revenge.' A half hour later, another time bomb was scheduled to go off.

Twenty minutes later, the door opened. Evans returned with two short-haired men in suits. One of them took a set of handcuffs off his belt. "Hold your hands together in front of you." He snapped the cuffs on Niko's wrists.

Evans sat across the table from Niko. "We know you released the information about Batman, Turkey."

"What?" Niko feigned surprise. "I don't know what you're talking about. What information?"

"Don't play dumb with me. What other information are you planning to release?"

"How can I release anything?" Niko raised his arms. "You've got me handcuffed in a room surrounded by guards."

"Talk now or you and Harris are going to prison for a long time."

Niko dropped his head to his chest and mumbled. "I didn't break my part of the deal." He looked up and raised his voice. "You said Secretary Grimes agreed to a shorter sentence. Did he decide to revoke that deal, too? Does he even know what you're threatening to do? I want to talk to Grimes. I want to talk to Bodnar."

"You're in no position to make any demands."

"You think sending me to prison is going to stop these leaks—whatever they are?"

The door opened. Niko couldn't see who was there, but Evans left the room.

The second time bomb must have gone off as scheduled—a message promising to expose a high-level member of Homeland supporting illegal torture in Turkey. Grimes should have received an email with an audio attachment. He was recorded discussing the death of a prisoner, and how to cover it up. That recording was only for Grimes—at least for now.

Within five minutes, Evans returned. She waved all the guards to leave the room and took a seat next to Niko. She grabbed the arms of his chair and turned it to face her. "Can you stop the leaks?"

"I told you. I didn't leak anything. I've been with you all day."

"Cut the bullshit. End the leaks now!"

Niko held up his cuffed hands. "Even if I could, why should I? You're going to send Lydia and me to prison."

Evans grabbed Niko by the shoulders. "Stop the leaks. We'll work something out."

"No prison for Lydia or me?"

"Agreed."

Niko shook his head. "Do you have approval to say this? Did Secretary Grimes authorize this?"

"I do. And the secretary authorized it."

Cat and Mouse
Chapter 21

Niko sat at the conference table in the offices of Crystal Intelligence, hands bound in cuffs, police monitor attached to his ankle, staring into the eyes of Victoria Evans, mere inches from her face. He had taken a chance—a dangerous one—and he came out on top.

Despite winning, Niko didn't trust Homeland. "Release me—Lydia, too. We'll see if we can stop the leaks. Get the immunity paperwork to Bodnar within the hour and send someone to remove our ankle bracelets."

Evans nodded and unlocked Niko's cuffs. "Stop the leaks—immediately." She stood and walked to the door. "You two work for me now. I expect you to do a good job, but you'll never set foot in this building again." She opened the door.

Vyper stood in the hallway, a worried look on her face. Her eyes opened wide and her face broke into a smile. Tears ran down her cheeks.

Niko rushed out and embraced her.

She buried her face into his shoulder. Trembling, she hung on with surprising strength.

Bodnar placed his hand on Niko's shoulder. "You'll have time for that later. We must be going."

Silently, they walked to the car. In the back seat, they fitted their soundproofing socks over their ankle monitors.

The lawyer handed his prepaid phone to Vyper who sent an encrypted text to end the time bombs:

Gr@nd-tH3fT Quiesce

Bodnar removed a small electronic box from the glove compartment. He used it to scan the interior and exterior of the car before sitting behind the wheel. "We can talk."

Niko gave Vyper a quick kiss. He sat back in his seat. "They're going to remove our ankle bracelets and monitoring software, aren't they?"

"I'll make sure they take care of everything within a couple of hours," said Bodnar. "You'll be free from all those restrictions."

Vyper handed the pre-paid phone back to the lawyer. "If Homeland backs out of this deal, we need to reset the time bombs. In the event I am unable to reset them myself, I need you to text the keyword 'Boom.' Then the whole world will hear Secretary Grimes' voice demanding American guards to cover up the death of a prisoner."

"Grimes won't take a chance—he won't screw up the deal. I'm sure Ms. Evans will come through." Bodnar started the car and pulled out just as his phone beeped. He handed it to Vyper. "This could be her. Check out the message."

She glanced at the phone. "This is not a text. It is a news alert ... Someone hacked into the Moscow Metro—a cyber-attack. All the signal lights on the tracks around the city are red. No trains are moving ... businesses and government offices are closed ... people cannot get to work. Russia suspects the CIA, but they do not cite any evidence."

Niko shook his head. "This isn't like the CIA. I'm sure they could do it, but not without high-level government approval. If Russia had evidence of American involvement, they'd consider it an act of war."

Vyper gave the phone back to Bodnar. "Whoever did this could have caused train crashes and loss of life, but they did not.

If it was CIA, they would deny it. Just like our deal. They want us to hack the Russians, and they want *deniability*."

"You're right," said Niko. "The government will never come to our defense. If we get caught doing something illegal, they'll throw us under the bus. So, deniability is important to Homeland—we can use it to our advantage."

Bodnar spoke up from the front seat. "You never stop scheming, do you?"

Niko smiled at Vyper. "Never. But don't worry. This is nothing like the time bombs. This is about Homeland letting us do our job without constantly looking over our shoulders. If Homeland wants deniability, they can't be caught communicating with us—monitoring us. They have to leave us alone."

Vyper raised her eyebrows. "Do I get my computers back? The network equipment? Everything?"

Bodnar took the ramp to I-66. "You two make a lot of sense. I'll make your demands clear."

Sterling, Virginia

Niko unplugged his laptop from the front of a network switch. He looked around Vyper's computer room with satisfaction. It had taken three days, but all her equipment was back where it belonged, wiped clean and rebuilt.

He opened the door and stepped down from the raised computer room floor to the living room. Vyper sat on the couch, computer in her lap. The TV on the wall displayed a large map of the Texas-Louisiana coast with colored lines connecting colored dots.

Vyper turned her head. "Sit down and take a break. How is it going?"

Niko sat down and leaned over to give her a kiss. He opened his laptop. "The last of the configurations are complete. It's time to run through final tests." He looked at the TV. "Looks like the oil fields. Is that what Cybercade's monitoring?"

"It is. I copied their data feeds. They will not notice." She set her laptop aside. "I have been checking out Runion and a few other dark websites, picking up chatter. There is more information on the Moscow Metro break-in. I am not sure who did it, but whoever it was, they included some of Prixster's signature code. It was not me, but the word is out—Prixster hacked the Metro."

"The world thinks *you* attacked the Russians? That makes you a target. Zatan was looking for you before Sokolov was killed. I can't see why he'd stop now." Niko held her hand. "If our government wanted deniability for their attack, this is one way they could do it. Maybe they know you're Prixster, and they're using you as bait."

Vyper pulled her hand away and waved it dismissively. "It is not the first time I have been pursued. Marko was the only person who ever discovered my identity. I will be careful."

"We have to take this seriously. What if he finds you? The Russians play rough—Sokolov did." Niko brushed her hair behind her ear. "You're prepared for virtually any kind of computer attack, but not for a physical assault. Just look at how helpless we were when the FBI broke in."

Her hand began to flap. "I was scared. They burst right in. We could not stop them. We could not hide."

"Let me take care of it. I'll beef up the security system and increase your home protection."

Vyper placed a hand on his cheek and kissed him. "You are the best." She placed her computer on her lap. "Right now, I want to check on my bots. They have been probing the pipeline and refinery systems ever since the FBI left us alone."

"Are you using your Groper program? Wouldn't it be detected?"

"Detected? Not my program. It does not look like a sustained attack. I spread the probes across thousands of bots located all over the world. And I have slowed it all down. It looks random." A text box appeared in the upper right corner of the TV screen. She pointed. "There—it found a server with old web software that was missing important security patches—the third one I have seen so far. I will install my monitor and tracker software on all of them."

Niko used his laptop to access the unpatched server. "I'll break in and grab the list of sign-on IDs." He tried a few hacker tricks. Soon he was browsing through restricted files. He copied the list of user names. "I'm going to monitor the sign-ins for a few days. See if there's any suspicious activity."

"This is odd." Vyper displayed a list of locations on the TV. "I've been collecting data from the Russian computers infected with my tracker. Most of them are located in Vladivostok. But three are accessing the internet from Phoenix, Arizona—three different computers on the same subnet. Not only that—two more are coming in from a location in the Bahamas—an office building in Nassau."

"Very suspicious. It looks like the Russians have collaborators in two more locations."

Vyper tapped away at her keyboard. "Let me see if these computers are accessing the systems in Texas or Louisiana."

While Vyper was occupied with the oil fields, Niko searched for home security systems—not just cameras and locks. He wanted something they could use to defend themselves as well. They could afford the best thanks to Sokolov's money.

The sound of typing stopped. Vyper stared silently at her screen.

"What is it," Niko leaned over to see her computer. "You look confused."

She nodded. "Five computers in the Phoenix site are probing a pipeline control network at Rockefeller Petroleum in Houston, Texas."

"Just as you suspected. We'll give Homeland the details. But something else is bothering you."

She turned the screen and pointed to a string of letters and numbers. "This is what they are looking for. They are trying to get a response from something. It reminds me of Stuxnet—only different."

"You think it's looking for a specialized computer? This site is a major oil pipeline hub. It could be looking for a system that controls pipeline operation."

"I agree, but I am not sure what to do next."

"That's why Homeland gave us the 'bat phone'." Niko took a cell phone from the table. "They like to hear from us every day. Now we have some significant information to pass along."

Niko called a special number connected to Homeland through two intermediate locations. He waited while the phones established a secure connection. After exchanging passphrases, Niko reported on the Phoenix and Nassau sites as well as the peculiar probes in Houston. He also promised to send the details in an encrypted, anonymous email. A terse acknowledgement from Homeland ended the call.

He shook his head. "Homeland is a pain in the ass. They should tell Rockefeller Petroleum they *must* tighten their pipeline network security. And someone from Homeland should check out Phoenix and Nassau. We have no idea whether they'll follow up on anything we send them. Marko never worked this way."

Vyper poked a finger in Niko's ribs. "Check this out. One of those Phoenix computers is probing the power grid in southern California. I don't like—"

A loud warbling sound interrupted Vyper. She pounded her fingers on the keyboard, paused, and pounded them again.

Niko watched without interrupting. This was the second time in two days she'd bumped into a hacker on a dark web router. Vyper had to act fast—wiping out evidence of her session before anyone could follow her through the network.

Her fingers stopped, and she looked up. "Someone is trying to track me. Maybe trying to track Prixster."

***

For the past week, Niko had sent a lot of data to Homeland, but the information flowed only one way. The guidance they received was, "Stay out of Phoenix and Nassau. It's not your job." Same thing with California. The Russians were trying to break into the electrical grid, and Homeland told Niko to stay out of it.

Vyper sat on the couch next to him. "I just planted another bug in the Rockefeller Petroleum engineering network in Texas. I discovered an admin logged into the system—from the Russian site in Phoenix. I killed his session, but he will probably return."

"Damn." Niko shook his head. "I told Homeland about this. Rockefeller users, including admins, are logging in from unsecured remote sites. If someone steals a password, they can log in from anywhere"

"Nothing we can do about it." She slid closer to him and glanced at his laptop. "What have you learned about the pipeline equipment? Have you found anything that would respond to the Russian probe?"

"Homeland hasn't told us shit. I've been reading some of Rockefeller's engineering docs. I found a flow computer that might be the target. It controls and monitors the flow of oil."

They looked through the specifications together, studying how the system worked. Anyone who modified the program could disrupt the movement of fuel and trick the monitoring system into reporting normal operation.

Vyper selected the source code of Groper. "I will add a probe to my program. We will see where all these flow computers are."

"I'll tell Homeland." Niko made a call on the bat phone, explained what they found and promised to send details in an email.

He was about to hang up when the man from Homeland said, "We followed up with Rockefeller on their lax security. They promised to enforce rules on admin signons. If they're not on Rockefeller's internal network, they're required to use the company's secure remote connection."

Being cooperative? They must want something. "That's great. Just a few minutes ago, someone from the Phoenix site—"

The voice on the phone interrupted. "We need your help. It's urgent. Have you seen the news about the power outage in Los Angeles?"

Niko searched the news. "Not really, just looking at it now. Seems serious."

"It's a cyber-attack on Valley Electric. We isolated their network from the rest of the grid. Our folks are still working on bringing them back on line."

Niko put the phone on speaker. "Vyper, Homeland needs you to restore power in LA. It was a cyber-attack—sounds like it might be related to the intrusion we reported last week. The one they told us to stay out of."

Vyper tapped away at her keyboard, then looked up. "I cannot access Valley Electric. Has anyone set up generators and satellite communication?"

"One moment," said a voice on the speaker phone. "I'm connecting you directly to our incident response team."

Niko turned on network news, where the anchor desk reported on the developing situation, speaking to on-site reporters via satellite phone. No video was available because emergency operations officials had commandeered all power generators in the area, including those from news organizations.

Vyper worked with the emergency team to establish a connection to the power distribution network and identify the systems that were affected by the attack.

"I wouldn't want to be in LA," said Niko. "Traffic snarls and accidents, mob scenes at banks and gas stations, looting, riots. Hospitals are running with limited power on backup systems. It's threatening patients' lives. Officials are reporting shootings ... some deaths. It'll be dark soon—officials ordered an immediate curfew."

By nightfall, Vyper had identified the cause and devised a plan. The power company had to isolate the major parts of the network so Vyper could repair each segment one at a time. They kept the malicious software isolated from the newly-repaired sections.

Each time Vyper cleared one segment, Valley Electric restored power to another section of the city. Within a few hours, the system was back to full capacity. The city was in shambles. Emergency crews would get no rest tonight.

It was after midnight in Virginia when Vyper closed her laptop. "I am exhausted. This is the first time I have had to fix a problem while people were suffering ... dying. The Russians have never attacked our country like this before."

Niko gave her a hug. "This tit-for-tat. Moscow blames us for the attack on their Metro, so they attack the power company in LA. Could be the start of a full-scale cyberwar. And our country has the most to lose." He kissed her. "You need some sleep. Let's go to bed."

They fell asleep almost immediately.

Whoop ... Whoop ... Whoop

Niko opened his eyes and glanced at the clock—2:15.

Whoop ... Whoop ... Whoop

Intruders! Probably not the FBI.

Defense
Chapter 22

Niko jumped out of bed and picked up his phone. On the screen, a night vision video showed the bright-green images of two men on the left side of the driveway and one on the right. He touched a drop-down menu and selected "Dog."

The sound of three barking canines broke the silence outside. The figures on the screen stopped, raised their weapons, and turned to a defensive position.

Vyper stood on the other side of the bed, stepped into her slippers, pulled on a nightshirt, and picked up her phone.

"Follow me!" Niko snatched a shirt and pair of shorts from the chair next to the bed, picked up the bat phone and his gun, and ran to the computer room, Vyper right behind him.

He held Vyper's hand. "Stand behind the door. It's bulletproof." He slammed it shut. "Call Homeland."

On the inside of the computer room door, a large video monitor showed the three green figures moving toward the house. Niko touched the screen and selected more menu options. A loud alarm screamed outside the house.

The video switched to full color as floodlights illuminated the lawn outside. Two spotlights scanned the yard randomly. Three men dressed completely in black, carrying assault rifles and a battering ram, suddenly stopped and tore the goggles off their faces. They sprinted to the outer edge of the lawn.

"They had night vision goggles," said Niko. "The light must have been blinding. Looks like they're wearing body armor."

Vyper yelled into the phone. "Homeland, this is Harris. Armed men are attacking my home. Send help now." She ended the call and touched an icon on her phone. "Data purge and computer shutdown started."

The lights blinked. Vyper glanced at her phone. "They cut power. We are on batteries."

Niko slipped into his shorts and pulled the shirt over his head. "It's okay. I connected the security system so it runs on emergency power."

Outside, two men spread out, ten yards to either side of the third, then all three sprinted toward the house. As the first man came within ten feet of the door, two strobe lights flashed intense beams at his face, stopping him abruptly. The other men came from the sides and ran up to the door.

Niko remotely fired the door-mounted mace cartridges at the intruders. Two men dropped to their knees holding their faces.

The other man picked up the battering ram and smashed it into the door. He rammed it a second time. The door lurched into the house and dropped to the floor.

Niko switched the video to an indoor camera so he could watch the men cross the threshold into Vyper's home. He remotely fired two more mace cartridges at the intruders as they entered. All three dropped to their knees, struggling to clear the liquid from their eyes.

Standing behind the computer room door, Vyper put her arm around Niko who held a finger to his lips.

They watched the screen as the intruders spread out to search the house.

One man walked to the computer room door and jiggled the knob. "Open door!" He jiggled it more. "Open door, now!" He stood back, raised his assault weapon, and fired a short burst of bullets at the door. None of them penetrated.

A second man joined him, carrying the battering ram.

Niko motioned Vyper to a corner at the far end of the room, while he stepped to one side of the door, raising his Glock and aiming it at the entrance. He inhaled and slowed his breathing.

Body armor. Aim high.

The door to the room burst from the hinges. As the first man appeared, Niko shot him once in the head, knocking the lifeless form against another man.

Someone outside the door returned fire. Niko turned and glanced at Vyper, who nodded and raised her thumb.

From outside the house came the distant sound of police sirens, becoming louder and more insistent.

Niko peered through the doorway and spotted two men gesturing to each other. He shot one in the head, knocking him backwards to the floor. Before the second man could raise his weapon, Niko shot him, too.

Flashing red lights pulsed through the open doorway. The sirens of several vehicles competed for attention. They had to be right outside.

Vyper ran to Niko's side and peered through the computer room doorway. "The front door is gone. And the men—they are not moving. Are they dead?"

Niko wrapped his arm around her. "I think they're dead. I hope there were only three."

A gunshot rang out, then two more.

A powerful voice from a bullhorn demanded attention. "FBI. Drop your weapons."

Another gunshot. The faint sound of helicopter blades beat louder, changing pitch before settling into a low hum.

Niko hugged Vyper. "The cavalry arrived. Let's wait in the living room."

Vyper walked around the lifeless men on the floor.

The bat phone rang. Niko answered it. "This is Zima."

An unfamiliar male voice responded. "Is Harris with you? Are you safe?"

"Yes, and yes. We're both here. Safe and alone ... I think. Are you Homeland?"

"Homeland sent us. Walk out the front door slowly, one at a time, holding your hands over your head. Leave any weapons you have behind."

Niko turned to Vyper. "We have to trust someone." He set his Glock on a table and headed outside, stepping into the blinding light, hands held high. Within seconds, two men frisked him while a third held a gun at the ready.

A middle-aged man in a business suit approached. "You can drop your hands." He took Niko's elbow. "Follow me." He walked away from the house.

Niko glanced at Vyper, who was walking behind them, accompanied by a young woman dressed in a jogger's outfit. He stepped on a stone in his bare feet. "Do I have time to get my sneakers?"

"Just watch your feet until we get in the helicopter. We'll get you some shoes later."

"Helicopter? What's going on? Where are we going? Who are you?" Niko tried to see beyond the bright lights. Something large was sitting in the field across the street.

The man slowed his walk. "You can call me Mister Smith. You're not safe here. We're taking you where we can protect you."

The faint outline of a large vehicle appeared when they reached the street. As they walked closer, Niko saw a small commercial helicopter, silver and black, no markings.

He looked at the man who called himself *Smith*. "Are you FBI? Do you know who tried to kill us?"

"We'll debrief you after our flight." He opened the door to the chopper and stood to the side. "Get in. Watch your step."

The vehicle was on runners, like a sled. A bar parallel to the ground acted as a step. Niko cautiously set one foot on it before entering. The inside looked like the seating area for a small corporate jet, a pair of seats facing forward and a pair facing the opposite direction.

Vyper got in next and took the seat beside him. She took his hand. "Do you trust these men?"

The engine started, and the blades began to turn, making enough noise to drown out normal conversation.

Niko leaned in close and kissed Vyper. He raised his voice. "Everything'll be fine."

I hope.

Secrets
Chapter 23

Niko peered out the helicopter window at the ground below, dimly illuminated by a crescent moon. He held Vyper's hand and looked into her questioning eyes, but he had no answers. All he could do was shrug his shoulders.

Who are these people? Where are we going? Are we in danger?

His mind raced through the clues. The people who attacked the house could have been Russians. Mister Smith and the others arrived after Vyper called Homeland for help. They probably stopped the Russians. Then someone called Vyper on the bat phone.

These have to be the good guys.

During the shooting outside Vyper's home, someone with a bullhorn had identified themselves as the FBI. But then Mister Smith showed up. He didn't act like someone in the FBI. And why did he use a fake name?

The helicopter took a turn. The sound of the engine changed. Niko spotted a body of water ahead, maybe a river. The chopper headed down, but the land below was all forest.

They landed on a circular concrete pad in the center of a clearing. The engine noise faded. Niko unfastened his seat belt and turned to Vyper. "We're here. Wherever that is."

She nodded her head toward the flight deck. "We have company."

Smith walked up. "A driver will be here shortly to take you to your temporary home. I'll see you in a few hours." He opened the door and left the chopper.

Niko shook his head. "Talkative guy. Looks like answers will have to wait."

Vyper wrapped her arm around his and laid her head on his shoulder. "Do you really think we are safe?"

He moved his mouth close to whisper in her ear. "I don't trust them, but I believe we're safe ... for now. Let's try to make the most out of it until we learn more."

A young man, not much older than Niko, approached. His hair was trimmed closely, and he wore a dark business suit. "I'm your driver. Follow me."

Niko took Vyper's hand, leading her outside.

The man stood beside a dark SUV and helped Vyper and Niko into the back seat before getting into the front.

Niko peered through the narrow opening separating the front seat from the back of the vehicle. "Where are you taking us?"

"Mister Smith will debrief you." A dark window slid shut, blocking their view of the driver.

These folks took security seriously, and so did Niko. He held a finger to his lips and slid next to Vyper. They rode in silence along a two-lane road through dense woods. With the front view blocked, all they could see were the trees lining both sides of the road.

Ten minutes later, they turned right, driving a short distance before they stopped. When they pulled forward, they drove through an iron gate attached to stone pillars, then onto a driveway surrounded by a manicured lawn, and came to a stop.

The driver slid the back door aside and helped Vyper out of the SUV. Niko slid across the seat and stepped out in front of a four-car garage.

Vyper held his arm.

Before Niko had a chance to look around, the driver took charge. "Follow me. Stay on the pavement. When we get inside, don't open any doors, and don't speak to anyone."

As they rounded the corner, a large stone house came into view, tall chimneys on either side of the sprawling mansion. A dozen windows dotted the first floor, with matching dormers above.

The driver walked ahead to a covered entryway and opened a large wooden door.

Inside was a foyer that looked like it belonged in a modern hotel. A stairway led up to the right, blocked by a "Restricted Access" sign on a chain. Straight ahead, a few wooden seats and bookcases lined the walls along the corridor. At the end of the hall, they turned into another corridor. Halfway down, the driver opened a door and waved his hand toward the entrance.

Niko and Vyper stepped inside. The room was large—a combination living room, dining room, and kitchenette.

"Make yourselves at home," said the driver. "You'll find fresh clothing in the closet. Don't leave before Mister Smith arrives." He turned around and left.

Vyper held a finger to her lips. She took a tour of the place, Niko at her side. She walked to the window and opened the curtains, revealing a small lawn leading to a wooded area. The door on her left opened to a full bathroom. The door on her right led to two bedrooms, each with a king-sized bed. In one closet, she found two pairs of pants and two blouses her size, plus some pants and shirts that would fit Niko, hanging above two pairs of tennis sneakers. Inside a dresser drawer she discovered underwear and socks.

Vyper chose an outfit to wear. "I need a shower." She kissed Niko and walked away.

Anything Niko did with his phone could be monitored, so he checked out the TV and turned on the news before settling into the couch. He thought about Smith and his people. They had been helpful and accommodating, but hadn't shared any information. Worse yet, anything he and Vyper discussed could be recorded. He hadn't gotten much sleep last night and his eyes were getting heavy. The local news droned on in the background as he dozed off.

Vyper's kiss woke him up. When he reached out to her, she jumped back, a smile on her face. "No hugs until you take a shower."

Niko stuck his lip out in a fake pout. "If you insist." He grabbed something to wear and headed to the bathroom.

The hot water and change of clothes raised his spirits. He was ready to face whatever challenges awaited them.

When he stepped into the living room, Vyper stood and wrapped her arms around him. She turned her head as though to kiss him, then whispered, "We cannot stay here, constantly being watched ... listened to. It is creepy."

In a low voice, Niko responded. "We must ... for now."

All alone in a strange place without their possessions, they sat together on the couch and watched TV.

When a chime rang, Niko got up and opened the door. "Come in, Mister Smith."

Smith nodded and entered, carrying a briefcase, wearing the same suit as earlier in the day. Something about him seemed a bit less intimidating—perhaps his loosened tie or the hint of a smile. "We have a few things to talk about."

Niko pointed to the breakfast island in the kitchenette. "Why don't we sit over there."

Smith sat on a tall stool, opened his case, and removed a folder. He looked across the table at Niko and Vyper. "Do either of you have any idea what happened tonight?"

When they both shook their heads, Smith continued. "A five-man team assaulted your home. Three men were found inside the house, dead."

Niko nodded. "They came after us. It was self-defense."

"We have no reason to doubt you. The FBI arrested the other two men, who tried to escape—one is hospitalized." Smith opened the folder and pushed a picture of Vyper across the table. "Each gunman had a picture like this in their pocket." He flipped it over, revealing a single word handwritten on the back—PRIXSTER.

Vyper's hand flapped and she began to rock. The front feet on her stool lifted and returned to the floor.

Niko put his arm around her shoulder.

Smith slid the picture back into his folder. "Neither of the captured gunmen would talk at first, but one of them finally agreed." He fixed his gaze on Vyper. "Alexei Sokolov hired them."

"No!" Vyper shook her head violently and flapped both her hands. "He is dead."

"We've received several reports that Sokolov faked his death," said Smith. "The man we interrogated seems to support those reports. The bodies of he and his wife were disfigured—shot in the head, and their hands were missing. It's possible this fooled Russian investigators, or perhaps they were paid off."

Niko held his grip on Vyper. "You're safe. He can't get to you now."

Smith placed his hand on Vyper's arm. "Are you okay? Is there anything you need?"

Her head stopped moving and she clasped her hands together. "I will be fine."

Niko whispered to Vyper, "I love you." He looked at Smith. "Who's Prixster?"

Smith raised an eyebrow. "Let's be honest with each other. Sokolov figured out Harris ... I mean Vyper, was Prixster. He sent these people to snatch her—alive. The suspect we're holding told us Prixster has something Sokolov needs, but he had no idea what it was."

Vyper sat up straight. "I cannot go home. He will keep searching for me. We need to hide."

"We can help you with that." Smith removed some papers from his folder. "In return, we need your help to stop the Russian cyber-attacks."

Niko leaned forward, hands on the breakfast island. "We appreciate your help, but I'm confused. We're already helping Homeland."

Smith pushed a document in front of them. "This is from the personnel office of Crystal Intelligence. You are no longer assigned to the Homeland project. They have reassigned you to my organization."

"They did this without talking to us? Suppose we didn't want to be reassigned?"

"Homeland can defend the country without your help." Smith slipped the document back into the folder. "The only way to stop Russia is to go on offense. And that requires overseas action—our specialty."

Niko exchanged a look with Vyper.

We're working for the CIA?

Part III: Offense

Making Plans
Chapter 24

Safe House, somewhere in Virginia

Niko's first night in the safe house had been a restless one. Twice he'd awakened in a sweat from a nightmare and reached out to Vyper. All he remembered of the terrifying dream was Sokolov's cruel smile and Vyper's screams.

After breakfast, he sat on the couch next to the woman he loved, the TV volume loud enough to make eavesdropping difficult. He leaned closer and whispered, "We have to stop Sokolov and Zatan before they find you. If the CIA can help us eliminate them, we should do whatever they ask."

Vyper wrapped her arm around him and nodded.

At eight o'clock, right on schedule, a chime rang at the front door. Niko greeted Smith who stood next to a large suitcase and held a briefcase.

The CIA man wheeled the suitcase inside. "I brought some of your clothes. We're keeping the rest of your things in storage for now. If there's anything you need, just let me know."

Niko was tempted to give him a list of demands but thought better. *First, it's time to listen.* He led the man to the island in the kitchenette where Vyper was waiting.

Smith sat and opened his briefcase. "Our conversation yesterday must have raised a lot of questions." He placed a folder in front of him. "Let me begin by saying that I trust both of you, and I hope to earn your trust."

Niko took a seat and glanced at Vyper.

Smith raised an eyebrow. "I can see you're not convinced. Nevertheless, we have to work together." He opened the folder. "Let's talk about your assignments." He slid a document across the counter to Vyper. At the top, it displayed the security classification: SECRET//ROPE2//SHADE. "This is your first assignment. It should be simple for someone with your talents. We want you to develop software that can penetrate a Linux system, using techniques that security experts have never seen before. Something that won't be detected by up-to-date security programs."

Vyper nodded. "I understand. You need a zero-day implant. What does this Linux system do? Where is it and how do I access it?"

"I can't divulge that. We'll use our field operatives to handle the insertion. The security precautions implemented on this computer are stringent. The document lays out all the details. In addition, we have a test computer, with the configuration of the target system, sitting in a lab."

"What is it for?" asked Vyper.

"As I said, I can't tell you. We operate on a 'need to know' basis."

Vyper leaned forward. "Fair enough. But why me? There are hundreds of people with the skills for this. Besides, you said we are going after the Russians."

Smith took the papers from Vyper and leafed through them. He handed them back, opened to a page labeled TARGET. "There's more. Once the program is operational on the Linux system, it must search for a specific industrial controller. Here are the specifications. Once it finds the target, the program should try to insert another implant onto the controller." He studied Vyper's quizzical expression. "No, I can't reveal what this specialized machine does. However, we have an identical controller in our lab to test this as well."

Niko rested his hand on Vyper's arm. "He wants you to plant a bug to take control of machinery. It might be a train, a power plant ... for all we know, it fires nuclear weapons." Niko turned to Smith. "Isn't it true?"

"You're asking about a hypothetical. You're not cleared for the details."

"Okay," said Vyper. "What else does this software have to do?"

Smith flipped through a few more pages. "It must open a communication channel to reach my team in a way that's difficult to detect. My team will use the channel to send software updates. And one final requirement." He poked at three words on the page. "Insert the phrase 'KILROY WAS HERE' inside the implant ... in English, disguised by weak encryption."

Niko resisted saying anything confrontational—it wouldn't do any good. The CIA compartmentalized everything. Perhaps even Smith didn't know what the program would be used for.

Vyper leafed through the pages. "Can I keep this, or do I have to commit it to memory?"

Smith reached under the breakfast island and opened a panel, revealing the door to a safe. "You can study it inside your apartment any time, as long as no one else is visiting. When you aren't using it, store it here. Press your finger to the scanner to open it." He moved aside. "Go ahead. Put it away."

After Vyper stored it in the safe, she frowned. "You did not hire us to write a program for you. Niko will help, but this is primarily an assignment for me. It'll only take a few days. What happens to us then?"

Smith removed a second document from his folder. The security classification was designated: TOP SECRET//STRAP3//TWILIGHT. He looked at Vyper. "You identified a Bahamian datacenter in Nassau the Russians are using to attack the Rockefeller Petroleum network. You also told

Homeland there were sections of the network you haven't been able to penetrate remotely."

"Correct," said Vyper. "They have configured their firewalls very well. So far, I have been unable to slip past them. I believe somebody needs to physically enter the site and insert a probe on the protected side."

A smile appeared on Smith's face. "That's exactly what we intend to do. The operation requires an accomplished con man. Someone who can gain the confidence of key operations personnel in Nassau. And this person will have to understand the technology nearly as well as Prixster. It would also help if they were familiar with Belenko, aka Zatan."

Niko had no doubt who Smith was describing.

The CIA man steepled his fingers and locked his eyes on Niko. "We know about your life in Sevastopol and Philadelphia. You have the aptitude and experience required to mislead people." He held up his hand. "Don't worry. My organization is not part of law enforcement. With some training, you could be the most qualified person for this job."

"You want me to be a spy? To break into a datacenter and attach a bug? Why me? Why should I do it?"

"You've asked more than one question," said Smith. "You're right. That's what we expect you to do. We'll put you through a fast-track training course to round out your skills. We have assets in Nassau for support. As to why we picked you—frankly, our people are perfectly capable of handling the job—but maybe not as well. But our government can't afford to be accused of an aggressive cyber-attack."

Niko looked at Vyper. "He admitted it. If I get caught, they can deny any involvement."

Smith nodded. "It's a dirty business, and you're right. We require deniability." He held up one finger. "Don't forget about Sokolov. He's after Vyper, which should give you a strong motivation to stop him. And we believe Belenko is not only working for the Russian government—he's also secretly supporting Sokolov. We nail Belenko, we get Sokolov, too."

Vyper laid her hand on Niko's arm. "This sounds dangerous. Maybe you should not do it."

Niko shook his head. "Sokolov sent five armed men to your home. He won't stop looking for you as long as he's free. We've got to nail him."

"Okay," said Vyper. "When do we move to Nassau?"

"You don't understand," said Smith. "Niko will work in Nassau, but you'll be working out of one of our CIA offices in Virginia or Maryland, where we can guarantee your safety."

Vyper's hands began to flap. She pressed her palms on the counter top and stared at her hands. A few moments later she looked up. "No! I go with Niko. You will not separate us again."

Niko didn't want Vyper to take the risk, but he knew her mind was made up.

Smith wrinkled his brow. "That's not the plan. Only Niko goes to Nassau. This isn't—"

"Change your plan." Niko stood and walked behind Vyper. "You need our help. Those are our requirements."

"It's not that simple."

"Then make it simple or find someone else."

Smith stuffed the papers into his briefcase and locked it. "Give me a minute." He grabbed his phone and walked across the room. He made a call, keeping his voice too low to hear.

Niko wrapped his arms around Vyper. "Are you sure about this? You'd be safer here."

She hugged his arms tighter. "I am the safest when we are together."

A chime rang out, and Smith opened the door. He took a silver suitcase from someone before shutting the door and carrying it to the kitchenette. "I'll rework the plan." He set the case on the floor next to Vyper. "Meanwhile, I want you to be comfortable here. Even though you're staying in a safe house, we agree not to monitor anything you do—visual, audio, or electronic."

Niko huffed. "We're supposed to believe you?"

Smith nodded. "After I leave, go ahead and open this suitcase from Mister Bodnar. He told me Vyper's fingerprint will unlock it. He didn't say what he packed, and I didn't ask." Smith turned to leave. "We can discuss the new plan and your training program tomorrow."

Once he left, Vyper opened the suitcase. Inside were their laptops, a game console, equipment to search for electronic bugs and hidden camera lenses, and a white noise generator to interfere with any long-distance surveillance.

Maybe they couldn't trust Smith, but Bodnar always came through.

Mission
Chapter 25

Warrenton, Virginia

Niko lay face-down on a table in the medical offices of Warrenton Training Center while a male nurse inserted a needle just under the scalp.

"That wasn't so bad," said Niko. "Can I sit up now?"

The nurse shook his head. "Stay right there. That was just to numb the area. I'll be back in ten minutes to insert the implant."

Niko thought about Vyper, probably lying on a table next door getting the same treatment. They were both here because Mr. Smith agreed to a revised plan for Nassau—one that included Vyper. He said the CIA was serious about their safety and security, which meant they had to allow tiny transponders to be inserted under their skin. The devices would be removed as soon as the Nassau operation was complete.

For the next seven days, they'd stay in the Tower Apartments in downtown Warrenton, only a short drive to the training center where they'd prepare for the mission.

The nurse returned. "You'll feel a little pressure. Your hair will hide the small scar."

The poking and prodding were annoying, but didn't hurt. The nurse opened a bottle and brushed something wet over the cut. "All done. The liquid bandage will keep it from bleeding. Don't wash your hair for a few days."

At nine o'clock, Mr. Smith arrived to take Niko and Vyper to their next appointment. They walked across the parking lot to an office building. After going through three security checkpoints, they arrived at a small conference room with eight chairs around a rectangular table.

Mr. Smith sat in front of the only laptop in the room. "We'll start the week with a mission briefing." He motioned for them to sit across from him. A large screen covered the wall at the end of the table. When he tapped a few keys on the computer, the CIA seal appeared on the screen with the word MKSIGMA in bold letters below it.

Niko shared a bewildered look with Vyper. The internet was rife with rumors about CIA projects, like MONGOOSE and STARGATE, but the name on the screen sounded too much like the notorious mind-control program, MKULTRA.

The CIA seal faded, replaced by a world map with a line connecting Nassau, in the Bahamas, to Vladivostok, in Far Eastern Siberia. A large bubble containing a network diagram appeared above each location.

Smith pointed a laser dot at the Siberian location. "Belenko, aka Zatan, is planning and coordinating Russian cyber-attacks from this restricted network in Vladivostok. The mission of MKSIGMA is to gain access to the restricted area, discover their plans, and neutralize the threat." The red dot circled a graphic that resembled a brick wall. "This firewall isolates the restricted network. It's configured like the Nassau firewall that Harris has been unable to crack."

"My name is Vyper. Nobody calls me Harris."

"Vyper it is." Smith nodded. "Physical security around the Siberian datacenter is daunting, made even more difficult because it's located inside Russia." The red pointer circled a connection to the firewall. "This entry point is privileged, allowing trusted networks more complete access." Smith moved the pointer slowly from the firewall to another one in the

Bahamas, following the line connecting the locations. "We'll break into the Siberian network from Nassau."

Niko shook his head. "You want me to walk into the datacenter and plant a bug on the privileged side of the firewall so Vyper can hack her way into Vladivostok?"

Smith displayed a more detailed diagram and moved the red dot to one of the switches. "You've got the idea, but I don't want you to plant a bug. Instead, you'll make a network connection between this restricted switch port and an open port on the wide area switch." The pointer moved between the two ports.

"No." Vyper shook her head. "They can detect everything I do. It will appear to be unexpected network traffic from the outside."

"We've got it covered," said Smith. "Nassau Telecom configured a private channel using a separate wavelength over the same fiber. The Russians will never notice the covert tap."

Vyper was full of questions and so was Niko. Smith provided detailed documentation and went over each point they raised.

Niko was convinced the technical aspects of the plan were solid. But none of it would work if he couldn't sneak in and make the connection. It should be easy. Just another scam. He took a deep breath to calm himself and let it out. "How are you going to turn me into a spy?"

Smith leaned back in his chair and closed the laptop. "Let's start with your cover story. You'll be a visiting professor from the Ukraine—always good to have a cover you're comfortable with. The school, New Providence University, will hire you to teach network security."

"What name do I use?"

"You'll be Anton Zhora." Smith crossed his arms against his chest. "Once in Nassau, you need to complete the following actions." He projected a list of bullet items on the screen:

- Human Intelligence
- Electronic Intelligence—Coral Computing
- Penetration—Network Access
- Electronic Intelligence—Vladivostok

The red dot moved to the item at the top of the list. "First, establish trust at the university while collecting information on everyone you encounter—students, faculty, anyone who shows interest in you." The dot moved to the next item. "Second, break into the Coral Computing Datacenter remotely and collect all the information you can. It's a multi-tenant facility, and Belenko is one of their clients."

The dot moved to the third entry. "Once you've collected enough information to develop a plan, go inside Zatan's datacenter and connect the switches." Smith moved the dot to the last item and looked at Vyper. "After the connection is made, you will break into Vladvistok from Nassau to discover what Zatan is up to."

"Sounds like it'll work, but I'm not a spy. You said I need to collect information about people ... do I take pictures?"

"One of my associates will be joining us later to demonstrate the tools available to you." Smith turned to face Vyper. "We got you a job as a security analyst for Charles Town Cloud—the largest internet provider on the island."

Vyper's hands began to twitch until she laced her fingers together. "Do you expect me to be a spy, too? I am not good with people."

Smith shook his head. "No. I want you to work your shift as a trusted employee, bringing no suspicion on yourself. Each day, after your shift is over, go back to your apartment and work for us. Your initial assignment is to hack into Coral Computing—

gain access to their cameras, their security systems, robots ... everything. Once Niko gets inside and makes the connection, you'll penetrate the Vladivostok network as we discussed. We also need your help with a couple of special projects, but we can discuss them later."

"You mentioned an apartment," said Vyper. "Where do we stay?"

"You and Niko will have separate apartments on the third floor of Island Village. I know you want to be together, but it's important for you to act as strangers. You'll each fly into Nassau on different days from different airports. Never go to your rooms at the same time and be sure to leave from your own apartment every morning. Keep in mind, the Russians could be watching you."

Smith stood. "We have to get moving. You are both scheduled for your first self-defense training session. Follow me."

Vyper shook her head. "No fighting. I do not like fighting."

Niko took her hand. "Think about it, Vyper. Sokolov's still out there. He's a violent man, and he's looking for you."

When she didn't respond, Smith opened the door. "We've got to go. They're waiting."

Niko kissed Vyper's hand. "Come and watch, then. You might learn something you could use if you ever get in trouble."

Smith led them to a gymnasium with two full-sized training dummies standing on wrestling mats. The only other person in the room was a short, muscular man in a sweat suit.

The man motioned them to sit on a bench. "Good afternoon. I am Mister Jones. I'll be your self-defense trainer. The methods you'll learn are from Krav Maga, a combination of martial arts and street fighting."

"Should we change clothes or anything?" asked Niko.

Jones shook his head. "Today will simply be an introduction. You won't do anything physical. Starting tomorrow, you'll need to wear more appropriate clothes." He spent an hour discussing and demonstrating the basics of the art.

Smith looked at his watch. "We've got another appointment." He turned to the instructor. "Thank you, Mister Jones."

Niko and Vyper followed Smith back to the conference room where they took their seats.

Smith opened a folder. "When my colleague arrives, she'll describe your specialized equipment, but she hasn't been cleared to discuss your mission. She doesn't even know where you're going."

His phone beeped. He glanced at it and stood. "She's here."

When he opened the door, a petite, gray-haired woman entered, pulling a shiny black suitcase behind her. She had a pleasant grandmotherly smile that seemed out of place at a CIA training center.

She took a seat and opened the case on the table. "I'm Miss Quincy, but most people call me 'Q' ... like in the Bond movies." She laid a cell phone in front of her and slid two more across the table.

"We already have Samsung phones," said Niko. "Why do we need these?"

Q raised her eyebrows. "These look normal, don't they?" She didn't wait for an answer. "If someone snatches your phone, they'll probably remove the SIM card to disable or clone it. But it's only a decoy. The card contains no data. The functions found on the SIM have been built into a chip."

Niko picked one up and turned it in his hand. "Interesting."

"That's not all." Q popped out the card. "When it's removed, the phone sends an alert to everyone working on the project. It also turns on the camera and mic, streaming everything to a web page. It keeps streaming until it runs out of batteries. Turning it off doesn't stop it."

"This doesn't have a removeable battery," said Niko. "The only way to stop it would be to destroy the phone."

Q nodded. "That's the idea. Anyone who removes the SIM card is potentially hostile." She removed an ID badge from her case. "These phones have a few more tricks. I understand you'll be working in a facility that uses this type of proximity card. When a legitimate user needs to prove their identity, they wave this within six inches of a reader to open a locked door or perform some other function. Your phone has an app that will copy the data from one of these badges if you're close enough." She held up a small box and some blank ID cards. "Later, you can use this device to create a duplicate badge."

Niko had worked in a datacenter that used cards like this. He thought about all the ways he could maneuver his phone close enough to someone's badge without them realizing what he was doing.

Q brought out special eyeglasses with tiny, hidden cameras on the frames. She explained the RF sniffer program on the phone that detected and mapped wireless communication. She demonstrated a tiny camera that recorded video and sound but didn't transmit.

Right out of James Bond. No wonder they call her Q.

"One final thing." Q set a device that looked like an old calculator on the table. "If you're checked for bugs, the implants under your scalps won't give you away. They don't transmit anything until one of these devices sends a request." She pointed to the calculator. "The transmitter in your implants are low power. Their range is a hundred meters. We have a second transponder for each of you with twice the range, and we'll conceal them in the lining of a purse or wallet."

Smith stood. "I'm sorry, but we have to cut this short. You can show them your other gadgets tomorrow." He led her to the door.

After Q left the room, Smith opened his laptop. "We have one more project to discuss today." The CIA seal appeared on the screen. Below it appeared the word MKRODENT. "This project has a higher classification level than MKSIGMA. Don't discuss this with anyone other than me. I'll limit my briefing to those details you need to know. It's similar to the project you completed—the Linux implant that crosses over to an industrial control computer."

Vyper nodded. "The one where I buried KILROY WAS HERE in the code."

"That's right." The CIA seal on the screen was replaced by a logic diagram. "This is a simplified version of the firmware that controls the triggering of a weapon." Smith pointed the red laser dot at one of the inputs. "Before this weapon can trigger, it must be armed." The dot moved to another spot on the screen. "But arming it is not sufficient to trigger it. That won't happen until sensors indicate it's safe and the target is in range."

Vyper's eyes widened. "What kind of—"

Smith raised his hand. "I can't tell you. You don't have a need to know."

Niko placed his hand on her arm. He looked at Smith. "I hope you don't plan to start World War III."

Silence was the only response.

Niko glanced at Vyper and shrugged. "Okay, Mister Smith. What do you want us to do?"

"We have copies of the firmware used for these weapons— the one currently in production plus four previous versions. I need you to reverse engineer it and determine how to set all the safety and targeting signals high—authorizing triggering. Don't make any changes to the arming signals." Numbers and capital letters filled the screen. "This is a snapshot of the code starting at the load point."

Vyper studied it briefly. "If this mysterious weapon uses the program you have requested, it will trigger the instant someone arms it. Is that what you want?"

"It is."

Nassau
Chapter 26

Nassau, Bahamas

Niko opened his eyes. Vyper lay next to him, still asleep, facing away. He was in her apartment, three doors down the hall from his own. The ceiling fan turned slowly, circulating fresh ocean air. The sun was still low in the morning sky. No need to turn on the air yet.

This is the life.

He arrived here a week ago, filling in as a substitute professor at New Providence University. Vyper arrived the following day. Smith had warned them to act as total strangers in public. If this had been a weekday, Niko would have gotten up before sunrise to sneak back into his room, but today was Sunday, and they didn't have anywhere to go.

When Vyper rolled onto her back, Niko propped himself up, resting his chin on his elbow, just high enough to study her face. He watched her chest rise and fall with each breath. Then he thought of Sokolov and the armed gunmen who came after her.

He'll never get to you. I won't let him.

Vyper's eyes opened. She smiled. "How long have you been staring at me?"

"Only a few minutes, but I could admire you for hours." Niko gently brushed the hair away from her face. "Did I ever tell you I love you?"

"Every day, silly. I love you, too." She wrapped her arms around his neck and kissed him. "What do you want for breakfast?"

"Only you." He slowly pulled the sheet aside. "Just lean back and enjoy."

Their lovemaking was tender at first, then their passions took over. They used every inch of the king-sized bed, trying out their favorite moves and experimenting with new ones. When exhaustion took over, Niko lay on his back with Vyper's head resting on his chest.

She ran her hand across his abs. "They say it is better in the Bahamas. I agree."

After sharing a shower, they sat at the dining room table enjoying coffee and bagels. The view through the sliding glass windows was tropical and serene. Palm trees lined the sea wall. The towering hotels on Paradise Island appeared in the distance.

Niko carried their empty cups to the kitchen, refilled them, and returned. He took a sip. "How's the job going?"

"It is boring. We wait around in case the cloud service develops a problem, but nothing happens on second shift. There are only two of us, and Junior plays video games all evening. Imagine a twenty-something Bahamian man who calls himself Junior."

"I'd love to visit you at work." Niko laid his hand on hers. "You get a dinner break, don't you? Maybe I could join you one night."

"You know we cannot be seen together in public—the Russians might notice. Fortunately, I do not eat with Junior. One of us must stay in the office to cover the shift. I always go to Blackbeard's Conch House. It is a dive, but the seafood is great—and the crowds disappear after the cruise ships leave."

"I'm sorry you have to eat alone." Niko swirled his coffee and took another sip. "So, tell me about Junior. Is he a good gamer? Can he beat you?"

"Junior likes video poker." Vyper wrinkled her nose. "I spend my time watching what the Russians are doing. They are still poking around the Texas oil fields. It looks serious, but Smith says we should let Homeland handle it. He wants us to work on our mission."

"Did Smith say anything about the firmware for the weapon?"

Vyper shook her head. "He thanked me for it. He never talks about the weapon, or the KILROY message. Says he is forbidden to share the information with us. It worries me."

"I know what you mean. That firmware is pretty complex for a simple weapon. It's got to be something expensive and dangerous. And that KILROY message—the CIA doesn't want it to remain a secret forever. I think they intend to scare someone—let them know we've penetrated their systems."

"We can only guess what the CIA is doing. No sense in worrying about it." Vyper went to the living room to get her laptop. "Let me show you how far I have gotten with the Coral datacenter."

Niko moved his chair closer.

When she typed in a command, a floor layout appeared. "This is the datacenter. I found it on an engineering database. Each of those rectangles is a client enclosure, with their internet address ranges in the corner." She pointed to a spot near the middle of the room. "The Russian hacking of Rockefeller Petroleum comes from this client—a company identified as Blue Koala Systems. I tried to identify the owner, but it was registered anonymously in Santa Fe, New Mexico."

"So, that's Zatan's computer center?"

"Yes, and I tapped into Coral's security camera system." Vyper displayed five rows of video snapshots on the screen. "I can even control recording and playback. Some cameras scan along a fixed path while others remain stationary. I can see all the open areas, but some clients have rigid containers to isolate their operation—they do their own monitoring."

A video filled the screen, the image moving slowly to the right. Wire cages stood in a line, each one containing racks of computer equipment. At the end of the line of cages was an enclosure made of smoked glass. Vyper pointed to it. "This belongs to Blue Koala. Somehow, you need to get inside."

Niko spotted a panel next to the entrance. "Is that one of those badge readers?"

Vyper nodded. "Clients manage the badge IDs for their own employees, but they use the same system."

Some kind of vehicle moved past the camera. It looked like a Segway but didn't have a passenger. Niko studied it. "What's that?"

"A robot," said Vyper. "That one is for security. It makes scheduled rounds searching for irregularities. It also checks most of the equipment indicator lights. They have other robots, too. Some swap out disk drives—that kind of thing." She smiled. "I can control them from here."

"You could start a robot rebellion. It would freak people out."

Vyper shoved his arm. "Sometimes I wonder how your mind works." Another floor layout appeared on her laptop. This version showed loudspeakers, smoke and heat detectors, and several small yellow boxes with red letters. "Everything is computer-controlled. Those boxes are the fire suppression nozzles. Not water, though. They use inert gas—displaces the oxygen."

"Wow," said Niko. "When I do get inside the datacenter, you'll be with me ... well, virtually. You'll be watching me and watching my back."

Vyper tapped on the laptop and the images of two faces appeared. "Do you recognize these men?"

"They're my students. Are those Blue Koala ID badges?"

"They are," said Vyper. "I downloaded the images you captured at the university with your eyeglass camera. I compared those faces against the ID badges at Coral. These are the only two who match. They work for Zatan."

"Fantastic." Niko got up and retrieved his laptop. He typed the names of the students. "I'll look them up on the internet later. Got to find a way to get close to them."

Vyper took the cups to the sink. "Smith should be happy with our progress."

Niko grabbed the plates, only a few bagel crumbs remaining, and walked behind her. "You know Smith would expect us to practice our Krav Maga."

She turned and scrunched her face. "I told you. I do not like it. I watched you practice, but I cannot do it. I hate violence—real or not."

"I wish you'd try, Vyper. Sokolov is after you, and he won't give up. You need to learn to defend yourself."

Vyper's hand flapped. She pressed her palm on the table. "No. All my life, I have avoided conflict. Even when I was abused, I always submitted quietly. It is difficult to change."

"What'll you do if Sokolov finds you? Will you submit to him? Do whatever he wants?"

"I ... I cannot let him win. I will try to resist."

Niko rested his hand on her shoulder. "Do you remember what they told us in Krav Maga training? What they said about aggression?"

Vyper's head drooped. "Fight quickly, violently. Do not stop until the enemy is down and helpless."

"Can you do it? Will you do it?"

"I ... I don't know. Maybe—"

Niko's phone rang. He waited for a secure connection and answered.

"Smith here," said the voice on the phone. "We need your help—actually we need Vyper's help."

"Wait until I put it on speaker," said Niko. "Okay, go ahead."

"There's a major fire at the Rockefeller Petroleum refinery in Harrisburg, east of Houston. Five storage tanks are on fire and emergency crews are trying to keep it from spreading to other tanks. Homeland believes it was a cyber-attack."

Vyper yelled at the phone. "Of course it is. We warned Homeland weeks ago. You said they would handle it. You told us to leave it alone. Now you ask for our help?"

Smith's voice was calm but firm. "So far, no casualties have been reported, but that could change. I need you to work with Homeland. I'm transferring you to the response team."

A man with a southern accent came on the line. "Williams here. They tell me you can help."

"This is Harris," said Vyper. "What happened. How did it start?"

"A large pool of gasoline at Lamar Refinery formed out of nowhere and ignited, triggering several explosions. None of Rockefeller's equipment detected any leak, but it should have."

"Did they shut down all the pumps moving flammable liquids throughout the refinery?"

"It's an extensive operation. They turned off everything near the affected area."

Vyper looked at Niko and threw her hands in the air, then she faced the phone. "If you suspect a cyber-attack, why did you limit the shutdown area?"

"Like I said, it's a large operation."

"Stop all the pumps—throughout Lamar. And block external network access. You must not allow it to spread."

"We'll do as you recommend with the network. As far as the pumps, I'll forward your request to Rockefeller management."

Vyper rolled her eyes. "Give me access to the network—a satellite link if necessary."

For the next two hours, Vyper worked with Homeland to inspect all systems in the Lamar network. The cyber infection was extensive, spreading to dozens of flow computers and other industrial controls. Despite her pleas, Rockefeller didn't shut down any equipment outside the affected region.

Niko watched the news coverage. Images of flames and thick black smoke played in the background while reporters interviewed local officials. Area roads were blocked. Residents in nearby Harrisburg were told to shelter in place.

Vyper yelled into the phone, "There is a new leak. Sensors show a sudden pressure drop but the computer is not reporting it to operations staff." She gave the details to Homeland.

A breaking news chyron ran across the bottom of the TV broadcast. A reporter explained the situation. "Emergency crews have been deployed to the site of a new leak. Officials have not identified the—"

An explosion appeared on the TV. Flames and black smoke shot up. The camera image jiggled, then shifted to a better view.

On the speaker phone, Williams from Homeland spoke. "We're shutting down all pumps at Lamar."

As the hours passed, Vyper helped identify and restore the software on all operational systems at Lamar. She also inspected systems in refineries throughout Texas and Louisiana searching for signs of an attack. It was after midnight by the time Homeland declared the Lamar fire to be contained.

Mr. Smith came on the phone. "I want to express my thanks, and the thanks of Texas and the nation, for saving lives and mitigating the damage. To protect you, we have concealed your identity, but we are in debt to you nevertheless."

Vyper shook her head. "It did not have to be this bad. Next time listen to what I tell you."

Niko moved closer to the phone. "Now that Vyper restored Rockefeller's service, is our Nassau operation over? Do we go home?"

"Definitely not," said Smith. "The Russians have already begun planning another attack. They won't give up until we stop them."

"Another attack? What's their new target?" asked Niko.

"It's getting late. I can brief you tomorrow." Silence hung in the air for a few long seconds. "I'll tell you this much. One of their targets is the Calvert Cliffs power plant southeast of DC."

Vyper raised an eyebrow. "That is nuclear."

"You're right." Smith ended the call.

Niko kissed Vyper. "It won't do any good to worry about it tonight. You're tired and I have to go to work in a few hours. Now is a good time for me to sneak back to my apartment."

***

Despite yesterday's excitement, Monday morning was a normal work day for Niko. As Professor Anton Zhora, he gave his 'Defense in Depth' security lecture to each class, making sure to capture images of his students with his eyeglass camera. He paid special attention to the two young men identified as Zatan's employees.

When he arrived home, he grilled a hamburger for dinner. It reminded him that Vyper would be eating alone at Blackbeard's Conch House right now.

Niko put away the dishes and sat on the couch. Just as he settled in, an alarm went off on his phone. He read the message:

CELL/A – SIM CARD REMOVED

Vyper! Someone's got her.

Vanished
Chapter 27

Niko's heart raced. He jumped up from the couch.

Someone has Vyper's phone.

He wanted to call her, but she wouldn't be able to answer if someone else had her phone. He made a secure call to Smith. "This is Niko. Someone removed Vyper's SIM card."

The CIA agent spoke calmly. "We know. We got the same alert. I've mobilized a search. Do you have any idea where she went tonight?"

Niko couldn't think. He took a deep breath and let it out. "Blackbeard's Conch House near the airport. She eats dinner there when she works."

"I know the place. We're tracking her phone. She's not at Blackbeard's now, but her phone's GPS history put her in that area at the time of the alert. If they have any security tapes, we'll check them out ... hold on a minute."

The line went silent. Time moved slowly as he waited.

Smith came back on the line. "I need your help, Niko. Set your fears aside and focus. Her phone is streaming video and audio—two men have it. I believe they're speaking Russian."

Niko's recent nightmares flashed through his mind. Sokolov smiling, Vyper screaming.

Smith's voice was insistent. "Niko, are you still there?"

"I'm here. Where's Vyper? Is she okay?"

"Listen to me. Her cell is streaming to the emergency web page right now. I can see one man speaking Russian, and I hear another man's voice responding. No sign of Vyper, but that doesn't mean she isn't there."

An alarm went off on Niko's phone:

CELL/A - NO POWER

"We received the same alarm," said Smith. "One of the men destroyed her phone."

Niko gripped the arm of the couch. "Did it give you a location before it died?"

"Along the north shore of Lake Cunningham, but I'm sure they won't stay there. I need you to watch the video of those Russians. Watch it from beginning to end. You might see or hear something we didn't notice."

"You can find her, can't you? She's got an implant in her scalp."

"When we get close enough, her implant will respond, but it's only good for a hundred meters. If her purse is still with her, it'll respond at two hundred meters."

"What good is that? You don't know where she is, do you?"

"We got a security video from Blackbeard's. It shows two men escorting her into a car. That same car just passed a traffic camera on Independence Drive. We've dispatched drones to the area to find the car. Better yet, they're equipped to detect Vyper's implant."

"You saw her at Blackbeard's?" Niko yelled into the phone. "What happened? Was she hurt?"

"She fell asleep or passed out while she was eating—probably drugged. Two burly men spoke to the waitress before carrying her out to their vehicle. We sent detectives to the restaurant. They'll find out what happened."

Niko grabbed his laptop and sat on the couch. "I'll check out the video. Call you back later." He tossed his phone on the cushion and opened the web page on the computer. A list of two videos appeared—one for the front camera and one for the back. Niko selected the one in the front.

Someone's hand appeared, resting on a dark T-shirt. The gruff man's voice spoke Russian over the muted sound of a car engine. "I got the SIM card." The image shifted abruptly to the face of a middle-aged, Eastern European man with a nose that must have been broken at least once. "I turned it off." The video moved in a jerk to his lap and remained dark.

Niko knew the phone would never turn off, but the Russian didn't know.

A different voice asked, "Is the girl still out? Do we have to tie her up?"

"No, she will stay asleep long enough to get to the house. Then she is Falcon's problem."

Falcon! Sokolov!

The name hit him hard. His worst fears had come true.

Neither Russian spoke for several minutes, then one of them broke the silence. "Pull over here. I'll ditch the phone."

It sounded like they pulled onto a gravel road and stopped. The image jumped from a view of the man's shirt to a car door, which opened. The video moved in a blur, then settled on a glimpse of the night sky before it was blotted out by the heel of a shoe. The audio and video ended.

Niko played the second recording—from the back camera. The audio was identical. The video didn't add anything new—only a stationary image of the inside roof of the car.

He called Smith. "Have you found her?"

"Not yet. The last camera their vehicle passed was at a bank near the mall on Marathon Road. They turned into the Highland Park area. We sent a drone to search from a low altitude. No signal yet. We've got agents in the area."

"They're taking her to Sokolov," said Niko. "They called him *Sokol*—that's *Falcon* in Russian and Ukrainian. It was his nickname in Sevastopol. I'm heading to Highland Park."

"We'll find her. Stay where you are."

Niko ended the call and grabbed his Glock. He checked the magazine and picked up two more full clips.

Then he remembered the interrogating radar unit Miss Q had given him. "It's best to use the directional antenna," she had told him. "The signal will be strongest when the antenna is pointed in the direction of the implant."

Niko rushed to the computer room and grabbed the unit before heading to the car.

***

Vyper awoke, unsure of where she was. She opened her eyes and stared at a sloped, off-white ceiling with a single light bulb hanging from the center. She was lying on a cheap couch with unmatched, fraying cushions. Her sundress was rumpled, riding high on her thighs. One of her legs dangled over the side, her leather wedge shoe still secured tightly by its straps.

A man shouted, "Sokol," in a gruff voice.

Sokolov! He is here!

She shifted her gaze to the sound and locked eyes with a short, husky man with closely trimmed hair. He shouted again, and another voice responded. It sounded Russian.

Vyper's mind instinctively blocked out everything around her. She flapped her hands and rocked her head back and forth. It was comforting.

She thought about Niko and smiled. Then she thought about her situation. This was no time to zone out. Niko would expect more of her. She stopped flapping and squeezed her hands into fists.

Krav Maga. What did they teach? Act vulnerable. Wait for an opportunity.

Vyper could not fight this man while lying on her back. And someone—Sokolov—was just outside the door. For now, she decided to watch and wait for an opening. She would have to strike hard—and keep striking. Her shoes might slow her down, or they could be used as weapons. She decided to keep them on.

The room was small. The only furniture besides the couch was a folding chair. Another man walked through the doorway. Vyper recognized Sokolov from the pictures she had seen. He was shorter than Niko had described but looked more intimidating. He held a large knife in his hand. His voice was gruff. His lips curled into a cruel smile. "You are awake, Prixster." He glanced at the other man and pointed to Vyper.

As Sokolov watched, his assistant grabbed Vyper by the hair and yanked her to her feet.

She he slumped in a submissive posture before the man she despised.

His assistant stood behind Vyper and held her arms tightly.

She panicked. Her struggle was useless, and her head began to rock. She went to that safe mental space where nothing around her matters.

Then she remembered Niko's words, "Will you submit to Sokolov? Do whatever he wants?"

Vyper willed herself back to reality. Alert once more, she would wait for the right moment.

Sokolov narrowed his eyes and moved in close. His hot breath smelled like rotten fish. His black eyes sent a chill down her spine. "You stole my money." He held his knife near her eye. The blade was half a foot long, sharp on one edge and serrated on the other. He turned it slowly. The curved point touched her cheek, sending blood trailing to the corner of her mouth. "You will return it to me."

Vyper averted her gaze, feigning submissiveness, and answered in a low voice. "I do not know who you are or where your money is."

Sokolov ran his finger through Vyper's blood and held it before her eyes. "It would be a shame to cut this pretty face." He stepped back and looked at her, moving his eyes from head to foot. He ran the point of the knife down to her shoulder. "Pretty dress. Such a pity it covers up a beautiful woman." He slipped the blade under each spaghetti strap, yanking back, cutting it free.

He is distracted. Strike now!

Vyper raised one foot and smashed it onto the instep of the man behind her. The man shouted in pain and freed her arms. She raised her knee, threatening a kick to Sokolov's groin.

He swung both hands down to protect himself, leaving his head vulnerable. Vyper clapped her hands forcefully on both of his ears. She butted his head with the top of hers and jumped forward, knocking him over.

As they fell together, she grabbed his head and prepared to smash his skull on the concrete. Before they hit the floor, she felt a sharp pain in her side—the knife.

***

Niko drove along the narrow streets of Highland Park, shacks and rickety fences on either side. Trash, old tires, and abandoned cars littered empty lots. His radar unit hadn't shown any sign of a signal.

The phone rang. Smith was on the other end. "Our drone spotted the building." He gave Niko the GPS coordinates. "It's a peach-colored shack with an old fishing boat around the back. I'm sending a team. If you get there before they do, wait. Vyper has a better chance if you don't try to be a hero. I'm dispatching another drone—this one with an infrared camera."

A few minutes later, Niko slowly approached the house, driving slowly. He checked the equipment tracking her implant. It consistently pointed to the same building.

Vyper's in there.

He parked across the street and walked toward a neighboring building which appeared to be abandoned. From there, he could watch the house. Weeds had taken over the yard, nearly covering the old boat Smith had described.

Three men in jogging suits, carrying gym bags, walked casually toward Niko, waving. As they got closer, one man held his finger to his lips and pointed to a cluster of palm trees. Niko joined him.

Each man squatted before his gym bag and opened it. They removed bulky goggles and fitted them to their faces. They also donned heavy vests.

One of the men, probably the team leader, handed a vest to Niko and whispered, "Put this on. It won't protect you completely, but it should stop a body shot. Meanwhile, stay here while we recon the situation."

The CIA team spread out, disappearing into tall weeds. A drone with four vertical propellers flew overhead, then turned around and flew back.

Soon, the leader appeared at the house where Vyper was being held. He motioned for Niko to join him.

The man spoke softly. "All the windows are covered with plywood, but infrared shows four people inside. One near the front door, probably a guard. The other three are together in one small room where the implant's signal is coming from. Only one of the three is standing. Wait outside until we call for you. Your presence should let the woman know we're the good guys." He handed Niko a radio.

Niko nodded. "I have a gun. I can help."

"No," said the leader. "My men have infrared scopes. We work well together. I don't want you shooting anyone on my team. You could be killed, too. We'll neutralize the enemy. If something goes wrong, and you have to defend yourself, assume they're wearing body armor. Shoot for the head." He pointed to one of his men, standing at the side of the house, aiming a rifle at the boarded-up window. "The assault starts when he takes out the guard."

The leader ran to the door and pressed his back to the wall, holding a rifle against his chest. Once the first shot rang out, he kicked down the door and ducked inside. The man at the window followed him. Four more shots rang out in rapid succession.

Niko's heart pounded. He wanted to believe Vyper was okay.

The radio chirped, and a voice announced, "All clear."

Niko rushed inside past the body of a man lying on his back, a bullet hole in his forehead, blood forming a pool next to his head.

The leader stood outside a room at the far corner, waving his arm for Niko to approach.

Niko ran up to him. "Is Vyper in there? Is she all right?"

The man nodded, a grim expression on his face. "I'm sorry—"

Out of the corner of his eye, Niko saw movement inside the room. He rushed in. One agent spoke on the phone. Another was kneeling next to three people lying on the floor surrounded by a puddle of blood. One was a woman, face down, wearing nothing but underwear—Vyper's underwear. A flowery sundress lay in a rumpled pile near her feet.

When Niko knelt down, he spotted the handle of a knife sticking out of her side.

Nuclear Threat
Chapter 28

Niko opened his eyes when he heard a door. He was alone in the Nassau Hospital waiting room—must have dozed off waiting to hear from the surgeon. He rose from the chair.

A young doctor wearing blue scrubs stepped into the room and walked over to Niko. "Mister Martin?"

Niko nodded. As far as the hospital was concerned, Martin was his name, and the patient was his wife. He searched the doctor's expression for any hint of Vyper's condition, but the man was impossible to read. "How's she doing?"

The surgeon's face softened. He extended his hand. "I am Doctor Hudson. The surgery went well."

A sense of relief washed over Niko. He reached for the arm of his chair.

"Please sit, Mister Martin." The doctor held Niko's arm until he settled into the chair. "Your wife was fortunate. The knife missed her major blood vessels." He took a seat. "Her abdominal injuries were limited to the small intestine. We repaired the damage, but the risk of peritonitis is significant."

"Isn't that an infection?"

Hudson nodded. "We have already started treating her with antibiotics."

"I understand she has a head injury."

"She suffered a concussion from a blunt blow to the back of her neck. It might have been a fist."

"When can I see her, Doctor?"

"Right now, she's in recovery. We'll notify you as soon as she can receive visitors."

When Hudson left, Niko checked his watch—nearly midnight. He planned to stay here all night if necessary. The magazines on the coffee table all catered to medicine and women's fashion. He spotted a remote control and turned on the TV, tuning it to an international network news network.

Videos of Sunday's fire at Rockefeller Petroleum appeared in the background while a reporter from Texas described the effect it had on the Houston area. After a commercial break, the news anchor introduced the story:

> Homeland Security released a statement earlier this evening, identifying a malicious computer virus as the cause of the Texas refinery fires. The Department has heightened the security posture at all major oil and gas suppliers in the United States.

Computer virus my ass. It was a Russian attack.

If Vyper were here, she'd tell him to stop moping and get to work.

Niko muted the TV, pulled out his phone, and logged onto a private network in Miami. He accessed Rockefeller Petroleum's corporate systems. Their security team was on high alert, in constant communication with Homeland. Rockefeller was aware of the details of the attack, but clueless of Russia's involvement. Niko checked two other Texas oil companies and discovered the same level of engagement.

Satisfied the refinery issues were being handled, Niko looked up the Calvert Cliffs nuclear power plant. Without his laptop, he couldn't penetrate their defenses.

The phone rang. Niko waited for the secure call to connect. Smith's voice came on the line. "Have you seen Vyper yet?"

"Not yet. The doctor said things went well but he was worried about an infection."

"She'll get the best care available, Niko. We're sending her to Walter Reed Medical Center in Maryland. Doctor Hudson said she should be able to travel soon, so we scheduled a flight for noon today."

"I'll be glad when Vyper's back home. She shouldn't have come here."

"We'll all feel better when she's back in the States. For now, Nassau Hospital's assigned her to a private room. I had it swept for bugs."

"Thanks." Niko turned the TV off. "Did we get Sokolov? I never got a straight answer."

"We got him. Actually, I believe Vyper got him. He was the man lying under her when we arrived. His head must have hit the floor hard."

Niko pictured Vyper's body lying face down—not on the floor. He remembered the knife, but he couldn't picture the person underneath. "He's dead?"

"In a coma … I doubt he'll ever regain consciousness. The other guys are dead."

With Sokolov near death, and never able to come after them again, Niko should feel safe—but what about Zatan. According to the CIA, he and Sokolov had been working together. That got him thinking. "How will the local news report the gunfight when we rescued Vyper? The neighbors would have noticed."

"As far as the public knows, the police raided the house to capture two drug dealers who died in the gunfight. No one else was there—not Sokolov, Vyper, or you."

"It sounds like you've got everything worked out. After I see her, I'll get ready for our flight."

"You don't understand, Niko. We're flying Vyper home. We need you to continue the operation. We don't know what Zatan's planning with Calvert Cliffs—and possibly other power plants."

"This was a two-person operation." Niko paced around the room. "Without Vyper, the plan won't work."

"We didn't want her to come to Nassau with you. We only agreed because she insisted. When she's feeling better, she can assist you from her hospital bed."

The door to the waiting room opened. A tall woman in a business suit walked in. "Mister Martin?"

Niko held the phone away from his mouth. "That's me."

"You can see your wife now." She waved her arm towards the open door.

He nodded then turned his head and spoke to Smith. "Gotta go. Talk to you later." He followed the woman down the hall to one of the rooms.

Vyper lay in a large bed surrounded by equipment. Two computer screens beeped in a rhythm to the movement of wiggly lines. An IV bag with dark red liquid hung from a hook.

He walked slowly to her side. A tube and several wires ran from the equipment to her bed, disappearing under her blanket. A purple bruise marred her beautiful face from her left eye to her chin. He stood there watching her breathe.

Vyper's eyes blinked and opened. She turned her head. A weak smile formed on her lips. "Niko." Her hand reached for him. "I knew you would find me."

He took her hand and kissed it. "I was so worried. I couldn't bear the thought of losing you." He brushed the hair from her face. "Are you in pain?"

She shook her head slowly. "The drugs must be working. I just feel tired." She squeezed Niko's hand. "You would have been proud of me. I defended myself ... at least I tried."

"I'm very proud of you. Sokolov won't ever threaten us again."

"Is he dead?"

Niko shook his head. "Not dead, but he'll never leave the hospital."

"I hope I can leave the hospital soon. Have they told you anything?"

Niko told her what the doctor said.

She nodded. "Sokolov had the knife, but I think the other man punched me—knocked me out cold."

"The CIA plans to take good care of you. They're flying you to Walter Reed. Your flight's leaving at noon today ..." Niko looked at his watch. "... in about nine hours."

Vyper raised her index finger. "I cannot go. We have to stop Zatan. He knows who I am. He told Sokolov about me."

"You have to go. They have the best doctors. Zatan can wait."

Her hand began to flap. She closed her eyes and the hand stopped. "I will go." She opened her eyes. "But you must stay. Help Smith. Find Zatan."

***

Niko had no classes today, so he stayed in his apartment and did online research while waiting for Vyper to call. He marked the time watching the long shadows of the palm trees outside his window shrink slowly from the west before stretching east again.

The phone rang—a secure call. He answered it right away. "Vyper, how are you doing? How was the flight?"

"I miss you, Niko." The sound of her voice made him smile. "I slept through the flight and slept even more in my room. Nurses pushed my bed to radiology for a CT scan. They seem to be satisfied with my operation in Nassau."

"I miss you, too. They say sleep helps you heal."

Vyper's voice was weak. "I want to see what Zatan is up to, but I do not feel like concentrating. I saw some news reports, but I did not follow up. Did Homeland declare a higher threat level?"

"They did." Niko selected the DHS web page on his laptop. "The alert is limited to oil and gas for now. No public mention of nuclear power plants, but I found suspicious Russian network traffic poking around Calvert Cliffs' computer systems. It looks similar to the early phases of the Rockefeller Petroleum attack."

"If Zatan's folks follow the same plan as Rockefeller, you know how to stop them, but they might be going after other locations. You will have to expand your search."

"I've already begun." Niko retrieved the notes from his recent research. "I've also been going through engineering documents from the Coral datacenter along with some of their clients. I've got a better picture of how everything works there. Of course, Zatan's network, Blue Koala, has tighter security. I'm having trouble fleshing out more details, but I'm working on it."

"Have you looked at the badge reader logs?"

"It's interesting. Blue Koala personnel work day shift only. The students you identified—the ones in my class—work Thursday through Sunday. That makes sense since my class is Monday and Wednesday. I'll see both of them tomorrow morning. Meanwhile, I've done some research online— Facebook, Twitter, and others. I plan to make friends with those guys."

"You are making wonderful progress. See, you do not need me."

"You've taught me a lot, but I need you now more than ever. And not only because—"

An alert popped up on Niko's laptop. "Holy shit! Something deadly serious is going on. Alerts have been sent to airmen stationed at two strategic bases, recalling all personnel to their duty stations immediately. One's Whiteman in Missouri—that's B-2 bombers. The other is Warren in Wyoming—that's missiles. They could have sent out additional messages. I just don't know."

"Could this be related to the Homeland alert? Or maybe Calvert Cliffs?"

"I don't think so. The worst-case scenario with a power plant would be a core meltdown. Something else is going on." Niko checked a web site known for tracking US defense posture. "Our military never tells the public about DEFCON levels, but I think we may have gone to DEFCON 3. Those bombers—those missiles—they're used for nuclear war."

Kilroy
Chapter 29

Bethesda, Maryland

Vyper felt sore this morning, but she didn't ask the nurses for pain medication. She needed her mind sharp.

Niko's words last night had scared her. *DEFCON 3.* When she was younger, she had heard stories from people who lived through the Cuban missile crisis—their genuine fear of nuclear war. That was ancient history—now the world could be facing it again.

Mister Smith knocked at the open doorway and peered into the room. "Are you accepting visitors?"

"I have been waiting for you." Vyper reached for the buttons that controlled her bed, raising her head a few inches. She looked around the room. "I presume it is safe for us to talk here."

Smith nodded and held out a laptop. "I brought your computer."

Vyper took it and placed it low on her abdomen. "Why are we at DEFCON 3?"

Raising an eyebrow, Smith responded, "Why do you say that?"

"You cannot mobilize troops at strategic air bases without the public noticing. What is happening? Are we having a nuclear standoff with Russia?"

"You know I can't tell you anything—even if something's going on."

Vyper pursed her lips. "If Russia causes Calvert Cliffs to melt down, will the military respond with nuclear weapons?"

"I can answer your question. Our nuclear policy continues to be one of proportional response. That's public knowledge." Smith plugged the laptop's power cord into the wall and handed the other end to Vyper. "Of course, the president can initiate the launch of these weapons whenever he feels justified."

"Does the alert have anything to do with the software I wrote? The one with the KILROY message—or the weapon firmware?"

"I hate to sound like a broken record, but you're not cleared to know what we used your software for."

Vyper plugged the power cord into her laptop. "Just tell me I did not give you something to start a nuclear war."

"Let's change the subject." Smith removed a cell phone from his pocket and held it out. "My team discovered this phone on Sokolov. We could use your help."

She took the phone. "You can get the FBI to break into it. Why do you need me?"

"We prefer not to involve the agency."

Vyper smiled. "The CIA knows how to break in. Why me?"

"You know why. My organization isn't allowed to do that kind of work inside the US."

"You want me to break into the phone using the cell service provider. That is illegal, you know." She opened her laptop and started an encrypted session with a private network. She powered on Sokolov's phone and studied the screen. "I will do it."

Once Vyper obtained full access, she searched for key information. "He was smart. Location services are turned off, so I cannot tell you where he has travelled." She searched for more information. "Sokolov has no contacts, and the internet history is empty. He used the Telegram app to send secure messages, and the 'self-destruct' feature is turned on. I cannot tell you what he texted, but I see a pattern. He texts to a different number every Friday. I will send the log to you, but I suspect these numbers are temporary."

Smith's phone rang. "Yes? ... Come on up." He ended the call. "I had a team go through Sokolov's house yesterday. We need help with his computer. My team broke into it, but there's a protected section of the file system we can't access."

"You found his house. Did Nassau Telecom give you his cell tracking?"

"The tracking got us close, then our agents identified where he spent his nights."

A man knocked at the doorway and walked in carrying a computer tower. He set it on the floor, plugged it in, and hooked up the keyboard and mouse.

Smith gave a USB thumb drive to Vyper. "We got this from his safe. Can't crack the encryption."

Vyper inserted it into her laptop.

"Aren't you afraid it could—"

"You think I will make some kind of rookie mistake?" She shook her head, copied the data, removed the thumb drive, and handed it back to Smith. Then she started the code cracking program. "This might take a while."

The man who brought Sokolov's tower to Vyper spoke. "I set it up for remote access. The sign-on—"

"I got it," said Vyper. She accessed the computer and ran the code cracking program against the restricted files.

Smith nodded for the other man to leave.

Vyper's laptop beeped. "The thumb drive data is available. It just looks like a jumble of numbers and letters to me—maybe bank account information. I will send it to you."

A few minutes later, the restricted files from the tower computer were ready. Vyper browsed through the contents. "This one is interesting—a list of Greek gods, but no explanation. Maybe they are codenames. Apollo and Hermes are highlighted." She typed a command. "I just sent you the files."

Nassau, Bahamas

A thousand miles south, Niko stood before his network security class. Fifteen students listened attentively as he spoke. Two men in their early twenties, dressed like they just came from the gym, sat next to each other in the front row. Niko knew their names—Ramon Roberts and Jalen Sawyer—both Blue Koala employees.

A network diagram was projected on the screen at the front of the room. It showed computers, firewalls, private network servers, and Onion routers.

Ramon asked a question. "Onion routers—you mean TOR?"

Niko nodded. "TOR stands for 'The Onion Router'. It's the most common way to access the Dark Net."

Jalen raised his hand. "TOR's anonymous, right? How's it work? Some kind of directory?"

"That's a great question," said Niko, "but well beyond the scope of this class."

Jalen scrunched his nose.

"TOR directory structure is a subject best discussed over a beer." Niko reached for the stack of papers on his desk. "But now it's time for our red-blue team exercise. Those of you on the red team will attack the networks defended by the blue team." He described the rules and handed out the assignments.

While the students worked to attack and defend, Niko started the badge reader app Miss Q had given him. If he could move his phone close to Ramon or Jalen, he might be able to copy their Blue Koala access badge. But he had to get within six inches of the card—and it wouldn't work if they didn't bring the card to class.

Niko walked among the students during the exercise. He looked over their shoulders, asked questions, and gave advice. Standing between Ramon and Jalen, Niko cupped his phone as he moved his hand low along the back of one chair and then the other. No signal.

Standing next to Jalen, he let his hand swing close to a front pocket. He reached over the man's shoulder, getting close to his chest. Nothing he tried returned positive results.

After the red-blue exercise ended, Niko did a wrap-up and dismissed the class.

As the students filed out of the room, Jalen hung back for another question. "Professor Zhora, you mean what you say?"

Niko shrugged his shoulders and smiled. "I said a lot of things, Jalen. And I usually mean what I say."

"TOR network directories—you tell me more over a beer?"

"Sure thing. I've only checked out a few bars since I arrived. You got any place in mind?"

"Me and Ramon go to Club Wahoo. Not jam up. We go Thursdays after work. You play darts?"

Perfect. This would be an ideal opportunity for Niko to copy their badges. "I play darts, but probably not as good as you. When do you guys get off work?"

"We work eight to eight. Always there by eight-thirty."

"Sounds good, Jalen. See you tomorrow night."

After class, Niko went back to his apartment. He was confident he could copy Jalen's badge, but there was a lot more to do. He studied the live videos from inside the Coral datacenter, then pored over the engineering documents for the center and many of their clients. He launched a network probe to identify the equipment inside each cage. Before going in, he would know more about this center than most of the people who worked there.

In the evening, he called Vyper. "Did they tell you how long you have to stay in the hospital?"

"Tomorrow is my last day. I am going back to the safe house in Warrenton on Friday." The excitement resonated in her voice.

"I'm surprised. I thought you'd be there a week."

"The doctor said something about my immune system. I will be glad to get out of this bed. All my computer equipment is in Warrenton. I want to make a few modifications."

"I'm glad to see you're back to normal." Niko laughed. "Thinking about your computers."

"Not just my computers. I asked Smith if our military is on high alert. He refused to talk about it. I think he used my software for something having to do with nuclear weapons."

"I think you're right. And don't forget the firmware you gave him. That was definitely for a dangerous weapon. But you know he can't tell us. And worrying about it won't change a thing."

"You are keeping something from me. You think you know what is going on. Tell me."

Niko had a few theories, but he never put it into words until now. "You remember when Smith told us we were working for the CIA? He said we would go on offense."

"I remember. But I do not think the CIA has done anything offensive. Maybe the Moscow Metro, but nothing since then."

"The Moscow trains were a small operation," said Niko. "A response to the Russian attacks on our action centers. When Russia escalated and went after LA's electrical grid and Rockefeller Petroleum, we did nothing."

"Why not?"

"I think the White House is afraid to escalate. The CIA may be planning a major response—something that threatens their nukes—and Russia may have found out."

"You think they used my software against Russia's nuclear weapons?"

"Maybe. The CIA could be prepared to unleash their attack—whatever it is—as soon as they receive government approval. If the Russian attack against Calvert Cliffs can't be stopped, the White House would probably approve the CIA plan."

Vyper was silent. She often did this during moments of stress. Niko could visualize her hands flapping, her head rocking.

While he waited, Niko ran a search for rumors posted on Russian-speaking websites frequented by ex-military.

Finally, Vyper spoke in a soft voice. "If the US suspected the software used for our own nuclear weapons to be under attack, we would take them offline immediately. Then we would rebuild the systems from scratch—using backup software known not to be infected."

Niko thought it through a few steps further. "If the Russian response was the same, their weapons would be useless until everything was rebuilt. They would feel vulnerable to attack from us. If they went on high alert, we would know—that could explain why we went to DEFCON 3."

"I have a bad feeling," said Vyper. "If the CIA managed to slip my firmware into the Russians' backup library, their technicians might load my version in response to the cyber threat. It could be loaded on some of their missiles."

Niko spotted something in the responses from the web search he kicked off earlier. "Someone on a Russian site mentioned KILROY." He typed in a few more commands. "They're asking others on the site if they know who KILROY is. They say KILROY hacked into their systems."

Final Preparation
Chapter 30

Nassau, Bahamas

Niko walked down a narrow cobblestone street in downtown Nassau. Ragged graffiti covered every inch of space on the walls of the shops and bars, most of the messages scrawled with a Sharpie, memorializing romantic relationships with hearts, names, and dates.

It was 8:30 on Thursday night. The streets were alive with tourists entering and leaving shops and bars. Locals hawked their wares, temping tourists to stop and buy. But Niko refused to stop, not until he found his destination. Then he saw it—a wooden sign with a smiling cartoon fish on a spear—his destination, Club Wahoo.

Inside, dozens of patrons in tropical shirts sat on high-top chairs around small tables watching baseball on large-screen TVs suspended above the bar.

As he walked closer to the back of the room, the ambience changed. A young Bahamian couple sat at a small bar decorated above by cheap strings of Christmas lights. Jalen and Ramon sat with a third man on pink chairs around a bright green table, their attention captured by the actions of another man standing with a dart in his hand.

Jalen cheered when the dart hit the target. He raised a bottle of beer to his lips and swallowed the remaining liquid.

When the man went to retrieve his darts, Niko walked over to Jalen and Ramon's table. "Hi guys. I found the place."

"Professor Zhora." Jalen stood and dragged a chair over from a nearby table, encouraging his friends to make room. "Have a seat."

"Please call me Anton," said Niko. "We're not in class."

While Niko took a seat, Jalen introduced him to everyone, including the man who returned with the darts.

Niko glanced at the bottles of Kalik on the table. He raised his hand for a waiter and ordered five more beers.

Ramon turned the conversation toward computers and networks. Jalen joined in asking Niko about the finer points of the TOR network. The other men at the table seemed uninterested.

When the second round of beers arrived, Niko excused himself to go to the men's room. On his return, he walked past a large Bahamian man, brushing against him lightly.

The man grabbed Niko by the shoulder and spun him around.

Niko looked him in the eye. "Sorry, I didn't mean to bump you."

The big man glanced at his friends with a smile, then glared at Niko. "You do not belong here. Leave now before you get hurt."

Niko pointed to the table with Jalen and friends. "I'm here with them." He started to turn around when the man made a fist and took a swing at him.

His Krav Maga training automatically engaged. Niko brought his left arm up to block the blow. He turned and grabbed the man's wrist with his right. "I'll bet your beer's getting warm. I know mine is."

The man's eyes narrowed as he tried to pull his hand away. "You punk. I'll —"

Niko twisted the wrist outward.

Surprise and pain showed on the man's face. His body tried to follow his wrist while his knees buckled.

Still holding the wrist, Niko pulled the man to his feet. "I really must get back to my friends now." He let go. "Unless you had something else to say."

"You'll pay for—"

Niko twisted his wrist once more. "What were you saying?"

"Nothing," said the man. He shook his head and walked away.

Niko took a seat. "What's with that asshole?"

Jalen shook his head. "Bad juju that one." He raised his bottle in a mock toast. "You taught him a lesson, you did. Where'd you learn that move?"

"High school," said Niko. "I was a wrestler."

Ramon laughed. "Must have wrestled some tough guys." He pointed to Niko's missing finger. "What's the story with that?"

Niko narrowed his eyes. "If I tell you, I'll have to kill you."

Everyone at the table looked confused, maybe even worried.

Laughing, Niko added, "Just kidding. I did something dumb with a table saw in wood shop."

Ramon confessed the dumb things he'd done in school, and the others joined in with stories of their own.

Niko got out his phone, took group pictures and selfies, then showed everyone the results. At one point, he got close enough to Jalen's pocket that the phone vibrated—indicating proximity to a security badge. A longer vibration followed, indicating a successful copy.

After his third beer, Niko said his goodbyes and headed back to the apartment. He turned on the TV to the local news, then he set up the badge-making equipment and created a copy of Jalen's ID with his own photo on the front.

A television reporter caught Niko's attention—something about new developments in the mysterious shootout Monday night in Highland Park:

> Police originally confirmed the death of two
> drug dealers, but our investigators obtained the
> photo of a third man, lying in a hospital bed. He
> is said to be alive, but comatose.

A picture of Sokolov appeared on the screen. He was lying in a hospital bed with his eyes closed, a respirator tube secured to his mouth. The reporter couldn't identify the man and police refused to comment.

The picture must have been taken while he was still in the Nassau hospital because the CIA had flown Sokolov to the States on Tuesday. Niko wondered if Zatan had seen the same the article.

He called Vyper. "Good evening, sweetheart. I'll bet you're happy to be leaving the hospital. I wish I could be there with you."

"I miss you, too." There was a sadness to her voice. "But we've got to finish everything with Zatan first."

"You all set for the trip?"

"I just lie in bed. Smith's people do all the work."

"Something's come up." Niko took a breath. If he remained calm, perhaps Vyper wouldn't be overly alarmed. "Sokolov's face appeared on the local news. It's a photo taken in the Nassau hospital. If I didn't know who he was, I don't think I'd be able to tell from the picture. No one has identified him, but local reporters are investigating."

Vyper's breath was uneven. She remained silent for nearly a minute. Finally, she spoke. "Zatan will not discover this right away. If he does, I am not sure what he will do."

"His first priority would be to bury the story. If the Russians learn he hid Sokolov from them, Zatan would be a dead man.

I'm pretty sure he'll go after Sokolov's money, too—assuming he doesn't already know where it is."

"You could be in danger, Niko. Zatan might come to Nassau."

"I've been thinking about it. If we abort the operation, Zatan will still be out there—a danger to you. Also, Smith is counting on us to stop the Russians. Maybe we can find a solution to this nuclear standoff."

"So, you intend to go ahead with the plan?"

"Yes. We have one more day to work out the details. Then Saturday, I go in."

***

On Friday afternoon, Niko tried on the dark blue coveralls delivered earlier by the CIA. The bright red logo of Zettabyte, a major computer storage vendor, was embroidered below the collar. According to datacenter records, Zettabyte personnel often delivered service to Blue Koala and other datacenter clients late at night and on weekends. Anyone in this familiar uniform would not raise suspicions.

He reviewed the details of his Blue Koala network diagrams. Most of the details were probably accurate, except for the restricted portion. For that section, he made an informed guess. Tomorrow, when he got inside, he'd have a bit more information to go on. He hoped he'd have a cable in his toolkit that could make the connection.

By sunset, he was ready. He called Vyper. "How are you feeling? Are you all moved in?"

"The CIA safe house is a lot more comfortable than the hospital. I got all my computers set up the way I like them. When you go in tomorrow, I'll be right there with you—well, virtually anyway."

Niko told her about the Zettabyte uniform and his other preparations. "Jalen's badge will get me inside the datacenter and into Blue Koala, and the uniform will get me past Coral security."

"I will use their cameras to watch everything you do," said Vyper. "Meanwhile you will be a ghost. Wherever you appear on camera, I will override the images for security. Their video will show the room to be the same as it was before you entered."

"Suppose I do something that sets off an alarm."

"I have you covered. I can control all automated equipment in the entire center. Alarms will come to me first. I will only send along the ones I want them to see. If anyone tries to enter where you are, I will lock them out."

"Vyper, you're amazing. I feel like we can't fail." Niko's phone buzzed. "I just got a text message from Smith. Zatan arrived at Nassau airport earlier today. Facial recognition picked him out. They aren't sure where he went."

"You think he spotted Sokolov's photo?"

"That's my guess." Niko's heart raced. Would Zatan come to the datacenter? Would he go after Sokolov's money? "I have to break into Blue Koala tomorrow. We can't let his arrival stop us."

"I think you are right. Zatan's team is up to something, too. The Russian hackers are still probing Calvert Cliffs. They seem to have stopped work on everything else. It is like all the computer experts are working on some higher priority project."

"Interesting. Let me check something." Niko searched several web sites known to be frequented by ex-military. At the air base near Kansas City, Missouri, B2 pilots went on alert, keeping half of the bombers in the air at all times. Similar actions were taken in Pensacola, Florida, and Abilene, Texas. "Looks to me like we just went to DEFCON 2. That hasn't happened since the Cuban Missile Crisis."

Dombarovsky, Russia

Halfway around the world in southern Russia, fifteen miles north of the Kazakhstan border, Lieutenant Colonel Pavel Burov led his comrade down a long, narrow concrete tunnel, fifty meters below the ground. Nineteen years ago, he had earned the honor to serve as a proud *roketchiki*, responsible for the physical care, security, and operation of ten nuclear missiles.

They approached the steel door to the launch center to begin their shift. Burov leaned into the retinal scanner and placed his right eye on the eyepiece, not blinking until the red light went out. He and his comrade stood before the camera and waited for the team inside to open the heavy blast door.

Even though they met this team every day, they never spoke to them. *Roketchiki* teams were trained not to form any personal bonds. Russian leaders didn't want to risk any coordinated resistance against pressing the button if the order were ever given.

Burov stepped aside to allow the other team to leave before he and his comrade entered. They performed the shift turnover tasks outlined in their checklists, then sat at their stations.

Normally, the next six hours would be uneventful, but four days ago, their commander had ordered them on high alert.

Blue Koala
Chapter 31

Nassau, Bahamas

Saturday morning, two hours before sunrise, Niko waved the badge he copied from Jalen in front of the reader. A green light appeared next to the door latch, and he entered. An armed guard looked up from his desk, glanced at the tool bag in Niko's hand and the Zettabyte logo on his uniform, and waved him through.

He entered another door into a large office area. Empty cubicles filled the center of the room. The cell phone in Niko's pocket vibrated. He checked the messages, all from Vyper:

> BLUE KOALA'S SERVER SENT A TEXT
> DO NOT KNOW WHERE IT WENT
> SUSPECT JALEN'S ID WAS DETECTED
> MAYBE SATURDAY IS NOT AUTHORIZED
> ALERTS STOPPED – I BLOCKED THEM

Niko went to the men's' room and sat inside a toilet stall. He placed his Bluetooth earbud in his ear and called Vyper. "I got your message."

Her voice wavered. "You must leave. Zatan probably received the message. He might decide to pay you a visit."

That had been Niko's first thought as well. "We can't back out now. If I leave, we'll never stop Zatan."

An uncomfortable silence hung in the air until Vyper finally spoke. "If you must ... then keep this call open so we can communicate. I will follow you on the security cameras, but they do not have sound."

Niko made his way to the door leading into the datacenter. A wave of his badge granted him entry. The inside looked exactly like the security camera videos he had studied. At the end of a line of wire cages was a smoked glass enclosure—Blue Koala.

Confident Vyper had frozen the video that security teams viewed, he rushed to the Blue Koala badge reader and waved Jalen's badge. He held his breath, hoping Zatan didn't block access.

I'm in!

The narrow aisles between racks of equipment were exactly what he expected. No one should be here, but he kept looking around anyway. He walked to the section where network connections to the outside world were accessible—this is where Blue Koala must house their telecommunication equipment.

Niko studied the equipment, the ports, and the cables inserted in the ports. When he was convinced he had found the right spot, he described it to Vyper. "Should I plug in?"

"Yes."

He set his tool bag on the floor, pulled out a tablet computer and long cable, and connected it to the Blue Koala network equipment.

"I see it," said Vyper. "Wait until I configure it ... Got it."

Niko picked up his toolkit "Now I'm going to look at the firewalls." He walked down the aisle, dragging the cable behind him like an umbilical cord attaching him to Vyper.

He reached into his tool kit and pulled out a special blue cable—the type primarily used by field technicians for administrative console access.

Niko plugged one end of the cable into a special console port on his tablet, and the other end into the admin port on one of the firewalls. If all went as planned, Vyper would connect through the long umbilical cord into the tablet and out to the firewall. "Is this the right one?"

"No, try another."

His second choice was also wrong, but when he tried the third one, Vyper responded, "Perfect. Now I will break in and modify the configuration. This might take a while."

Niko waited. Vyper would be working as quickly as she could, but he needed to get out of here as soon as possible.

"I got it," said Vyper. "Now you can make the connection." She described the port.

Niko disconnected the umbilical cord from his laptop and plugged it into the location Vyper designated. "Are you in?"

"One minute ... That is perfect. Now pack up and leave."

As he packed up his equipment, Niko smiled. "You were worried—"

"Get out!" Vyper shouted. "Zatan entered the building. He is with another man ... No! He is heading to Blue Koala's door. Hide!"

Niko glanced at the door.

It opened, and two men entered. One was Zatan, dressed in a Bahamian shirt and shorts. He looked physically intimidating—more than he did in his photos. The other man wore a dark blue uniform. He held a weapon in his right hand.

A gun? That's crazy.

Niko stood with his tool kit in hand. "Good morning. I'm with Zettabyte. Just finishing—"

"You are not Jalen Sawyer," said Zatan. "What are you doing here?"

Pointing to his logo, Niko replied, "Like I said, I'm with Zettabyte."

The guard raised his weapon.

Niko stared at the barrel of the gun. But it wasn't a gun. Sparks and confetti shot out. He felt a sting in his stomach, and then in his leg.

Taser.

He saw the thin wires a moment before excruciating pain shot up his leg then throughout his body. He shook, and his knees buckled. He collapsed, unable to control the movement of his arms or legs. This was the most pain he ever experienced.

The pain stopped suddenly, and his muscles relaxed. Zatan and his guard stood over him.

The sound of Vyper's voice in his ear demanded attention. "Get ready."

Ready? For what?

Zatan glared. "Cut the bullshit. Who are you, and why are you here?" He waved at the Taser. "You will answer me sooner or later."

A whirring sound drew Niko's attention to a robotic unit on tracks behind the two men, heading toward them.

Zatan and his guard glanced back just as the robot ran into the man with the Taser, knocking him down.

Niko jumped up and kicked the guard in the head with all the force he could muster.

Zatan stepped around the robot and assumed an offensive stance, legs flexed, arms raised. Niko could only hope his Krav Maga lessons were enough to handle this man.

The robot's arm suddenly extended into the side of Zatan's head, knocking the man to the floor.

Vyper's voice screamed in his ear. "Get out of there. I will lock them in. They will not leave."

Niko glanced at the small wires connecting him to the Taser. He spotted two small metal cylinders dangling from his uniform—one on his stomach, and one on his thigh. He gripped the one on his stomach and pulled it straight out. It was painful, but nothing like being tased. He removed the one in his leg, grabbed his tool kit, and left.

Warrenton, Virginia

Vyper sat before her laptop, flapping her hands and rocking her head. The stress of the morning had gotten to her, but she managed to stay focused while Niko needed her. She had allowed her anger to get the best of her, too—knocking those horrible men down with the robot, locking them in, and unleashing inert gas inside Blue Koala's enclosure. If they suffocated, they would have deserved it. She notified Smith— those men were his problem now.

When she stopped rocking, and emerged from her mental safe zone, she got down to business. Using the access Niko had set up, she navigated her way into Zatan's network in Vladivostok. This should be where he kept his most secretive tools and plans.

She remembered the list of Greek gods' names she found on Sokolov's computer. Apollo and Hermes were highlighted, so she searched for both of them. One of the results included a list. At the top of the list was:

APOLLO: CALVERT CLIFFS

She browsed the list further and discovered another entry:

HERMES: INDIAN POINT

Since Calvert Cliffs was the nuclear power plant Smith was worried about, it seemed likely that Indian Point was another plant—a fact she verified with a simple internet search.

It was one thing to identify the targets. It was another to discover what the Russians planned to do. Any truly destructive cyber-attack would likely target an industrial processor. That was Zatan's approach with the Texas refineries and the LA power systems. All of Zatan's malicious programs contained a few telltale patterns—unique, like a signature.

Vyper searched through Zatan's software and discovered two programs intended to infect industrial computers. Further analysis uncovered a nefarious feature—they attacked the monitoring systems to conceal unsafe conditions. If this was used on a nuclear power plant, the operators would not be warned in advance if something dangerous was happening.

She made a secure call to Smith. As soon as he identified himself, she blurted out, "Zatan is targeting two nuclear plants—Calvert Cliffs and Indian Point. You must shut them both down immediately."

"Calm down, Vyper," said Smith. "We knew about Calvert Cliffs. You say he's also targeting Indian Point?"

"Yes, those code names we found on Sokolov's computer. It identifies both sites."

"Why do you want us to shut them down? You know how many people will lose power?"

"Zatan has a program that will hide dangerous conditions from the operators. Do you want a power plant to overheat without operators responding?"

"I see your point. Three-Mile Island and Chernobyl have taught us what could happen."

Vyper's hand flapped. She made a fist and resisted the urge to zone out. "Will you shut them down?"

"These plants all have physical gauges. We'll demand that both sites check the status of their gauges instead of relying on the operators' consoles. If we discover a problem, we'll shut them down."

"I guess that will work."

"It'll work, Vyper. You and Niko may well have stopped one or two nuclear meltdowns. Those plants are located near Washington, DC, and New York City. If either site had a meltdown, we'd have a national disaster to deal with. You also stopped Sokolov and Zatan. The world owes you both a debt of gratitude, but they'll never know what you did for them."

Dombarovsky, Russia

The alarm surprised Lieutenant Colonel Burov. His partner sat across the small launch center, his eyes wide with anticipation. Burov picked up the phone. "*Da.*"

This was not a drill. They just received the command to arm ten missiles.

Burov and his partner independently reviewed the codes in the book against the codes they just received. They matched.

Each man inserted their keys and entered the validated codes. Within seconds, a green light appeared. The weapons were armed.

The next time the alarm went off, they would be given the order to launch.

Uzhur, Russia

Seven hundred kilometers north, in the heart of Siberia, another team received the same orders. They both inserted their keys and entered the valid codes. They watched and waited for the green light.

They didn't live to see it.

Aftermath
Chapter 32

Warrenton, Virginia

Vyper ended the call with Smith and breathed a sigh of relief. It was just this morning when she told him about Indian Point. Technicians at the site discovered an alarming temperature rise that did not show up on the operators' consoles. In response, they shut down operations until all systems could be certified free of malicious software. Calvert Cliffs had no such problem, but the situation was being monitored closely. Inspection and mediation were planned for all nuclear power plants across the nation.

With Sokolov and Zatan out of action, she hoped cyber-attacks would stop for a while. Of course, they would never stop as long as the US refused to go on offense.

It was time to relax and wait for Niko's call. She grabbed the game controller.

Her phone chirped, and she looked at the message. Something happened in Russia. She grabbed her laptop and searched for more information. The International Space Station identified an anomaly in Siberia. Earthquake monitoring stations reported a significant event at the same location. Reporters speculated the Russians performed an underground test of a nuclear warhead.

The US government said nothing, so Vyper searched ex-military sites. Homeland Security and all military services were on high alert.

Vyper retreated into her mental safe place. She rocked back and forth and flapped her hands. Nothing bothered her now.

Austin, Texas

Niko admired the view of the Colorado River from their balcony. Vyper sat in a chair by his side, a computer on her lap. They had decided to visit the best cities in America for young people, in search of a place to settle down.

He was inclined to limit the search to America. Their experiences in Nassau, only two weeks ago, had soured him on leaving the country.

Vyper set her laptop on a low table. "Do you think the Russian nukes exploded because Smith slipped my firmware into them? They blew up inside their silos."

"I think so, but Smith won't tell us." He reached out and held her hand. "Even if it was your program, you shouldn't feel bad. The Russians must have decided to arm those missiles. If it hadn't been for your firmware, they probably would have launched them as the US. It could have been a nuclear war."

Vyper sipped on an iced tea. "I thought about that, but I do not understand how Russian leaders think. Why would they want to start a nuclear war?"

"All I can figure is they felt threatened. When your KILROY message popped up in their missile systems, they thought the US compromised all their nukes. I'm pretty sure we only penetrated a few, but the Russian Army may have thought differently. When our forces went on alert, they were afraid we'd launch before they had a chance."

"That is crazy. But somehow, this cycle of cyber-attacks appears to have stopped. I wonder how long that will last."

Niko stood at the railing. "Cyberwarfare will never stop. We let the genie out of the bottle, and he won't go back in."

"You are so cynical." Vyper opened her computer. "Did you see this? Bitcoin's value dropped fifty percent overnight."

"You don't own any Bitcoins, do you? It's not real money, you know."

"No," said Vyper. "I do not gamble. But something is going on. Bitcoin is dropping like a rock." She typed in a few commands. "Hackers broke into three major exchanges and stole nearly two million coins. North Korea is the prime suspect."

Note from the author:

Our younger son, Neil, is amazing. He's also autistic. He inspired me to introduce a major character on the autism spectrum. This is my way of supporting autism awareness.

If you enjoyed this novel, I would appreciate your review on Amazon or wherever you buy your books. I'd also love to hear from you via email (mark.pryor@pryorpatch.com), and I invite you to visit my website to keep up with my writing (www.pryorpatch.com)

Read on for the first chapters of my novel, Noble Phoenix, available on Amazon.

Preview: Noble Phoenix

Available on Amazon
- Kindle: www.amazon.com/dp/B07465QGCW
- Paperback: www.amazon.com/dp/1548434922

Viktor
Chapter 1

1998 - Prague, Czech Republic

Angry young men with spiky haircuts and shaved heads transformed a cheerful crowd of music lovers into an angry mob. Fourteen-year-old Viktor Prazsky had invited Delia, the prettiest girl in his class, to the Global Street Party. Now they were caught up in the middle of this developing riot.

Delia clung to Viktor's arm, her dark, penetrating eyes shrouded with worry. "I don't like this. Let's get out of here."

Viktor nodded. He searched for a break in the crowd, but the throng of protesters propelled them forward.

An hour ago, Viktor and Delia had been enjoying a music festival at Peace Square. Viktor's father, a lieutenant in the federal police, had warned him not to go, claiming the festival was organized by anarchists. So, Viktor lied to him, saying he was taking Delia to see *Titanic* at the Old Town Theater. They were having fun, even when the bands stopped playing and the party moved to the streets.

Now, they were hemmed in by a gang of young men, raising their fists, shouting, "Reclaim the Streets," and waving signs with slogans expressing the same sentiment. Some men marched with red and black flags, carrying a three-pronged symbol reminiscent of the Nazi swastika.

Most of the protesters were older than Viktor — bigger and taller. Despite the cool day, many were shirtless. Some tied handkerchiefs around their faces, leaving only their eyes exposed. They looked like bandits.

Viktor moved forward with the crowd, Delia in tow, when he spotted something. He turned to her and spoke loud enough to be heard. "The museum is up ahead."

As they threaded their way through the mob, Delia cried out. "Leave me alone." Her grip on Viktor's arm tightened.

He stopped and looked back to see a tall man in a red ski mask holding Delia's other arm, screaming at her. "Black swine! Gypsy whore!"

Viktor's body stiffened, and his heart raced. *He thinks she's Roma — Gypsy.* Actually, Delia was Greek, but her dark complexion must have drawn this man's attention. *They hate Roma.* Two Czech men had killed a Roma woman a few months back. The story had been big news in all the papers — telling how those men assaulted her, then threw her into the river.

As the man in the ski mask continued his tirade, the crush of the crowd eased. People moved away from the confrontation, while continuing to march through the streets.

Viktor and Delia stood in the center of a small opening in the crowd, along with the man who towered over them, refusing to release her arm.

Delia struggled and screamed, while Viktor's mind searched for a way out. Police sirens wailed in the distance. He doubted they'd arrive in time. He had learned a few Taekwondo moves, but he was only a novice.

Moving protectively close to Delia, Viktor faced her assailant. "Leave us alone. We don't want trouble."

Crooked, yellow teeth formed a smile that showed through a hole in the ski mask. The man reached into his pocket and fished out a knife — about twice the length of his hand. *Click.* The blade snapped open. He waved it in Delia's face and pulled her closer with his other hand. "Get out of the way, boy. Your damn Gypsy whore isn't worth it."

Gotta do something. Viktor lifted his right knee and delivered a snap kick to the man's groin, causing him to drop his knife and collapse, writhing in pain.

Someone grabbed Viktor from behind and held him in a bear hug.

Where'd he come from? Viktor shouted, "Run, Delia." He struggled to free himself. Despite his attempts, the man at his back held him tighter.

As Delia ran off, the man with the yellow teeth grabbed his knife and stumbled uneasily to his feet. "Bastard!" He pointed the blade at Viktor's face. "I see you met my brother. He seems to like you."

Behind Viktor, a scornful laugh burst out. "You ain't goin' nowhere."

In front of Viktor, the yellow teeth smiled through the mask. "Gonna cut you, boy."

Only one way to break this hold. Viktor twisted to the left. As the man at his back moved his right leg forward, Viktor twisted right again, and stomped his heel on the arch of the man's foot.

With a howl and a curse, the man released his bear hug and shoved Viktor forward — directly toward the knife in the other man's hand.

Viktor instinctively turned his face to the right. *Shit! Too late.*

Something slammed into his left temple. Everything went black.

****

Fifteen minutes earlier, Lieutenant Eduard Prazsky jumped into the passenger seat of the patrol car and buckled up. He knew the street party would turn violent. He was glad he had warned his son, Viktor, to stay away.

Josef Filipek, his new partner, started the engine and turned on the siren and flashing lights as he pulled into traffic. He glanced at Eduard "Wilsonova Street near the opera house. Ten minutes, maybe quicker."

"There could be a lot of foot traffic in that area. You'd be better driving around—"

"I've been driving these streets for years, Lieutenant." Josef kept his eyes on the road. "I can't afford my own chauffeur, so I probably know my way around better than you do."

Chauffeur. Eduard often heard comments like this, but it always made him uncomfortable. "If you want to request a different partner, that's up to you. For now, let's focus on the call."

Josef glanced briefly at his partner and then back to the street, before turning the wheel sharply to the right. "Tell me. With all your money, why do you even bother to work? Can't your friend, President Havel, find something more challenging for you to do?"

It was clear his partner wasn't afraid to speak his mind, so Eduard decided to do the same. "I do this because I hate terrorists as much as you do. The Anarchists of the Black Trinity have been turning these street parties into violent riots all over Europe. They need to be stopped."

Josef continued to speed through the streets and take sharp corners.

Eduard wanted to make this partnership work. They needed to communicate and trust each other. "Listen. I grew up with money and I know our president, but that doesn't make me soft or ignorant. I also spent eight months in Kosovo clearing mines and hunting down war criminals ... so, can you stop being an asshole, and start treating me as your partner?"

A smile appeared on Josef's face. "I think you and I will get along just fine."

The radio came to life with a woman's voice. "Unit twenty-seven, this is base. Assist emergency medical responders heading to National Museum on Wilsonova Street."

Josef made a hard-left turn and accelerated. He flipped a switch to trigger an urgent, wailing siren.

Eduard grabbed the microphone. "Base. Twenty-seven responding."

"Affirmative, twenty-seven. Man down, possible stabbing. Assist with crowd control."

An ambulance came into view from behind, pulling up close, tailgating their police vehicle. Up ahead, a crowd appeared as they approached Wilsonova.

Josef slowed down to avoid hitting any of the desperate crowd scurrying away in all directions, but he didn't stop. He continued to move forward aggressively, forcing people out of the way.

Eduard took the microphone. "Base, this is twenty-seven. Arrived at Wilsonova. Will assist responders on foot."

Josef stopped the car. The ambulance stopped directly behind.

Both officers donned their riot helmets and grabbed their radios and clubs. Eduard grabbed an air horn. They got out of the car and faced a moving sea of young people, marching down the street, most with faces covered and fists in the air.

Two emergency responders in solid blue jump suits rushed toward them from the ambulance, each carrying a red duffel bag. Two more followed, pushing a gurney on wheels.

The man in front shouted at Eduard. "You two lead the way. My partner and I will follow. Don't worry about the gurney team. They'll push their way through. We can't let them slow us down."

Eduard nodded to Josef and pressed noise-suppression plugs into his ears. He aimed the air horn forward and released a loud wailing blast. People moved away from the sound as quickly as the crowd allowed, while the four of them pushed into the empty space.

It took two more blasts before they reached a large opening near the museum. Ten meters away, a man lay on the street. A young couple stood in front of him, obscuring their view. Eduard couldn't tell if he was injured or dead.

The emergency responders rushed forward and knelt beside the victim.

The young couple ran over to Josef, both of them talking at once, saying something about two men wearing masks, an argument, a fight, and a knife.

Eduard glanced at the victim. He looked a bit like Viktor — even wore the same clothes — but the young man's face was turned to the side. A pool of dark liquid stained the street. Then Eduard saw the knife, or rather the hilt. It stuck out of the man's temple. *It's not Viktor. It can't be. He went to the movies.*

The team with the gurney arrived. All four of the emergency responders positioned themselves around the injured man, preparing to slide him on a backboard and lift him onto the gurney.

As they lifted the victim up, Eduard saw his face.

Oh, my God! Viktor!

Desperation
Chapter 2

1999 - Brno, Czech Republic

Nine months later, Eduard Prazsky sat beside his wife, Magda, in Doctor Logan's office at the Moravia Fertility Clinic. The availability of discarded embryos made this the perfect location for Logan's research.

Eduard brushed a stray lock of brown hair from his wife's face and whispered, "I love you." She looked so beautiful, so hopeful — so determined. A highly respected cardiologist, she had reached out to her American colleagues for advice on treating Viktor. One of them told her about the experimental use of stem cells. Before long, she came up with a plan.

Eduard had agreed with his wife, gambling their son's future and his family fortune on the promises of Doctor Logan. All because of two violent degenerates, inspired by hate, who nearly killed his only child, Viktor. *Those bastards should be dead—not just rotting in prison.*

The doctor arrived and settled behind the desk facing them. "Good morning," he said, speaking English with a strong Scottish accent. "I hope you haven't been waiting long."

English. One more reason Eduard didn't trust this man. Any doctor working in the Czech Republic should learn the language.

Despite his wife's optimism, Eduard saw no progress. "What's happening to Viktor? Why do the tumors keep coming back?"

Logan glanced briefly at Magda before focusing on Eduard. "I know this is frustrating, Mister Prazsky." He leaned forward and placed both hands flat on the desk. "The stem cells we injected are creating new nerve cells in his brain, but sometimes they also create teratomas – tumors. This time there's only one small tumor, and Doctor Kaplan will remove it with radiosurgery. No knife."

"That's what you told us last time," Eduard said. "He's not getting better. The stem cells are killing him."

Doctor Logan ran his hand through his thinning hair. "We're fortunate Viktor survived the attack. Even though the knife penetrated deeply into his brain, it didn't affect any life-sustaining functions. Nevertheless, without these cell replacement treatments, he'll be permanently disabled."

It was true. Their son had been lucky — miraculously lucky. The doctors in Prague had brought him back from almost certain death. Eduard and his wife had called Viktor their phoenix — until the extent of his injuries became clear.

Magda held her husband's hand on her lap and looked at him with her deep blue eyes. "Please, dear. It does no good to second-guess our decision."

Eduard relaxed at her touch. He knew his wife understood this much better than him, even though it wasn't her specialty. "I don't know—"

Magda didn't wait for him to finish. "We knew Viktor had no chance for a normal life unless we tried this. We took a gamble ... a serious gamble. No one has ever done this before. Doctor Logan is taking a big risk with us. He could lose his license, even go to jail."

"Your wife is right, Mister Prazsky. It's still early in his treatment, and I believe this is working. But I can't offer any guarantees."

Eduard sat back in his chair and let out a breath. "I know you're right, but this seems so ghoulish. Viktor just lies there, doesn't open his eyes, and doesn't respond when we talk to him. A few months ago, he was a normal teenager. He laughed. He played football." Eduard choked back tears. "Our son doesn't even smile."

Magda squeezed her husband's hand. "Doctor, we're both worried about Viktor's progress. How soon before we see some response? How many more treatments are required?"

"I plan to grow enough stem cells for two more treatments. I wish I could tell you how soon he'll be responsive, but we are in uncharted territory here. There are no past cases to go on."

The door opened, and the faint sound of yells and chants of an angry crowd interrupted their conversation. Most of the sounds were unintelligible, but two words stood out — 'baby' and 'kill'.

A nurse stepped in. "Doctor Logan. There's a rowdy group of people at the front desk demanding to talk to you. Shall I call the police?"

He looked at the nurse. "No, Dana. Tell them I'll be right out." Logan looked at the Prazskys. "Sorry for the interruption, but there are people who don't approve of our work at the fertility clinic. This shouldn't take long." Logan left the Prazskys alone in his office.

Eduard turned to his wife. "Are we fooling ourselves? Does Viktor have a chance?"

Magda pulled a hanky from her purse and brushed it under her nose. "Our son doesn't stand a chance without this treatment — none. Very few people understand stem cells, but Doctor Logan does. He's the only one willing to treat Viktor."

"It feels wrong. We've given him millions of crowns. Hundreds of millions. And we can't tell anyone about the treatments, even though Viktor lies there lifeless. How do we know Logan's not just swindling us?"

"I don't think—"

A loud bang interrupted them.

"Gunfire!" Eduard said. "Quick. Behind the desk."

Magda grabbed her husband's arm and crouched beside him. "The door isn't locked." Her grip tightened. "They can get in here."

Eduard nodded and started to rise.

Three more shots. Screams.

His wife pulled him down. "No! It's not worth the risk. Stay here with me."

Rapid footsteps approached. Maybe only one person, certainly not a crowd.

Dana flung open the door. "Doctor Prazsky!"

Magda poked her head above the desk. "What happened?"

Dana's voice shook as she rocked from one foot to the other. "Doctor Logan's been shot. I think he's dead."

"Where's the shooter?" Eduard asked, moving from behind the desk.

Dana started to cry. "Everyone ran away ... Please help him."

Magda ran toward the door.

Eduard followed her.

****

The following afternoon in their hotel room, Magda dropped the phone and collapsed on the couch. She didn't sleep last night. Doctor Logan was dead. The police had questioned everybody in the clinic, and they asked more questions this morning. Then she pleaded over the phone with Doctor Kaplan at the clinic.

She turned to her husband, tears in her eyes. "Viktor's treatments are over."

Eduard sat beside her and held her hand. "How can they do that? Didn't Logan train anyone?"

"He didn't share his research or methods with anyone. He was afraid he'd be arrested for treating Viktor."

"What about Doctor Kaplan?"

To Magda, this was obvious, but her husband wasn't a doctor. "Kaplan is a neurosurgeon. He doesn't know anything about stem cells."

"He knows what Logan was doing, doesn't he?"

"He claims he has no idea." Magda let out a sigh and shook her head. "He's full of shit. He knows what was going on, but he doesn't want anyone else to know."

"Can't we force him to help Viktor? Would money help?"

Magda stood up and hugged him. Her husband was used to solving problems with money, but she knew it wouldn't work this time. "He can't help." Then she broke down and wept.

Eduard held her until the tears stopped, then brushed the hair from her face and kissed her.

Grateful for the loving support of her husband, she looked into his dark eyes. "You don't understand, do you?"

He shook his head.

Magda looked down at her feet. "Doctor Kaplan can't give Viktor the treatments. No one can." Slowly, she raised her head and stared at the ceiling, tilting her head slightly.

"What are you thinking?" Eduard asked. "I recognize that look."

A weak smile formed on her face. She paced around the room slowly, rubbing her neck. Finally, she sat in a chair. "He's already had five treatments. That might be enough."

"You really think so? Why isn't he better?"

"If Viktor's body has accepted enough stem cells, they're already creating new neurons."

"What do we do now? Just sit around and wait for him to get better?"

"Let's get Doctor Kaplan to remove this tumor, then we can take Viktor back to Prague. I work with several doctors who can deal with teratomas. Logan said he's still at risk. If any tumors appear, the doctors in Prague can remove them."

"Don't they need to know about stem cells?"

"No, they don't. Besides, this treatment isn't approved for clinical trials. We could get in trouble."

As a police officer, Eduard knew the risk. "You're right. I think we should keep this a secret ... forever."

Madrid
Chapter 3

2004 - Alcalá, Spain

Even though the cell replacement treatments ended five years ago, Viktor's health and quality of life steadily improved. It was truly a miracle, one worthy of celebration, but behind it all was a secret that could ruin his family. His parents paid for an illegal medical procedure. They broke the law.

This morning, Viktor completed a series of medical tests at Alcalá University Hospital, near Madrid. After lunch, his parents accompanied him to the office of Doctor Moreno, the most respected neurologist in Spain.

As they pulled up to the curb, Viktor reminded himself to use the name Oliver Klima, the false identity for his medical appointments. He hated the deception, but he knew there was a risk the doctors could discover his illegal treatments, putting his parents in jeopardy.

Viktor stepped out of the taxi and opened the door for his mother.

Magda reached for her son's hand and winked. "You're looking handsome today, *Oliver*."

"Thank you, Mother." Viktor helped her out of the car.

They entered the modern three-story office building and headed for the elevator. Viktor knew his way. He had been coming here for two years. This was his fourth visit, and he hoped it would be his last.

The 'Klima family' arrived in the reception area and were directed to the doctor's office where a gray-haired man, wearing a white lab coat, met them at the door. "*Buenas tardes.*"

Magda responded in English. "It's good to see you again, Doctor Moreno."

The doctor directed them to the chairs in front of his desk while he took the seat behind it. He glanced at his computer. "I have your test results, Oliver." He looked at Magda and continued, "If you have any questions, Doctor Klima, let me know."

Moreno glanced at the file. "Let me begin with Oliver's vision."

Viktor pointed to the small black patch covering his left eye. His curly black hair was long enough to cover the remaining scar on his temple. "I see nothing with this eye."

The doctor nodded. "The damage to your optic nerve blocks the information between your left eye and your brain. But, you seem to have adapted well to the limitations of your vision."

Viktor's blind eye never improved after the attack, and he had difficulty judging distances with a single functioning eye. Despite this, his parents always requested tests, hoping the stem cells could produce another miracle.

He rubbed his scar. Something he often did when nervous. "I see well enough, but I hate it when people stare at my patch."

"I'm sure your friends and family are used to it. Would you prefer they look at your lazy eye?"

Viktor shook his head and looked at his father. "No, it looks creepy. I prefer the patch."

Eduard spoke up. "He's had eye muscle repair surgery. Both eyes moved together properly for a while, but within a few months they lost the synchronous movement."

The doctor nodded. "That's a common problem with complete vision loss in the eye."

"What about the MRI?" asked Magda.

Moreno turned the computer screen so Viktor and his parents could view it. He pointed with his pen. "On this image, you can see the empty area on the left where the injury occurred. That area is smaller than it was on the scans from previous years."

Viktor studied the image. It was comforting to know the stem cells were still working to heal his brain, but they couldn't let the doctor know the reason for this miraculous growth. Fortunately, his mother knew how to handle this.

Magda nodded. "You mentioned this during our last appointment, but you said we should wait to see how things developed over the next six months."

"That's right, and the damaged section has continued to shrink every six months since our first MRI. We don't know if the same thing happened during the time Doctor Durant was treating Oliver. Those scans weren't conclusive due to the surgical procedures he performed."

Durant. He had been the French doctor Viktor first went to after the stem cell treatments ended. Four times during those three years, a tumor formed and he needed surgery. When Durant's questions threatened to uncover the illegal treatments, his mother decided to change doctors.

Eduard shrugged his shoulders. "Is this a problem, Doctor? Isn't it good to see the area of his injury shrink?"

"In any other part of the body, healing like that would be a good sign. But neurogenesis, the growth of healthy nerve cells, has never been observed in the temporal lobe of any adult brain. The good news is, we haven't detected any growth of unhealthy nerve cells during the entire two years I've been seeing Oliver."

Nothing unhealthy. That's what Viktor wanted to hear. *Two years. Nothing wrong. No more tests!*

Magda took her husband's hand and looked at the doctor. "Are you telling us Oliver has gone two years with no malignant growths, and you're concerned because you suspect his brain is creating healthy cells?"

"That's right. But this kind of new cell growth is unheard of, and I'd like to do some tests."

Magda nodded and rose from the chair. "Thank you, Doctor. We'll have to think this over. Could you give us copies of the results?"

Viktor and his father stood, preparing to leave.

"Certainly, Doctor Klima. The nurse will give them to you on your way out. But I need to tell you about the results of the electroencephalogram."

"The EEG? Did you find something?" Magda took her seat again. Eduard and Viktor did the same.

"Oliver's results are normal ... except for one thing. His brain waves have a higher amplitude than normal — about ten times the average person."

This was nothing new to Viktor or his parents. Doctor Durant noticed this anomaly, too. His mother believed this was most likely a symptom of his newly acquired ability — one they must keep secret.

He had first noticed this ability a year after a man plunged a knife into his head. Whenever Viktor's mother was near him, he knew whether she was happy or sad. The same thing happened with his father, his friends — everyone. Eventually, he realized he was sensing other peoples' feelings.

Magda raised her eyebrows. "You said Oliver's EEG results are normal, but you're concerned because his brain waves are stronger than expected?"

"That's right. The brain consumes more energy than any other organ in the body. Oliver's brain demands even more."

"Is that a problem?"

"We can't be sure without more testing."

"More testing." Magda frowned, then stood. "All right. If you think it's required. We'll set up an appointment with your receptionist."

Viktor knew she would agree to the appointment, like she did with Doctor Durant. But he also knew they weren't coming back. They'd never see Dr. Moreno again. To do so would only draw attention.

****

A few hours later, two blocks from the university hospital, the Prazsky family finished dinner in their hotel and went upstairs for the night.

Viktor sat on his bed talking on the phone with Karla. The door leading to his parents' adjoining room was closed. "We're heading home tomorrow. I'll be back at school on Friday."

He had met Karla the previous fall, when they began their sophomore year at Charles University in Prague. Two months ago, in January, they started dating. They became almost inseparable, getting together or talking on the phone every day, sharing their dreams and aspirations.

There was one passion, however, that Viktor had never shared with Karla, and he wanted to tell her now. She knew he spent time at the gym, but he hadn't explained what he did there. "I'm taking my black belt test next week. Would you like to come?"

"Black belt?" Karla sounded surprised. "You're a black belt?"

"Taekwondo. It's a Korean form of karate. I'll be a black belt when I pass the test. People often bring their family and friends to watch."

"That sounds exciting. When is it?"

"Wednesday evening. It's at a gym close to Prague Castle."

"I'd love to. Is the testing hard? Are you nervous?"

"I used to be nervous when I tested for lower-level belts, but not anymore. It's just a matter of demonstrating what I've practiced."

Viktor's thoughts drifted back six years to the terrible day on the streets of Prague with Delia. That day he had been helpless against those men, and he never wanted to experience that again. When he started Taekwondo, the moves came easily to him, even though his non-functioning eye proved to be a challenge. His limited vision, however, was offset by the strength of his newly acquired sensitivity to emotions. He realized he could detect his opponent's intentions almost before they did, making his defensive reflexes lightning fast. If anyone ever threatened Viktor today, he knew he could defend himself.

Karla's voice brought him back to the present. "I can't wait to see you do your karate stuff."

Viktor heard the faint sound of a second female voice talking to Karla.

"My aunt just arrived. I gotta go. See you in school Friday."

Ending the call, Viktor hopped off the bed and knocked on the door before walking into his parents' room.

His mother turned to greet him. "You get taller every day, and better looking, too. I'm glad you could join us."

Viktor plopped in an overstuffed chair and faced the television. "I'm packed, and it's boring sitting in my room."

"Make yourself comfortable," his father said with a chuckle. "Did you lose your razor?"

"It's the five o'clock shadow look, Father. Women love it."

Magda rubbed Eduard's cheek. "Not this woman. Too scratchy." She turned back to her son. "How does Karla like it?"

"She thinks I'm hot."

His father poured drinks, dark Alhambra lager for himself and Viktor, and a glass of Àn Tinto wine for Magda. "We have something to celebrate."

They all raised their glasses.

Eduard offered a toast. "To our son. Two years. No tumors."

Viktor took a drink, savoring the flavor, and set his glass on the coffee table. "No more tests. No more doctors."

His mother smiled. "It's a good idea to go for testing every five years or so, just to be sure."

Viktor was a keen observer of body language. His mother's smile was broad and genuine, showcasing her pearly white teeth. Her eyes were radiant. But he also sensed her emotions, something she didn't show on her face. "You're worried about my brain waves. The EEG results."

"I can't hide anything from you," said his mother. "Even though you appear to be healthy, I worry. The doctor might be right. Your brain uses so much energy, it could be harming you."

"You mean my headaches, don't you?"

Eduard set his glass on the nightstand. "I'm no doctor, and I can see it. Those aren't normal headaches."

Viktor worried about it, too. Sometimes he got so dizzy he nearly passed out. "It only happens when I get upset. I've learned to control it." There were also things he hadn't told his parents, like how his vision often suffered — objects became blurry, and sometimes he saw double. The thought of losing sight in his only healthy eye was frightening.

His mother nodded. "I hope you're right."

Viktor looked at his father. "What is it? I can tell something's bothering you."

"That's the problem. You can tell. You know too much about other peoples' thoughts." Eduard reached out and held Magda's hand. "You can't let anyone know what you're capable of."

"I don't care what the EEG shows." Viktor tugged nervously at the edge of his eye patch. "I can't read minds."

Magda looked at her son. "We never said you could read minds. But sensing someone else's emotions is unusual."

His father shook his head. "This is serious. Do you want people to be afraid of you? You scare the wrong people, and you could be locked up — or worse."

Viktor didn't share his father's concern about sensing feelings. He stood up and scratched his scar. "I'm going to bed. What time is our flight tomorrow?"

"Eleven o'clock," said his father. "But we need to catch the seven o'clock commuter train to Madrid. It's a short walk to the train station, but we have to leave early."

"Do they serve breakfast on the train?"

"We can get something at the station — maybe juice or a pastry. When we get to the airport, we'll have time to eat a real meal."

Magda took her husband's hand. "Remember. We have a dinner date tomorrow night."

"Oh, that's right," said Viktor. "March eleventh. Happy Anniversary in advance."

****

In the early morning, Viktor shoved his gloved left hand into the pocket of his winter coat as he pulled his luggage with the other. Alcalá Station was only a hundred meters away.

His father wrapped one arm around Magda as he pulled their bag with the other. "You'll warm up once we get inside the station."

"I know." Magda wore a cashmere coat, with a scarf wrapped around most of her face. "Which train are we looking for?"

"There are a lot of trains to Madrid. We're going to the same station we used yesterday on our way here — Atocha."

Warm air welcomed them when they entered and headed toward the lighted board displaying train schedules. Viktor was still learning how to cope with his sensitivity to emotions. The man to his right was excited, but the woman with him was worried, and she held the hand of a young girl who was confused. Their emotions, as well as the emotions of everyone else within a ten-meter circle, assaulted his mind from all directions, as though everyone was yelling at once.

He recognized the 'emotional signatures' of his parents, but the feelings of the strangers around him seemed to blend together. All except for one person whose emotions screamed for attention.

Hatred. He sensed intense feelings coming from someone in front of him. He studied the people until he was fairly certain he knew who it was.

He looked at his father and pointed ahead to the left, about two meters away. "The man with the blue hoodie is angry at everyone. More hate than I've ever felt before. And he's struggling with a heavy gym bag."

"He probably doesn't like crowds. Keep moving. Tell me when you see which platform our train leaves on."

"You don't understand, Father. I've gotta stop him."

Viktor's sensitivity to feelings often proved to be an advantage, but it would be of no use in stopping this dangerous person. He'd have to intrude into the man's emotions – another ability he acquired from his illegal medical treatment. It wouldn't be easy. And then there were the headaches.

The man in the hoodie was close but moving away. Viktor had to act fast. He focused on the strong hateful emotion, then he amplified the intensity and projected it back. He could sense the increase in hatred coming back from this man. It worked. Viktor had control.

He shifted the emotion from hate to fear and then terror. He concentrated on strengthening it as much as possible. Suddenly, pain struck Viktor like a hammer, right in the center of his forehead. It was the headache that always came, punishing him for his strong emotions. *My curse.* He wasn't even sure if his efforts paid off.

Fortunately, they did. The man he targeted let out a scream, dropped his bag, and clutched his head with both hands.

Viktor's eye moved from the man to the bag on the floor. Two wires, red and green, hung out of the side. Ignoring the pain in his head, he shoved the suspicious satchel out of the man's reach with his foot and yelled. "¡*Bomba!*"

He sensed his mother's fear and saw it in her face. His mind must have affected her as well, but not as much as the man with the bomb.

Screams erupted from the crowd. Everyone tried to get away.

Eduard grabbed Magda by the arm and yelled, "Let's get out of here. Now!"

Viktor sensed the fear from his parents and the people nearby. *I did this. Caused their fear.* He concentrated on calming himself. As he did, his headache began to subside.

The man in the hoodie must have recovered as well. He leaned over and reached for the bag.

The bomb! Viktor raised his right knee, pivoted toward the man, and delivered a round kick to the elbow. *He won't pick it up now.* Momentum sent the man to the ground, falling on his injured arm.

Eduard grabbed Viktor. "Let's move!"

The shrill sound of a whistle announced the arrival of two police officers. One of them ran over to the man lying on the ground. The other one inspected the fallen gym bag.

Viktor's vision blurred, and he felt dizzy. Nevertheless, he did his best to follow his parents as they moved away from the officers.

His father pointed to the overhead board. "There's ours — Atocha Station on platform two."

As they waited in line to access the platform, an official closed the gate.

"*Atención! Atención!*" a man's voice bellowed over the public-address system. "Alcalá de Henares Security orders everyone to leave the station immediately. All trains have been cancelled. Repeat. Everyone leave the station immediately."

Angry voices erupted throughout the station. Men and women turned toward the exits, pulling their children with them.

As Eduard approached the exit, he leaned close to Viktor and kept his voice low. "Did you make him drop the bag?"

Viktor thought his father was unaware of this part of his ability. "I had to. I'm sure he had a bomb." He ignored the weakness that followed his headaches. Fortunately, his vision began to clear.

They exited the station and his father pressed him further. "How'd you do it?"

He knows. Mother must know, too. Viktor had no idea how to explain it. "With my mind. Something else I have to keep secret."

"Whatever you did, it affected me, too."

"*Atención! Atención!*" The announcement was repeated.

"What do we do now," asked Magda. "We'll miss our flight."

Viktor heard someone mention *bomb*, but he didn't hear any explosion. He pulled out his phone and searched for news. "Holy shit!" He looked up at his parents' concerned faces. "Bombs exploded on trains all over Madrid. They hit Atocha Station. A lot of people died ... dozens."

"Atocha Station?" said his father. "That was our stop! We would have been there if we hadn't missed our train."

****

Eduard sat in front of a desk in their hotel. "If you can't get me two rooms, one will do. Just get us some place to stay for the night." All trains and flights were cancelled, and there was no telling how soon travel restrictions would lift.

"Yes, Mr. Prazsky." The hotel concierge nodded and picked up his phone.

Magda tugged on Eduard's arm. She pointed toward the bar. "The TV ... uh ... look at it."

A large crowd gathered around the bar, staring at the news report on the large screen. The banner on the newscast read *Terrorist Attack in Madrid.* Eduard couldn't hear the announcer, but he saw videos of destruction in the background. Train cars with gaping holes. Torn metal, all kinds of debris, and what appeared to be bodies were scattered everywhere.

All three of them rushed toward the bar, struggling to get close to the TV. As they approached, Eduard heard the news report.

> *Ten bombs exploded simultaneously on four commuter trains in Madrid during morning rush hour today. Officials report at least one hundred people died and hundreds more were injured. This is the deadliest terrorist attack in Spanish history.*
>
> *Authorities blamed the Spanish separatist group ETA, but our sources say it was the work of Muslim—*

Eduard strained to hear every detail. If not for Viktor — his special ability — the three of us would be dead.

Béziers, France

Over six hundred kilometers north of Alcalá, a man stood in a richly appointed room next to an immense stone fireplace. His neatly trimmed beard revealed a hint of gray, and his stern expression conveyed the arrogance and authority you'd expect from the grand master of a secret international society. When he had been selected to lead Arcadian Spear, he chose the moniker Perseus.

His attention was riveted to the same newscast the Prazskys were watching in Spain.

> ... *separatist group ETA, but our sources say it was the work of Muslim terrorists.*
>
> *Spanish Prime Minister José María Aznar said, 'March 11 now has its place in the history of infamy.' The government declared a three-day mourning period, all parties have called off their campaign events, but the general election will proceed Sunday as scheduled.*
>
> *A man was apprehended in Alcalá station carrying an explosive device, which police neutralized.*

Perseus looked at his aide. "Excellent work, Brother Girard. Other than the bomber they stopped in Alcalá, the Madrid attack was a success."

"Thank you, Your Grace." Girard, a muscular man in his late forties with closely cropped hair, nearly two meters in height, was the personal assistant to the grand master, a man fifteen years his senior.

Perseus grasped the body of a carved ivory dragon mounted on the handle of his antique Greek cane and raised it in the air toward five large computer screens hanging on the walls. Each screen showed graphs of selected investments, updated in real-time. "The stock market is plummeting, as we planned, but our security and defense investments will move up." He looked up at Girard. "Our partners are pleased."

Girard bowed slightly. "Several groups are organizing protests. I'm not sure which party will benefit in the election."

"I don't give a damn about Spanish politics. It's the rest of Europe and America that matter."

"Every Western government has made public statements of support," said Gerard. "I'm sure they intend to increase spending on security."

"As they should. But, we can't leave it to chance. Make sure Germany immediately calls for a European Union security meeting while tempers remain high. Make sure our man Huber is engaged."

"I've spoken to Huber. He expects the chancellor to be receptive."

"Good. But we need to keep up the pressure."

"Yes, Your Grace. We have everything in place for the attack on the high-speed line — three weeks from today."

About the Author

After living most of my life in Pennsylvania working in technology, my wife and I moved to sunny Florida. I've always been interested in science, world issues and beer. In 1971, Uncle Sam sent me to Tonkin Gulf on the USS Midway. I programmed my first computer in 1966, then worked in the computer industry for my entire civilian career.

Nowadays, my wife and I love to travel. I've been to 44 of the 50 states, and 35 countries on five continents, visiting breweries and brewpubs along the way.

Made in the USA
Monee, IL
26 June 2020